The Inner Channel: The Keepers' Histories Part 1© by Kate-Lois Elliott 2023. Published in contract by Rebels of Summer.
Conditions of Sale
This book is sold on the condition that it shall not, by way of trade or otherwise be re-sold, hired out or otherwise circulated in any form without the written consent of the publisher and author. It may not be published in any form of binding or cover other than that which it is published and without a similar condition being imposed on the subsequent buyer without written consent.
Written by Kate-Lois Elliott. Cover design by Kate-Lois Elliott.
Inside map illustration by Oliver Lavery. All rights reserved by Kate-Lois Elliott and Rebels of Summer. First published 2023.

For Kim

The Inner Channel

The Keepers Histories:
Part 1

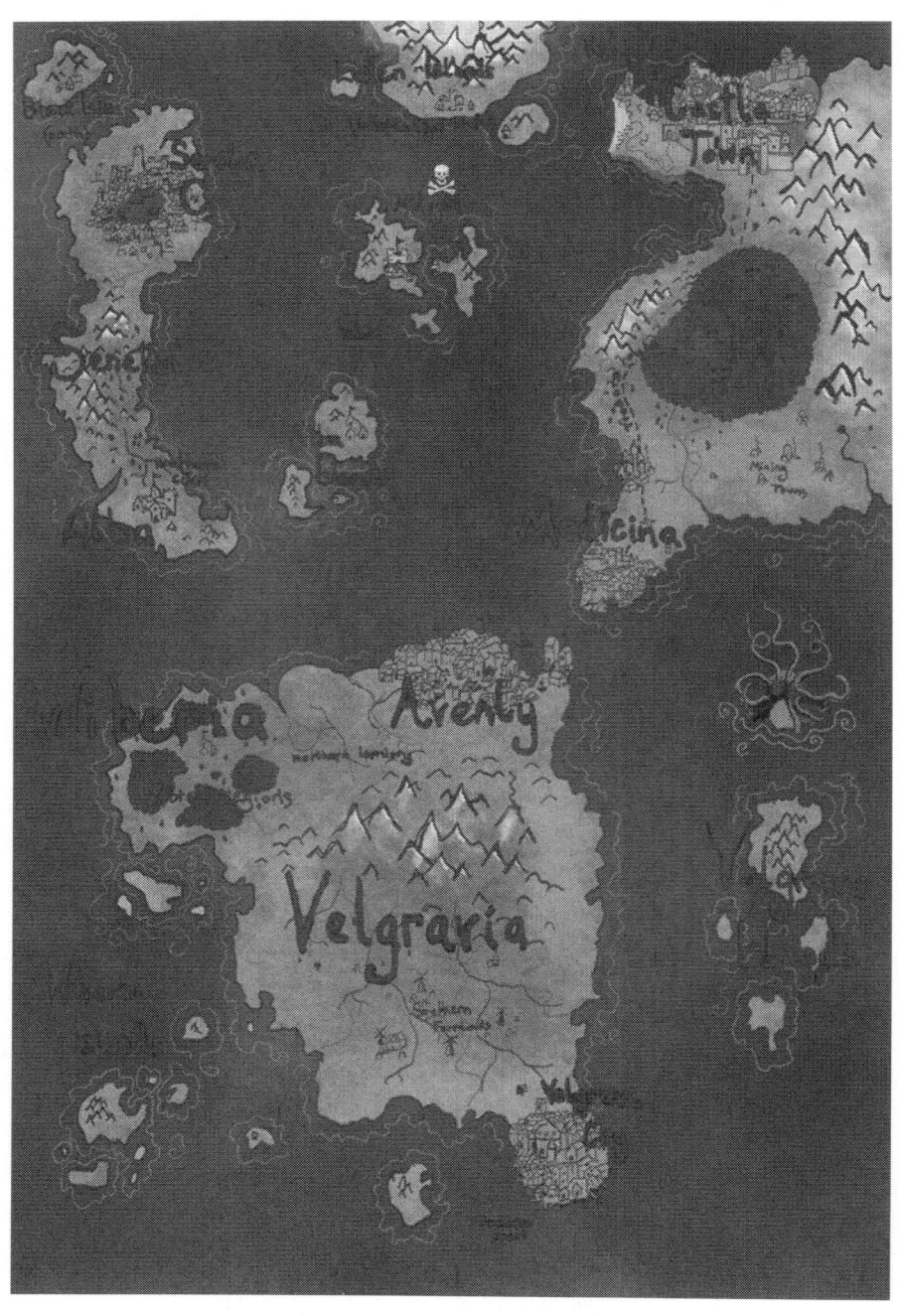

Image by Oliver Lavery

Prologue - The Final Turn

Shanaki was tired. Not the sort of tired that a person feels at the end of a long working day, but the sort of tired that brims lightly below the surface for an age until the bearer no longer has the strength to hold it back; a prolonged, lingering tiredness. Yes, Shanaki was feeling it today as he walked his daily walk from his rooms to Menagerie Square. What added to this was that today the heat and humidity had lifted the pollen out of the air and drenched the atmosphere with drowsy inactivity. The cats that sat on the walls clawed and stretched their shapes, and rolled into the shade as the sun slowly worked its way across the sky. The nobles, in their layers of proper clothing, huddled behind silk parasols or under rooftops, and the workers daydreamed away the afternoon under the sluggish sky. Though Shanaki was in the winter of his life, he had a strange feeling that morning, a feeling that only shows itself on rare occasions in a single lifetime; a fateful signal that an important change was about to begin. He looked up in the direction of the clouds, waving his finger to feel the flow of the breeze, and he felt the tension build. The calm before the storm feels much like the calm after, and as a seasoned performer, he knew a pathetic fallacy when he was in one.

The ancient city of Senelin is famous for its labyrinthine streets. These streets pile on top of each other with winding staircases that lead you down to its logic-defying underbelly - where the less fortunate are forced to dwell - or up to the great gardens, or further still to the bridges and towers that view the metropolis from the sky. These citadels towered over him as he made his way to the centre, to a glass building on top of a hill.

The building in question was one of the few pieces of architecture left over from before the modern wars and was yet to be renovated for some stately purpose or business from the south. The square used to be a menagerie of sorts, hence its name, where the old kings once kept tropical birds that had been brought back from their travels to the southern cities. Now it was filled with the bustle of early morning shoppers, underneath its wide and deep glass frame with a skylight roof.

At the centre of the building was a large Elkien tree. It had a trunk greener than any leaf in the forests surrounding the city, florid with glow as if it were bathed in moonlight and not captive in its oversized greenhouse. Its branches reached all the way out of the building, through the hole in the top and right out into the sky. If you didn't know any better, you might feel like it was breathing. It was, of course, breathing - in its way - but that is something that can only be explained by complicated magicks that make all living things breathe. But anyway, that is a story for another day.

On the far side of the square were grand raised beds with flowers from all over the northern islands and provinces: deep purples, reds and greens, and winding shapes that intermingled with each other all the way to the ceiling. To the other side was a cluster of proud-looking shops, old specialist sellers with the most peculiar stock. One of the shops sold nothing but watches and in another was every single book ever written by the southern scholars on the game of Sailor's Squares. Collectors would come from far away to visit these little shops, but they made most of their money from passersby, who often browsed the stores curiously and perhaps picked up the odd keepsake or two. On the corner, as you entered from a street, was an ice cream and coffee parlour, which shipped in ice from Black Isle every morning in the summer and was ever so popular with the local gentry.

Today, like most days, in a perfectly worn-down curve at the bottom of the Eiken tree, Shanaki the storyteller would dwell.

Shanaki was an old man with ruffled grey hair that once was black as night. His eyes showed his years, as if they could tell a thousand stories in a blink, yet all the while something in his countenance gave a whimsical air that made it very difficult to tell his age. He was a careful storyteller; he would never lead you down a dark path without planting a light at the end of the road, and he would never tell you a story of grief without putting mirth somewhere in the middle. If you were listening hard enough, you might even wonder if he himself was descended from one of the fair folks who'd once inhabited these lands a millennia ago. The very folk he told stories of today.

Travellers didn't exactly come from far and wide to listen to Shanaki's unique style of storytelling, but once inside this famous square they'd often stay to hear him speak. They'd linger at the back, whilst the local children gathered together on the moss and mismatched marble in front of the Eiken tree. Travellers in Taverns would say 'You must visit Senelin City if you travel far north enough, for the strange old buildings, and the art, and the winding streets, and the food, ' and as an afterthought, they might add, "... and if you do happen upon the King Tristain Square, stay and listen awhile to the charming storyteller. I do hope he's still there."

That same storyteller sat for a while today before starting his turn, watching the crowds gather, and when the muffled tones had dulled to a soft hum, he took a breath and drew them in with a clear-cut and undiluted storytelling voice that pierced the air like a bird at dawn.

"There were once four tribes protecting the world," he said, "There were the Healers, the Warriors, the Seafarers, and those who saw beyond what eyes can see. These tribes once lived in harmony and connected the world through supernatural gifts that were bestowed upon them by a higher power. In this world, communities lived far apart, and little was known of the inner workings of the world. There were struggles and hardships but, still, the people lived their lives mainly in peace. The four clans communicated from the four corners of the lands, as the Channels were clear and they trusted the natural order of things. When they died their knowledge and experience went into the ether, and their spirits guided the living through the power of the Tor. There was a door that provided access to all the known powers of this world, and this door was sacred, but this door was hidden…"

"No, come on!" said a boy at the back, before Shanaki had even had a chance to put his own twist to the tale, "Don't tell us old children's tales that we can learn in a temple! Everyone knows that story. Tell us something real, as true as you can make it."

Shanaki was not at all surprised that the oldest myth in the world wasn't going down particularly well that morning. Everyone did know that story, but not everyone knew that his version was quite different. He considered starting a tale about the northern privateer trades, as there was a group of young people who were on their way home from the schoolhouse who he knew were quite partial to an adventure tale. He looked around, some shade-chasing travellers had paused by the stream and were sitting, smoking pipes, vaguely aware that they'd walked into the start of something and waiting to decide whether to set their load down for the afternoon. Even some locals who had heard his stories many times were scattered around the square. The nobles who were nursing coffees had turned their chairs away from each other to face him.

It won t be a bad haul today, he thought to himself, *if I can find the right story for it.* He fiddled with his beard as he checked the coins in his hat and looked out at his audience. He could stop in at the local tavern on the way back home for his dinner and a mug of ale if all went to plan. It was, he suspected, partly his forty years of travelling the world, telling and collecting stories, and partly the heavy rain that now started to build, pattering against the glass all around them, that gave his audience all at once a sense of safety and comfort within the warm walls of the menagerie, and a sense of unease at the thought of leaving the building, with the quickening tempest so plain in their sight.

He was just introducing the main character of his chosen piece, Captain Creet, when through the mutters and light echo that was cluttering up the cavern, came a deep, booming voice from the back wall, "Tell us about the tales of Adrianna, the woman who ended the world."

Shanaki stood up from his crevice in the tree trunk and looked around at the crowd, others were looking around too, some rolling their eyes or tutting, "Who speaks?" asked Shanaki.

A drunk man, gin bottle in hand, slowly approached the tree. He stopped behind the students and, with the utmost poise one would expect from an old trooper, he took a bow.

"I do know the tale of Adrianna, my friend," said Shanaki, ignoring the disdain from the crowd at the tables, "Though it is an old tale. I have only heard it once or twice," he lied, "I am afraid I would not do it justice. Besides, it is not as commonly loved as my other stories. I fear it would not be popular amongst my gentle listeners," he said with an air that he hoped sounded earnest. No harm in investing in a bit of light flattery to get the numbers up.

The drunk man lifted his hands as if he were about to dance a jig, "Oh everyone knows the tale of Adrianna!

> THERE WAS A DIFFERENT TIME MY FRIEND
> WHEN ADRIANNA WALKED
> SHE SPOKE THE LANGUAGE OF THE TREES
> AND WITH THE GODS SHE TALKED
> IF YOU WANT TO KNOW THE STORY
> OF WHEN SHE BROKE THE SKIES
> YOU'LL HAVE TO FIND THE MOUNTAIN
> WHERE ADRIANNA LIES
> IF YOU WANT TO KNOW THE SECRET
> OF WHEN THE WORLD WAS NEW
> YOU'LL HAVE TO LOOK INSIDE THE EYES
> OF ONES WHO SHE ONCE KNEW
> THEY WHO LIVE AMONGST US
> BUT DO NOT KNOW THEY ARE
> THE ONLY WAY TO FIND THEM IS TO
> KNOW BEFORE YOU START
> OHHHHH ADRIANNA... ADRI..."

"That's quite enough of that, thank you, sir," said Shanaki with feigned irritation, as the crowd of students giggled.

"I would like," interjected a softly spoken man from the group of travellers, who had an accent that sounded like he came from the eastern lands, "...I would very much like to hear the story of Adrianna. I have heard of it, but not in the same way as they say. In my country, we call her Adrienne, but I do not know the full story. Only pieces." The crowd offered murmurs of agreement that Shanaki was now unable to ignore.

Shanaki sighed into his worn cape; he felt old, achingly old, older than the building in which he'd been sitting these past many years. He wondered if he could in fact do this. Stories, after all, get adapted throughout the years in order to stay relevant to modern audiences. He didn't have to tell it exactly as it had happened, did he? He could still tell the story without running the risk of being censored by the king's guard.

Shanaki was known for being very popular with the local children. He was known for not adapting his stories to meet less sticky ends for the young people who hung around the square; he would not shy away from the gruesome details of the Warrior Lothian, who journeyed up to the abandoned forests of the North and met with monsters in the mountains, or the Pirate, Little Jill, who travelled all the way from Black Isle Cove down to the southern farming lands on a rowing boat, only to be arrested for piracy as soon as she crossed the southern border. Shanaki spoke the truth, the way adults tell stories late at night when the tavern is asleep and only a few souls are awake, loaded with whisky, and eager for a tale that will make their blood rush. But this was different, this was everything.

No, he thought. This story, above all, if ever told in full again, deserved the attention to detail that he was known for. *The irony of it all,* he mused, *is that this requires the energy of a young man, yet when I was a young man, I would not have dared to venture upon such territory. And of the story? If only they knew... but if not me then who? If not now, then when?* He looked down at his crinkled hands and sighed; he was indeed tired. *If not now* he resigned, *then never.*

Shanaki got up to stretch his legs and take a turn about the room, processing the scope of the task before him and taking in the clientele once more for luck, to gauge how to pitch his tale. This would be his final curtain.

The strong smell of freshly made coffee and pastries wafted through the room, past the smartly dressed gentlemen and ladies in crinoline sat up like dolls at the tables facing his makeshift stage. It passed them and seeped right through to his pit, where the young and rootless waited on tree branches. Boys and girls dressed up to the nines and boys and girls in beggars clothing sat together, distinguishable only by the superficial clothing upon their backs. They sat there, chatting and waiting for the story to start, nibbling on walnuts and apples from the stores outside. For now, they were unburdened by the labels that time and society would eventually imprint into their status, and dictate the small domino-shaped decisions that they made each day: who should I speak to, where should I choose to sit, who am I in relation to you?

For now, the smell of coffee represented nothing, but one day they would wake up to it, either as an unquestionable entitlement or as a painful reminder that they would forever remain on those branches, stuck down to the sides whilst the porcelain dolls rose up. The young had all the time to bring their make-believe status about, but for this small moment of time between now and adulthood, where they knew of the world but were not conditioned yet to know the ways of it, they could remain anonymous amongst their peers; they could be anyone and they were equal.

It was to them that Shanaki addressed his story, not to the punters in the coffee shop, not even to the weather-worn travellers at the sides, or the traders sheltering from the rain, but to the young, for stories have the greatest impact on those whose minds are not yet made.

"We all think we know the story of Adrianna," said Shanaki, "How her father killed her mother to escape for the Consortium, and brought her up on an invisible island where he taught her illegal, powerful magicks, and of how she eventually brought the world to its knees, destroying all power and order, but this is not that story. So firstly, let me tell you how it was before, in Adrienne's small corner of the world, before her world went dark. Let me set the scene…"

Chapter 1 – Wiberia

The corridor was dark, lit only by a fading torch at the foot of the stairs. He had asked to have the Keeper's Lamps replaced the day before for this very reason. The apartments lay over Velgrave Square, and at night you could see movement in the hallways facing the east of the city if you were walking in the public gardens below. He skulked along the hallway and knocked on the brass handle of the door to the furthest chamber. The door opened ajar and he pushed it to, just enough for him to slip inside, and barely tapped the stone wall as he closed it.

A woman was sitting in an old leather chair. She looked solitary, pensive perhaps, as she weaved a small piece of material by a low burning fire.

"Have they arrived?" he whispered.

"Yes," said a woman, "a messenger came not half an hour ago. They are here."

"Good," he said, "fetch the girl."

It was a humid summer night in Velgrave, but the lateness of the hour meant that the only people about would be those who wished for their comings and goings to be hidden in the darkness of night. All who did so surely were up to nothing good. They didn't ask and you didn't look, that was the deal.

They took a cart to the southern edge of the city. The girl was wrapped in a blanket and hidden at the back, along with the few possessions that he'd seen fit to bring along on the journey. Each casket was hidden inside a gillie box, the sort that was used in trade and would need to be shipped back to Avenly Port, where they could be filled with goods headed for Velgrave's markets.

They stopped at the checkpoint. A gangly old guard, who by his tone wasn't pleased to have been left alone on the night shift, peered inside the vehicle, and then back at the man and the woman who were driving the horses.

"What's your business?" he croaked.

"We've plenty to pick up in Avenly," said the smuggler, "I'm hoping to get a head start before the commercial ships arrive in the morning. The summer is very much upon us, and I want to pick up premium goods for the social season. I'm sick of having to settle for makeshift vessels because my servants are too incompetent to make it there in time," he said as vituperatively as he could, so as to mimic the most self-important of Velgrave's courtiers.

The man held his stare, and for a moment it seemed as though he might ask to search the cart. The smuggler reached his hand inside his pocket to grab his blade, ready for the worst.

"That will be fine," said the old man, and sat back down into his seat, taking a sip from his flask.

The cart rolled on for another hour in silence. Neither the man nor woman spoke but occasionally looked at each other with uncertainty. After a while, the air started to taste like the ocean, and the sound of light waves grew ever-present. They stopped the cart at the beach, where three sailors were waiting for them.

They unloaded the contents of the cart, including the girl, who yawned and sneezed as they moved her onto a small fishing boat. Two of the sailors then mounted, leaving the third behind with the cart. This third man was young, and not dressed like a sailor at all, with the straight back and strong presence of someone of a much higher status. The smuggler farewelled him warmly, handing him a gold-plated book and a small wax sealed note. "For your keeping only," said the smuggler to the boy. The boy nodded and nervously clasped the package to his chest.

The smuggler and his accomplice then boarded the boat, and with that they set sail: drifting out to sea under the cover of nothingness, never to return that way again...

The homestead stood on one of the eastern islands offshore of the Wiberian forests, the coast was not half an hour's ride from the nearest house on the mainland and three hours' ride from there to the nearest market town. Though the Central Lands were a well-established island region of the world by then, there were still many uncharted islands within its reach that had not been settled on. As we know, the southern powers in Velgrave had taken advantage of this and placed experimental, New Order 'communities' on them, and this settlement was no different. The Great War had been in stalemate for many years by then, and the privateers who were hired by both the north and south kingdoms tended to keep to the trade routes and rarely ventured this side of the southern mainlands. It was as far away from society as if it had been five regions away.

The base consisted of a number of small stone buildings built around an older house, with three stories, balconies and whitewashed walls. Out of the context I have given you, you might imagine it to be one of the smaller houses of the southern farmlands, with its oversized porch and rickety balconies encasing its frame, but this house was not like those grand southern houses. This settlement was alone on the island of unmanned forest, deep and dark at night and full of flourishing nature by day. The island didn't even have a name and didn't stand out on any maps, it was a green spec off the coast of Wiberia. Back then, Wiberia wasn't populated like it is today; it was an extension of the forest region, with the occasional valley occupied by little hamlets dotted amongst the wilderness. Next to this, the island that lingered on the coast was an uncharted pothole of a place, and other than the ten or twenty people who dwelt there, there was not, and is not still, another human to see.

Ten minutes 'walk from the settlement was another building, which went unnoticed in this unnoticed place. It had once been used for servants, ostensibly, and though the outside of it was barren and unkept, the inside was warm and contemporary for the times and its occupants had filled it with evidence of a life well-travelled.

There were objects scattered throughout from all over the Central Lands; a worn down rug that had been brought from the grand shops in Velgrave, art from Senelin City and strange vessels from Keeper's Cove that now sit at the back of antique stalls for collectors to marvel at, but in those days these items served practical purposes for modern magicks. At the side of the house was a used study, with books from the four corners of the world and papers scattered over surfaces. There was a small but hearty kitchen, with a Forever Stove (one of those said vessels) and the sound of the seagulls flying away from the shore drifted inwards on summer days when the shutters were left wide open.

This was Adrienne's home, and it was the only home she could remember with genuine clarity. It was a feral place, where the wildlife roamed free and the game was plentiful. She spent her afternoons hunting with a crossbow or catching fish off the rock pools to the north of the island, which every child - no matter where from - would learn to do at an early age; back then the island nations took pride in their surroundings.

For two hours every morning, Adrienne would receive schooling from her father: they would drill through ancient languages, geography, and northern history, and towards the later hours of the morning he would teach her to make things out of wood and string and materials from the forest, a favourite pastime of his. Kernavin taught her the ways of the land; how to tell the changing of the seasons by observing the movement of animals and birds; how to catch a fish and build a shelter; how to weave a basket out of reed; how to start a fire.

This was all done with patience and without the restrictions that she would have received if she'd been under the eyes of the Consortium. Yet other than this, he distanced himself from her, always so preoccupied with his work and planning his travels to Senelin City in the north - an event that happened three or four times a year when he would leave Adrienne completely alone. The love he showed was in providing her with the skills she needed to survive, but she would only feel the benefits of that much later.

Instead of seeking the attention of a seemingly reluctant parent, Adrienne became accustomed to hanging about in the kitchen with the serving lady, an old friend of her father who had journeyed with them to this place at the start of it all. Adrienne watched her source herbs to create tinctures and healing creams, and this was not at all a fruitless use of her education, as Adrienne learned that it was not good to rely on apothecaries for such things: the more things are done for us, the less we know of the world. She discovered how to heal a wound using things you can find in any woodland, and how to create the perfect tincture to calm fear or give confidence or encourage trust.

Adrienne mirrored her father's behaviour, keeping herself to herself. She became solitary and did not mix with the children in the settlement. They were forbidden to eat with anyone who hadn't pledged themselves to the order, and besides, she found their ways amusing at times and troubling at others. She found that the children did not seem to think or question unless instructed by the elders. They would sit and muse upon the Channel, referring to their books, but Kernavin said that these conversations sounded more like quotations than musings. The Channel was to be respected, not worshipped.

And so, in her early days, Adrienne's world was filled with the unpredictable love of her father, and the unconditional love of a friend, who lived with them and whose presence kept both father and child afloat. Upon meeting the lady, you might think it impossible to tell how old she was. From the looks of her she couldn't be more than fifty years of age but her hair, raven black, was full and luscious and her eyes, which saw right through you, looked simultaneously bright as a newborn and old as the world itself. She had a sort of spritely elegance about her, sometimes a flicker of mischief that though she had hidden well came out when you would least expect it. The lady's name was Elsen, and though her story is ten times as long and unusual as you would expect, this is not her story.

Adrienne made it her mission to tease out stories from Elsen about the great Laten Islands, far northeast from here, where the woman had grown up. Adrienne longed to know of the towering mountains and great caves, of the volcanic rocks and the great castle in the cliffs, as for now, in this quiet corner of the Central Lands, all she had were stories.

This is the thing about stories. Every person you meet on the street has one, whether they see it or not. And every time we start to tell a tale of one, we are constantly tempted to go off on a tangential tale of another, as each story collides and meshes with our own. For what are stories without other people, other choices and other lessons touching our own?

Then two things happened next, which changed Adrienne's relationship with her father and put into place the building blocks for *our* tale. Firstly, Adrienne became particularly interested in the way objects functioned, she was forever taking items apart and putting them back together again, a new activity which bonded them together, with their mutual interest in the workings of things. Secondly, as she got older, she became better at noticing the intricacies of her father's behaviour. She observed at times that many of the adults in the settlement came across as strange to her, and Elsen explained that something truly awful must have happened to them to make them like that. In turn, she noticed how tormented her father was, how preoccupied he seemed, and how secretive. With that, she started to develop her own ways around his perceived coldness. She became accustomed to sitting around in her father's study in between lessons; asking questions, often picking things up and turning them upside down to see the cogs and wires that kept them together.

Her father didn't often use the Revolter; it lay in the corner of the study gathering dust and occasionally acted as an extra surface for the constant migration of papers and books around the room. Adrienne could probably pinpoint every single time she'd seen it work, with the dark shadow of someone's profile and their voice speaking a message within its small stone walls. However, there was one message that she'd seen over and over. It was a short message, and it hadn't even originally been sent to this Revolter or intended for her. Her father had journeyed with it from Velgrave on that dark night so many moons ago. It was a message from Adrienne's mother, sent to them the week before her ship went down and she'd disappeared forever, 'I have arrived safely, cannot stay long, but please tell Adrienne that I love her.' It was short, and you could barely make out the shadow of her figure standing and waving her last goodbye, but it was something.

"But how does it work?" Adrienne asked, prodding at the buttons of the great stone machine.

"It's complicated magicks," he said, pouring hot water into his tea cup, whilst the dog shuffled at his feet. He cleared the Revolter of the paper mess that had accumulated on it during months of lack of use. "Imagine a single moment in time: you speaking a message to me. Well, the Revolter harnesses the energy of that single moment. Every Revolter is made to the exact same form as the very original, sans the code on the front, which is changeable. You change the code, and you connect with the Revolters who match the code as well. This is why you should always keep the code closed when it's not in use. The machine can be susceptible to spying from those others who have your unique code. It's no good for transporting sensitive information."

He pointed out a metal dial and the twelve interchangeable metal symbols on the front of the large stone casing. "When the Revolter harnesses the energy of the message, so too does any matching Revolter. So, whoever is on the other side automatically receives the message, which gets copied from the original source - you - and then is erased at the original Revolter…"

She seemed weary of the object now, "You get destroyed?" she said incredulously.

"No, unless you put an object directly into the Revolter, it can't destroy anything at all, just the memory of the message," he said, "A Revolter can't hurt you as long as you use it correctly."

Adrienne looked at the empty box of dark slate-like stone, "It's quite big actually." She poked her head inside the square shaped stone casing, "What's it made of?"

Like a shot, Kernavin reached forward, "No!" he jumped up and pulled her back, "Do not, not ever, put yourself or anything you value inside of that machine. It's dangerous. What did I just say?"

Her heartbeat sped up at his reaction; he could be blunt indeed, but he rarely got angry, and it shook her. She sat down on the floor next to the dog and put her small arms around its neck, looking up at her father.

"Even if you were my age," he said in as kindly a tone as he could muster, whilst holding back gritted teeth, "I still wouldn't allow you to put anything in the Revolter. It's not built for that. What can happen to a living being is unthinkable."

"You said it was safe! And I've seen objects…" She questioned defiantly.

"Objects are not people, Adrienne. There is more to a person, or an animal, than our physical being. Humankind playing God will lose its humanity."

He put his arms around her shoulders and leaned in. "In the end, we must trust our own understanding of the world, we must give ourselves the chance to see clearly what others cannot, but we must respect the nature of magicks. You can search all you want inside any contraption but without the energy from the Channel, it won't work."

He picked the dog up and put him on Adrienne's lap, "But for now!" he said, and she laughed a mildly embarrassed laugh, as he donned a cloak and put on a theatrical voice.

"Let me tell you a story about the Keeper's Cove, in the dark forests of the mountain regions of the north, just a day's walk from the bohemian port of Medicina. Yes, that's a rugged old town, full of old sea folk with strange stories of mermaids and sea beasts. If you ask them, they might tell you about Keeper's Cove, but only after the tavern is quiet and the lights are low, and the whisky bottle is nearly empty will they tell you about the Danaan. Keeper's Cove is home to the Gedogin people, or Keepers in the common tongue: the oldest people in the northern lands. But the forests there are filled with bandits, ogres, witches and worse… Some say, the Danaan - who disappeared from our world without a trace - walks in darkness. You will not hear them coming. It is said they can float in and out of the Inner Channel, that they can read your mind, control your thoughts and turn plants into magick that can cure any disease... or send a person into madness."

Adrienne had heard this story time and time again, and though she was no longer a child she was at least grateful for the intimacy that she craved. Though the act itself was the same, her experience of it now was quite different. There was something in her father's expression that she had not noticed before. It is funny how much a look can mean to an adult who has felt adult things, and it was an adult that Adrienne was now becoming. What was in that look though? Was it pain? Regret? Fear? Or maybe a mixture of all three? She couldn't tell.

Either way, something about that moment triggered Kernavin into teaching Adrienne more than he'd intended. It was here, in this home in the middle of the wilderness, that Adrienne first learnt about the Inner Channel. The real Inner Channel. This wasn't anything like the old tales of the Channel and myth of the great clans; nor was it the Channel that emerged out of the heads of would-be monks who inhabited the grand house in the square, with their manipulated tales of the new order; nor were they the old wives tales told around campfires when all voices able to hold a tune have dried out. This was the real Channel. The Channel that fills the spaces in between, fuels our intuition and seeps into our dreams. Even in those older days that I speak of now, many would have brushed it aside, but some still lived it for real, some still felt it for real, and believe you me, there were solid reasons why anyone back then might have found it far easier to cast it aside. For these were the days when dancing tree roots swimming out of an open fire were not just a spectacle: they were a window from the blinking world into what was lying just underneath, as alive as ever.

These lessons were simple, more than anything, Kernavin's goal was to open Adrienne's mind to the idea that these things were in fact impossible, to counteract what was spoken of in their small world on the island: the idea that we accept a Revolter for what it is because we see it work all the time. What is it then that stops us from believing that other Magicks work and exist in the world?

Chapter 2 - The Silent Lessons

It was dawn when they first arrived here. Blinking in the morning light, Kernavin carried his daughter off the boat at the estuary; their belongings following them in watertight chests carried by tired sailors.

They had lived in a house in the grand city of Velgrave in the south. His wife was a serious woman, with golden hair and a southern tan, but by far anything you might expect from a kept woman of the south: an important woman in court and stately matters to say the least. She had been a member of the Consortium, the organisation that the southern crown had supposedly put in charge of 'state welfare and security for both the northern and southern kingdoms.' Regardless of anyone's political alliances, this woman had done good work to maintain peace between the Consortium and the Gedogin, and it could not be denied that she had prevented many rifts that would have done great damage throughout the central lands. This was also how Kernavin and her had met.

Her sudden loss had a great impact on many things, including the safety of her daughter. She had been the daughter of a great and powerful lord in Velgrave, whose influence reached much further than the court of the southern Kings. Adrienne's father, who was a free-thinking northerner and - not being on the list of people she'd be permitted to consider marrying - was not so much in favour with southern society. As with all stories of this nature, they fell in love in spite of this, and with high disapproval from all at court, had married. This elevated Adrienne's father's status and lowered her mother's, though neither cared much for that. Yet her death had left in question who was responsible for the child's future, the father or the grandfather.

In those days, the options that a family of adequate wealth had to educate their children were limited. Often children were taken away from the diversions of the south to conduct their education elsewhere: they would be versed in all courtly things in a southern farmland plantation, or they would be sent to a Consortium-run school in the city.

The other option, the new path less taken, was to send children to one of the outer islands where the new religious orders were forming. This was done in the hopes that they would grow up to understand the Channel in the right way, though it was said that the Consortium had a bigger hand in this than they were letting on, and the real aim was to seek out those who displayed great abilities and might be of use to their regime. However, this too was not without its downsides, as there is a thin line between respecting the Channels of nature and indoctrinating yourself into a new and poorly researched, dogmatic way of living, where power corrupts just as it did on the mainland.

Kernavin's father-in-law had sought to send Adrienne to one of the southern farming families, where she'd learn to be a lady and prove useful to him in court. It was suspected by all who knew the family that Adrienne's father could not bear to lose his daughter and wife at the same time, and so had escaped to one of the villages in the Wiberian mountains with her. They had often searched for him there to no avail.

Kernavin chose the lesser-known option and took up with the pious people on this island, offering them a bribe and hiding in plain sight.

On the final day of her childhood, before her Midmoon celebration, Kernavin had taken Adrienne away in a carriage with his wife's devoted friend, Elsen. They packed up as much of their things as they could and travelled overnight to a boat, which took them all the way up the coast. He wasn't even able to give her a proper celebration for her Midmoon night: not the bonfire, feasting and dancing on the main street of the central courts of Velgrave that were afforded to other young women when they turned of age. Instead, they celebrated that night, with a small fire and a box of Tricken cakes that her father had brought with him. He held a small pouch of Keeper's dust in his hand, took out a handful and ceremoniously blew it into the fire. Light shot from the fire in thunderbolt shapes and ended with a small spark at the end that looked like a fairy dancing. This is why they called it Keeper's dust, for it looked like the famous cove, home to the Gedogin Keepers who guarded the secrets of the inner Channel beneath the quiet of the forests.

Over the years, Adrienne had grown into a tall, handsome woman, with dark hair and deep eyes. She wore her hunting knife, which had once belonged to her mother, around her neck in a golden clasp, alongside trousers and shirts for hunting that had naturally replaced her muddling dresses from Velgrave. If she'd stayed in Velgrave she might have become quite skinny, but her time in Wiberia, hunting and working on the land, had made her uncommonly athletic in appearance. She was so much so that when she did reach seventeen, she started to feel self-conscious around the other girls at the settlement, who barely chose to talk to her already. *And why would they?* Adrienne thought. She took her tutelage in private and chose to be alone in her breaks, scouting the island, hunting and hiding with no one but her dog to accompany her.

Though they were technically pledged to the new religious order, they were left pretty much to themselves in their outpost. They were not required to attend meetings, and only occasionally socialised with the people who lived there. It was widely understood that Kernavin had donated a large sum of money, which granted him and his daughter anonymity. As a result, the few children on the island treated Adrienne with something like disdain.

If you'd met Adrienne at that time, you may have thought her quite odd. A quiet girl, so far from the world in which she'd been prepped to inhabit, not socialised in the way that most Velgravian girls would have been since their Midmoon celebrations and initiation into the fold of debutants. If you'd taken her back to Velgrave, she might have been shy around boys her age, and uncomfortable around those very people who she was meant to befriend. But even if she'd overcome all this, she wouldn't have wanted to fit in, not anymore. She no longer belonged in that world, nor did she belong in anything other than in between, waiting patiently for her purpose. She grew unassuming, an observer and then a doer, trying out thoughts and activities with curiosity, scepticism and openness that allowed her to see the world around her with fresh eyes.

Adrienne's relationship with her father did change as she approached adulthood, especially with her lessons becoming far more interesting to both parties, but it became a working relationship, one built on respect more than overt affection. When Kernavin did show his love for Adrienne, it was fleeting and almost childlike, too fast for her to catch. He was a calm man, but distant, and there was something about the quiet way of life on the island that appeared to soothe him, if only in a melancholic way. He told her that he had been born a farmer, and he would end his days as a farmer, though he had not lived as one. It meant that he was entirely alone, and his daughter, in those crucial years, was alone too. He was haunted by his demons, ones that he could not share with his daughter other than when they forced their way out. He was prone to fits of grief, which a person could be forgiven for blaming entirely on themselves.

She longed to see more than this little island, to visit the greater north, the great industrious stronghold of Keeper's Castle and the mystical lights of Keeper's Cove. She longed to visit the Laten Islands and the mining towns to the east. Her father had told her of the northern city of Senelin, home of art masters in the winding city, and eventually, after much pressure from her, her father had given in and began to take her with him to his meetings in the north. Alba City was the home of the academics, the universities and the court of King Tristain. The fastest route to the north was the great port of Avenly, where all boats headed north and south passed through, and because of this Adrienne got to see the Wiberian forests all the way up to the north coast and the port too.

    Alba City, however, was not to Adrienne's liking. This was mainly because she was seldom allowed to see any of it, and instead was confined to the same house of her aunts with the same set of adults at their seasonal gatherings. Adrienne often found these visits wildly unsatisfying as the adults would generally huddle together in private meetings and instead of going outside to explore, she was forced to sit in on them.

    She would patiently wait in her corner of the room, listening in on conversations with lords or important Gedogin members, discussing court gossip or recent news from the war. They always ended in a dinner where each and every person would drink and spill even more gossip of a distant cousin's shame or an affair at court. This happened about three times a year for about three years, and after this long, she no longer looked forward to her trips away and often begged to stay at home with Elsen, but it was no use. She was required; it was the only thing her father required of her. She did, however, enjoy the dinner parties that preceded these events. Diplomats, it would seem, were much more fun and much less guarded, with a bit of meat and ale in them, even if the gossiping was vulgar to her.

    Adrienne missed her mother, but her memories of friends from the South had faded. In a way, in trying to keep Adrienne safe from the world, Kernavin had inadvertently taken a part of her childhood away. She did not spend much time around people her age, and as a result of being surrounded mainly by adults, learnt to speak and behave as one, especially when living in the woods required her to fend for herself much more than any young lady at court: both practically and in terms of finding her own amusements.

Aside from this, and by all other accounts, this home was not far from idyllic. Nothing, however, weighs up to its romantic ideal, and therefore many of these moments were lost on Adrienne, as she in her inexperienced youth was not aware of this one important fact: that it would end. Life itself is only valuable because we know that eventually, it too will leave us. It is finite and anything finite is running slowly and steadily towards a loss.

"Your aunt has left for Senelin City, Adrienne!" Kernavin reasoned with her one late Autumn evening, "Going back to Velgrave will steal your sense... you'll get trapped in their narrow minded..." he looked at her quite seriously, "Or they'll try and take you away. I can't risk your grandfather trying to..." he was angered now but regained his composure, "I want a better life for you."

"A better life?" she exclaimed, "You don't like anyone here! The nearest town is a two-hour ride away!"

Her father considered this for a moment, pulling off his glasses to polish them in the light of the misty morning window, "Do you think you know less of the world than a child in a grand house in the city? Do you think they know anything about what happens out there?"

She stared at him, confused.

"Why do we always journey along the canals to get to your aunt's home?" He asked.

"Because the lower streets of Senelin are dangerous, the people have very little and..."

"Did you know that there's a bridge that will take you all the way to the top level without having to look at the filth and poverty that so many people have to tolerate?"

"No, I didn't know that."

"The war is between who?" he asked.

"The north and south central lands, over trade routes," she replied.

"But who really?" he egged her on.

"The Consortium enterprise is encouraging the war on either side because they want to use it to gain back control over the Gedogin at Keeper's Cove, who are essential for trade and magickal advancements."

"Good." He said, "Last time…"

"…but what about the Consortium," she interrupted, "there are lots of people who say it's they who are essential for magickal vessels and trade."

"There are those that do," he said, then briskly changing the subject, "Last time we visited Alba we met with who?"

"The Laten Islands Ambassador," she promptly replied.

"And what can you tell me about him?"

She lay back in her armchair, ready to play the game, "He's a good dinner companion, very funny. He speaks the common tongue perfectly. His wife breeds horses," she continued like a tedious courtier, "He's furious that his island's needs are being practically erased by the Consortium. The Privateer's island is on the Midpoint Islands, which is Laten territory, but the northern islands refuse to help. Laten Island trade is expensive, but that's not because they have to get so much taxed and shipped in from abroad that they have to balance it out, although that's only part of it."

She was silent for a moment.

"Go on" he gestured.

"The reason they're being treated terribly by the northern king is that the North wants to control them. Their islands would be an important base in the war if the south were to make it that far: they are the closest to Keeper's Cove, but King Tristain's court still won't acknowledge the Laten people and their king, because they don't see them as entirely human... they call them Radan"

"Good," said her father, resting his case.

Adrienne looked a little unsettled, struggling to find her words, "Are they though?" she asked.

"Are they what?" he blinked.

She looked away, "Human?"

"Of course they are," he said, seriously, "they were isolated on the island for a millennia, and because of the food they ate and the resources available on the island, only the smaller people survived. It's the natural order of things. They have a complex history, based on older political alliances than this, but the argument lately has been that they don't merit the same rights as other northern states because they aren't... human enough. Not quite beasts, not to be imprisoned or feared, just not human. But you should never use the word Radan, Adrienne. It's not a term you use in polite society."

"What does it mean, really?" she asked.

"It means what I said, Adrienne," he was looking away from her now, "It means not human enough, and it's a foul word used by foul people."

"But the ambassador used it when talking about his people!" she said.

"He did, he's allowed to use it, he was defending his people. If you were to use it back to him, well, it would take the power away from his people rather than grow it," he said.

Kernavin picked up his papers and made for the door of the study. "That'll be enough studying for today,

Adrienne," he said, "take the afternoon to go out with the dog, or help Elsen with the herbs, whatever you wish, but make sure you take some time to think about what we've discussed today. I don't want it going over your head."

With that, he left the room and went upstairs with a flourish.

There are truths, which are so universally accepted, so ingrained into our language, that to pinpoint the exact moment we learn them is as difficult as to remember our first thought. There are truths so complex that it's hard to know if any single person has the exact same understanding of its complexity as another: as if there are infinite numbers to learn and each individual conceives their share of those numbers, never all of them, but enough to establish a shared language; enough to know that blue is blue but not to know that we see the same blue. The Inner Channel is one of these concepts, but in order for you to know Adrienne, I must explain how she saw it. The Inner Channel, part myth, part proven magick, part undiscovered bounty, was once the source of all the world's energy. It was a Channel of connection that stretched throughout the world in lines, invisible to the naked eye. It was fuelled by a collective energy, and knowledge, of us and of our ancestors who we still send to the skies today in the hopes that they will reach it. It was the cause of all our intuition, instinct and gut feeling, it was harvested by those who knew how, it was turned into pure energy, and it was stored in vessels that powered magickal objects for the common people. Those vessels were created at its source, the great Tor of Keeper's Cove. This was what Adrienne knew at the start before a new door was opened for her.

It was mid-Autumn, back in the south; the farmers would be bringing in the last of their harvests, and the villages and towns would be preparing for the harvest dances and feasts, thanking their ancestors for the food and strength to pass through the winter unharmed. The days had been growing longer and felt more drawn out than usual, and though the forest was quiet, lately there had been a tense silence engulfing the area.

    Adrienne was lying in the small, unoccupied bedroom of their wing, where her mother's things were kept. Her arms stretched across the ancient four-poster bed, looking at the untouched ornaments on display. Courtier's clothes stood in the wardrobe, and a woman's dresser was left untouched on the far side of the room, as well as a woman's travelling clothes hanging on a coat hook. She had taken to coming inside a lot lately, as something about the energy of the woods made her uneasy. Elsen had told her many times that everything impacted everything, down to the last tiny movement of a leaf or the cry of a cricket. By that logic, whatever was happening on the island and in the forests of Wiberia was the result of something bigger happening beyond. The war between the north and south provinces of the Central Lands was affecting the cities; she knew this from the many times she'd been told so whilst away with her father. Though there were no battles, it was present wherever they went. But realistically, the dark smog of war in any form could hardly be impacting the birdsong, the movement of insects or the flow of water in the stream, could it?

    Adrienne was watching the magpies dance outside the bedroom window, on the branch of the tree that stood tall to the side of it. She'd always loved watching the magpies. Many times her mother had told her an old wives tale that magpies used to be magic folk, who were given great knowledge to help protect and nurture their species, but they used their powers to gain worldly wealth and so had been banished to the skies, cursed to never overcome the need to hoard gold for the sake of hoarding gold. They now used what was left of their foresight to signal onlookers of their luck, in the hopes that they might eventually redeem themselves. Lately, she'd seen many lone magpies, and it had filled her with unease.

Kernavin and Elsen were downstairs in the kitchen, arguing over whether to turn the plums into jam or chutney. This was a regular occurrence, and as long as the season's spoils were plentiful, they'd both state cases for more chutney or more jam: they'd argue over the complications of making both, conclude that both had their merits and would eventually come to the conclusion that a few chutneys and jams would do but the rest could be used for wine. These were the rare pockets of time when her father would wake up a different man, where she saw glimpses of what her father once was, a gentle man who cared about inconsequential things like jam and merriment. They would last no longer than a few days here and there, and he would soon sink back into his darker moods, yet she cherished them more than she was even aware.

Adrienne walked downstairs and past the kitchen when her father called to her. "Adrienne!" he shouted, his mouth full of half cooked plums, "I have something for you, come!"

She followed him into the study, where, scattered around, were objects from a different life: old used Stair Books from the southern Velgrave Court that had been displayed in cabinets for the intricate metalwork etched into the covers, a state-of-the-art stone Revolter made using the most modern technology, that could receive messages from the furthest islands of the northern lands within minutes of being sent. On the rosewood desk were several open books, *The Modern Magicks of Medicine, The Scholars of Alba* and *The Magickal Research and Advancements of Keeper's Cove*. There were drawers full of thick wads of parchment, a branch of ivy that had slowly grown its way through the ancient window frame without the room's occupant noticing, and a chair next to the desk that was covered in dog hair.

"I had been waiting to give you this when you were older," he said, rushing to his desk, "but I guess you're older now." He closed his eyes and gestured for her to copy him by playfully placing his hand over her eyes.

"Now listen," he said, picking up a small, shell-like ornament from the desk. At the base of the object was a crest made of metal, it had a convex symmetrical shape in the middle, surrounded by what looked like fire flashing from the centre of the circle outwards. Shaking it, he told her to put its open end to her ears.

Adrienne heard a buzzing. No, she wasn't actually hearing it, it was as if the noise itself had bypassed her ears and gone straight from the atmosphere into her head, where she heard it clearly and distinctly.

"What is that?" Adrienne was astounded.

"That's the Channel," he said, "The great Inner Channel, the source of all magickal energy, of our own, of our ancestors, and of the world. We are all tuned into it to some degree, but if anyone is using it for a specific reason, then there will be an upset in the vibrations and you will be able to hear it through this. It's called a Noch."

She took it from her ear and began to turn it over in her hand, taking in the shell-like quality and heavy weight that clearly indicated it was metal.

"Remember that most people don't know that Channel is there at all," said Kernavin, "In the world, if you speak of it, they will think you are telling ancient tales. Most people see it as a concept more than anything, and yet unbeknown to them, they are still driven by its nature. They subconsciously take it in but are not aware of it. Some people, lately more and more, shut themselves off to it completely, relying on new ways to harness it, using man-made vessels from Keeper's Cove," he paused, "And it is said that there are some rare few, who still do not need these methods in the slightest."

"The Danaan aren't real," said Adrienne, "They're a made up story and even if they were real, they died off long ago," she said absentmindedly, inspecting the crest on the bottom of the object.

"Perhaps," said Kernavin "But that's not to say that there are people out there who can learn to listen to it. I'm just trying to explain," he seemed to struggle with his words, "Using a vessel without appreciating its source is like extracting the goodness from a plant without any respect for the plant and all the other properties that are needed. In moderation, and when necessary, vessels do great good," he gestured to the vials of tinctures lying on the dark oak cabinets in his office, "We understand the principles of magick but humanity turns it to poison, abusing its power, and disrupting the Channels it is governed by. You should never disconnect something from its source. This can have irreversible effects."

She handed him the Noch, but he closed her hand around it and pushed it back to her, "I know one thing to be true," he said, "I will show you ways to tap into the Channel lucidly and even so it may never come, but if it does, above all you must remember not to doubt it. That is the first and most crucial lesson. Do not doubt that it is there, even in your darkest of moments."

Chapter 3 - Childhood's End

As Adrienne was approaching her eighteenth moon, the occupants of the settlement moved on. Their movement was growing in the south, and they had been called to a larger, more public dwelling off the coast of Velgrave, where their message could burn brighter and their recruits were easier to access without the long journey west through the forests. Though the search for harmony with the Channel was the goal of many, it could not be acquired through following strict, man-made rules. Their fruitless cause, which searched in all the wrong places, provided the people of the South with an excuse to give up their freedoms at the promise of salvation and purpose: something long lost in the years of losses behind them. To not have to think, to not have to be held accountable for your choices, well, that can be desirable. And it was desirable to many people back then, as the great war between the North and the South had been raging quietly onward for the better part of a lifetime.

The only people who stayed on were Adrienne, her father and Elsen, though now Adrienne was nearly an adult, there were ever whisperings between Kernavin and Elsen about whether it was time for them to leave themselves.

Adrienne was by the house, watching the fish swim upstream, her dog swimming along for sticks across the water. There was a strange energy in the air, as there had been for weeks, but something else far more immediate was about to take its place. In that moment, a loud crack awakened the dog's senses; he stopped playing and barked a loud bark that startled the wildlife in the bushes before him. Instinctively Adrienne picked him up and searched the horizon. She moved forward and hid deep in the underbrush, then climbed to the top of an oak tree, looking towards the house. There was another loud crack, and she heard the front door to the house open with a thud. Elsen and her father were both inside, but something told Adrienne to stay put. No one called out or knocked. There were intruders, but who? And how on Earth had she not heard them coming? She looked towards the front of the house and could just about make out three shapes of men, with no horses or cart to speak of. Another loud bang came from inside the house and the three men turned to walk towards the house. She held her breath, though she was too far out of earshot for anyone to hear her.

    Other than an occasional sailor with a message arriving once in a blue moon, there was seldom another soul to visit them, yet here they were. She could just about make out banners on their cloaks, red with clashing purple. Privateers? Pirates? Her father had told her that pirates were poor souls who had been banished from society, forced to commit crimes in order to survive, hardened by the cold and hunger they faced daily. He said the only difference between pirates and privateers was the law and a solid wage on top of their plunder. He'd told her that understanding them made it easier to forgive them, but harder to kill them, which was sometimes necessary: there was no reasoning with an untouchable soul.

    She tried not to let her imagination run away with her, telling herself that there were many cases indeed before the worst-case scenario. There was something though, a feeling in her gut, the energy had changed, the energy that her father had told her so many times to trust beyond anything else. She climbed higher, up onto a branch that was sheltered by leaves. There was something clinical about the smoothness of this operation, as there was no shouting or chaos. These were not messengers, but they were not bandits either. She tried to control her breathing to calm herself. Her tiny dog was barking at the foot of the tree, so she skulked down and picked him up and hid behind the trunk.

She looked around the corner and saw that the riders were now standing still outside of the house. The Noch started glowing brightly in her pocket with a white light; she picked it up, but before she was able to put it to her ears, she heard the buzzing directly in her ears. *"Adrienne."* She heard what sounded like Elsen's voice in her head, but it couldn't be? *"Stay where you are."*

There was a loud thud from the centre of the settlement and more shouting. Though Adrienne tried to hold onto the dog, it was too late. He barked loudly and bound out of her arms towards the house, up through the open kitchen door and again there was a loud crack, twice more, and then silence. Not the silence she'd felt before, a more immediate change of state that signified everything. Two more loud bangs engulfed the area.

They always say that when the big moments come, they never feel like we think they're meant to - the big ones that is - and Adrienne, observing that thing, which ripped her life apart, felt as though she was watching an event happen to someone else entirely. She breathed heavily into her cloak. All around her was unnerving, thick tension. It was too sudden; too like the aftermath of a broken pot on the kitchen floor; too deep a space between watching it fall in slow motion and the task of tidying it away. The synapses were too far apart, so she just sat there in the empty space in between.

A flicker of thought landed at the forefront of her mind, and then it was gone: was that Elsen speaking to her, or had she imagined it in the height of the moment? At the time Elsen's words had entered her mind like an absolute, yet now she was questioning them. Had her father heard it as well? And if so, did he hear her words in time? In time for what? Was it real or had she just wished it, a fantasy in a moment of deep, deep confusion? And then, before anything could land long enough to stay in her memory, she forgot it as if it were a dream.

In a state of shock, Adrienne walked slowly and purposefully to the house, where an uneasy quiet filled the space. She turned and walked into the kitchen, slowly. She sighed as she saw no blood, nothing broken other than a chair that had clearly been thrown across the room and knocked down a couple of jars off the wooden table. This had all happened all around her. The dog was dead at the foot of the door, tumbled into a pile of fur and blood.

As she passed the door, she knelt down beside the dog's limp, lifeless body, and for a split second, she felt her heart sink. She gave herself a moment to lament the loss of the poor animal, who had never hurt a soul, who was loyal and innocent and who had no hand in any human corruption, who didn't deserve this. Somewhere at the end of that brief second though, another part of her had taken over: the part that acts out of necessity. The survival instinct she'd never known was there.

"Adrienne," said a voice. She turned to follow it and walked toward the stairs, Elsen was lying with her back propped up against the wall, bruised and beaten, heavily breathing. "Adrienne you must get to Keeper's Cove: it's the only place that's safe for you now. Get word to the Gedogin, you must tell them that the Seldelige..."

"The Seldelige?..." Adrienne repeated back to her, "It was pirates Elsen, they destroyed the place..."

"You've never seen the Seldelige, Adrienne, it was them..."

"Neither have you! Seldelige are great, terrible creatures. These were men."

"Yes," whispered the woman, "...they found us!"

"Yes"

"... they took your father," Elsen whispered in a faint voice, "Tell the Gedogin Alliance what has happened. You must seek them out, the message must come from your mouth only, no one else can hear it. Find your aunt in Senelin, she will protect you. Keep the Noch close... don't let anyone take it... don't trade it..." she was delirious beyond question.

"What do you mean?" said Adrienne.

"Something else," Elsen pulled Adrienne closer to her as her voice lost its power, "No matter what you hear, no matter what you learn about your father or me, we did everything we knew to be right. I loved your mother...!"

"I know you did..." Adrienne held Elsen's head up as her breathing lessened, "It's OK," and then the woman went silent, completely.

Without thinking, slowly and methodically Adrienne, an eighteen-year-old girl who had only ever witnessed the death of game that she'd hunted and eaten, took in the scene. It was like something out of a tale of old, the only difference being that in a tale of old she would rescue her father, swear revenge and chase after the pirates, wiping them out one by one. But Adrienne was not in a tale, and she was suddenly, entirely alone in the world.

She ran through the settlement to the sea and looked out at the ocean. The small fishing dock had no sign of use, what's more, there was no way of knowing if the privateers had even used it. You could dock anywhere on this island on a rowing boat, and the north-facing cliffs meant that you could get a ship right up to the edge and away in the time it would take Adrienne to run there. She walked the perimeter of the island, searching for any sign that might lead her to knowing where her father had been taken, but to no avail. There were no footprints, nothing left behind on the island other than the chaos they'd caused in the centre of it. But what was she thinking? Even if they had still been there, she couldn't take on a ship of armed men! Her father was gone and there was no piece of knowledge she could acquire, no valiant risk she could undertake. She was powerless.

She walked back to the house, the adrenaline that had led her to the beach was slowly fading, only to be replaced by sluggish exhaustion and uncomfortable, shallow breathing.

She resisted the urge to weep, pushing down her pain quickly before it bubbled to the surface and took over. Fighting through the growing ache that pushed on her chest, she pulled Elsen out into the garden, wrapped her in cloth and laid her down beside the dog. She knew what needed to be done, but it seemed to take all the strength she had left in her to get even this far. She laid them out in the flowers and sat with them for a while, her hands holding onto the grass as if it was the only thing keeping her up. She sat with them for so long that the sun had long gone down before she even noticed it was nighttime. She protected them with another layer of woollen blanket and left her next task for the following day. She then walked, like an inhuman shell, into the parlour room, crawled onto a chair, pulled a rug over herself and slept.

She woke in the early evening, though she had no way of knowing how long she'd been there, or for how many hours or days. Her empty sleeping mind stayed with her for a few moments as she woke, and the sun glided in through the trees onto her forehead. And then a cold wave of pain worked its way through her body when she remembered again all that had happened here; the sweet escape of sleep did not last long enough, in spite of the haze of numbness that was growing in her.

She walked into the kitchen and gulped down a large glass of plum wine. She took all of the items off of the long wooden kitchen table - dirty dishes, a vase of wildflowers, salt and pepper bowls - and placed them carefully on the countertop. She pulled the table out of the kitchen door and over to where the fire pit was, out into the woods a little further off in front of the house. She picked up the dog and placed him on the foot of the table. He was heavy and stiff and felt alien to her. Then, with all her might, she dragged Elsen through the flowers and rolled her along the wooden top of the table. She stocked up the fire pit with wood from the wood store and straw from the stable, and she sat down in front of it. She gave herself another long while to sit with them, staring blankly at the logs and listening - just listening out for anything from the Inner Channel, like her father had taught her to - not even knowing if this was the right way, but hoping she might hear a sign from somewhere, that Elsen was still with her, that she was not alone. But she felt nothing. Instead, she took a matchbox out of her pocket, stuck one against the side and threw the burning match into the fire pit. When the fire was burning bright she walked back into the parlour room, lay back down on the sofa again and slept some more.

Adrienne awoke the next day and gazed up at the tall ceiling of the parlour room. Sunlight was shining through the windowpanes onto her skin. The heat made her face feel tight as if something was cracking on its surface. She touched her cheek and felt the cracked blood that had dried down the side of her face. It was not her blood. For the first time since she'd been alone, she became aware of the state she was in physically. She'd been sweating and shivering, and her hair reeked of soot and smoke. She felt certain that there was a clammy layer of dirt and mud that covered every inch of her. She sat upright into the dust that the sunlight had uncovered with its rays and dragged her unwilling body to the stream to bathe. She washed her dress and undergarments in the stream too and left them to dry on the vines at the side of the study window. Afterwards, she walked up to her father's room and started to dress in her mother's travelling clothes: a pair of dark ladies' trousers and a shirt and cloak. She had never been allowed to wear them on the grounds that they did not fit. But now they did, perfectly.

    She walked back outside and knelt down on the grass. She felt refreshed by the warm sun drying her clean skin as if it had almost washed away the events that had led her to reach this morose state. She walked into the kitchen and downed another glass of plum wine, this time with a crust of bread with butter, and some old cheese left on the countertop. The food tasted dry and inconsequential in her mouth, but she forced it down. Then she walked back into the parlour room and lay back down in the same spot she'd woken up in and fell back into a deep sleep.

    She woke again a few hours later feeling famished. She went straight for the kitchen and took out everything she could find: salted meats that were hanging from the ceiling in the pantry, an old fruit cake kept from last year, plum jam on stale scones, bread and crackers, apples. What food she couldn't eat was wrapped up and packed into her satchel - not acknowledging that this would lead to her eventually leaving the place, just going through the motions with as little consciousness as she could muster. If she came across other items from the kitchen - a hunting knife, bandages or homemade ointment - she would absentmindedly tuck this away in the satchel as well.

    In her day-to-day life, Adrienne was good at breaking tasks down, chipping away at them so that by the time she came to really focus on them, the menial parts were done. She was the sort of person who would hide something valuable in such a safe place that she'd forget she'd done it. In some way, maybe she knew that she was preparing to leave, but acknowledging anything right now was too painful. Her subconscious mind was preparing her, but her conscious mind - her rational thinking, her emotions - was somewhere else; dark, recharging and absent.

Adrienne had no way of knowing how long she'd been in this state, but things were starting to seem a little clearer. She'd packed enough food to last her two weeks at most, and it would last. If she was careful, and only ate the food that would keep good for the least amount of time, she could keep the majority of it for emergencies.

The study was completely destroyed, as was the dusty Revolter that had lived, barely touched, in the corner for so long. She walked into the empty stables by the side of the house, which was where they kept outdoor camping and hunting gear. Underneath was a chest that her father had kept stocked in case of emergency. It contained a small medicine kit full of herbs and healing tinctures, scissors, and a tinderbox. There was also a small axe, a cooking cauldron, a compass, a map of all of the Central Lands, a pouch for water, and a blanket. From the study, she took two books: The Inner Channels and her father's journal.

The journey from the mainland estuary by river boat up to Avenly Port usually took them three days, but that was with three of them, she would have to take full charge of the oars this time. She reckoned, maybe optimistically, that she could make it in four days. The route was familiar to her, and the war hadn't reached this far as to make any single traveller she met on the way suspicious of her. The hunters that often travelled from the southern farmlands into the forests didn't come near the river so as to avoid hitting fishermen. Wiberia was a wild land, but it was still inhabited enough by people to need rules to protect them. Geographically in the south but legally part of the northern provinces, Wiberia was the only place in all of the Central Lands that was impartial in the civil war between the two states, which had been going on for as long as Adrienne could remember.

She stood, holding all she could possibly think to carry in her satchel and travelling cloak wrapped around her, and faced north. In moments such as these, we can do three things: we can fight, we can play dead or we can run. Knowing there was nothing left in this place for her to either fight or hide from, Adrienne did the only thing she could - she ran. As she took the boat to the mainland and clambered through the forest on the shore. Nothing seemed real, as she stopped and got her bearings, accessed her options and checked the surrounding area for extra food. Adrienne checked her pockets to make sure her father's purse was still safely tucked inside - nothing had yet sunk in. Not even when she woke on the cold ground covered in dew and grass after taking shelter amidst some trees for the night, not even then did it hit her. Only when she had walked across the stream on the seventh day and spotted the first signs of a town at the foot of the mountains, after the first new gulls from the north coast had flown over the cliffs in plain sight, did the truth sink in: the Seldelige, whoever these men were, had taken her father away, and she no longer knew if he was dead or alive.

Adrienne stood on the crest of the hill with her pack at her side. Before her lay Avenly Port, 'The gate to the north 'as the southerners called it. Here, contracts for voyages were signed in the distinguished boat houses, and on these streets, every single day, the ships recruited crew. It was here where sailors stopped over between journeys to regroup, and it was the premiere port for journeys by sea either north or south. The air was muggy, and the climb had been relentless. Sweat dripped down her side, and as she wiped it from her brow, she realised what a state she was in. Her sweat was mixed with dirt and grease from the journey, and her hair still smelled of burning. She decided to leave it as was, as she needed to look less like a southerner and more like someone who had been jobbing on the ships if she was going to get the ride she needed north.

Many ships passed through Medicina port to drop and pick up trade from Keeper's Cove instead of heading up the coast. The privateers who were stationed nearby often disrupted anyone heading near, regardless of which province they belonged to, so many took the longer but safer route up the dirt road and through the woods to the Keeper's Gates. It was a place she had heard much of but never seen with her own eyes, and she longed to see the bright cliffs light up at night: the illustrious markets run by the townspeople and the castle where each invention of the modern world was created.

It was hard to admit to herself whilst in the midst of such confusion and despair, but now with some distance, she felt it: she hated herself for not being able to save Elsen; she hated herself for hiding; but most of all she hated herself for not believing she would prevail, that her father was lost forever. Brief moments when she remembered the power that lay where she was heading gave her sparks of hope, and even though she knew it was the type of hope of a child who was promised that they would see something extraordinary if they could just hold on from one moment to the next, it was all she had. She couldn't trust using a messenger to send word, and a messenger would only take the journey she was now embarking on. The Revolters could be watched, especially if she used a public one, and she would have to pay someone else to work it for her, and she couldn't trust someone else. There'd been talk of giving out licences so they could monitor what happened on the public revolter routes, which was no good for what she needed it for, even if she could find someone to help her. She couldn't risk her message running into the wrong hands or not reaching the

Gedogin altogether. She had to soldier on because this was also the only chance she had to rescue her father.

For the first time, perhaps in her entire life, she realised how little she knew of what those men and women in the Senelin meetings had actually been doing there. It had never seemed important to ask, or interesting to know, but now, pulled into the centre of a seeming storm, she had wished she'd listened more. Whoever had attacked the house, whatever they had wanted with her father, it was not a black-and-white situation. It was messy, that much was clear. She'd have to keep her cards close to her chest for now and hope that Keeper's Cove had the answers she so desperately needed.

Chapter 4 - The Philosophy of Hoods

It was late when she arrived in the town, and most of the terracotta buildings had closed their shutters to the artificial light coming from the Keeper's Lights on the street. She followed the sound of clanking metal tankards and sea waves crashing against stone across to the promenade on the beach, where the taverns and alehouses were still open.

On the street were all sorts of entertainers, some who worked in the town, but many who had come onto the harbour from the troupers 'ships that were docking here to ready themselves for the coming season. She walked past a plethora of fire breathers, acrobats, storytellers and warlocks and then joined a crowd who had gathered around a spectacle in the corner of the road. At its centre was a tall, lanky man in a silk robe who was muttering pseudo magicks to himself and wafting his hands in the air as if summoning something from the great beyond. It was a well-known myth that any magicks could be created using this sort of spectacle, but performers often liked to milk it, pretending that they had great Danaan magicks at their fingertips. He flicked his fingers and lit six large candles with them, before bursting into some strange, lively song, which caused the onlookers to cheer and whoop. This was the sort of thing Adrienne had seen in the market towns time and time again. A man would simply hide a vessel under his coat to make it look like he was using old magicks. Everyone knew this, or at least they knew that there was no such thing as a Danaan warlock, but nobody wanted to think about that. Once the supernatural was tarnished, so was the mystery and the spectacle, and that was the fun of it.

As Adrienne walked around the corner, she found herself on an entirely empty road. She remembered this road, it was usually filled with market stalls, but there was nothing but a broken chair outside an abandoned store, and not a soul to be seen.

She made her way past an inn called The Hunter's Shoe. This was the place she'd stayed with her father and Elsen on their travels to Alba City, and she knew that the people there would treat her fairly and protect her from any less than honest sailors who might think her an easy target for theft, but she couldn't risk being recognised. If there was one thing she'd learnt from all those hours surrounded by diplomats, it was that you never knew who was working for who, and she was pretty sure this translated to the streets of Avenly, where the whispers were sold to the highest bidder. The sheer fact that she had no idea who she was running from or what her mission was meant that if she did end up in a sticky situation she wouldn't be able to trick or talk her way out of it.

So, instead of docking somewhere familiar for the night, she kept going and walked into a busy inn called the Port Arms. She'd been to this inn once or twice, and it was run by a madam, named Sue Proctor, who looked after some of the brothels on the other side of the town as well as a few other businesses. The brothels at Avenly had a good reputation for staying on the side of the women, and Adrienne knew for certain of one other business owned by Sue, which was on the main street: a charitable organisation for women who had escaped dangerous ways of life or unwanted marriages. It was well circulated that though some of the intake did end up moving on to the more reputable brothels, many were guided towards help in other ways, and the madam, therefore, had a clean and respectable reputation. This inn would therefore be a safe haven for the next few days. Somewhere she could hunt for a ship and, in the meantime, stay out of any trouble.

A boy was shuffling around at the back with empty ale tankards while the smell of a hearty broth was rising up between the floorboards from the kitchen. Sailors and business owners were scattered around the room, bartering and sharing intel. She walked up to the boy and handed him a copper Tadall coin.

"A room please, if you will?" she said in what she believed was her most weatherbeaten sailor's voice.

"I'll have one made up for you, miss, if you don't mind waiting down here in the meantime whilst we get it cleaned up? Will you be having supper?" he asked.

"Yes, I'll eat," she said, handing him another two Tadalls, "I'll also need pen and paper, and a messenger ready to send a letter off tonight."

The boy nodded and took the other two copper coins out of her hand.

"Another thing," said Adrienne, "Can you tell me what happened to the market on the harbour? It appears to have been abandoned, there wasn't a fire was there?"

"No ma'am," said the boy. "Attacked by the Consortium's soldiers, the Seldelige. They've been operating around these parts lately, it's not good for business I'm afraid. Apparently, they appeared out of nowhere and attacked the stalls. No one has a clue why, and most people are too shook up to talk about it."

Now, the Seldelige are long gone in the modern Central Lands, but at this point in our history, they were entirely new to the world. What people knew of them was about the same: great monsters rumoured to have been discovered in the iced mountains of the lands beyond the north - though no one could tell you where this account had come from. Apparently, they were broken in by the Consortium to do their bidding; unlawful and unruly, without an inch of humanity in them.

But why would they be in Wiberia? she thought.

"Do you know anyone who was there who might be willing to talk to me?" she asked.

"Only this gentleman whose stall was attacked," said the boy, "he was badly hurt and they had to put him up in rooms next door. He's been talking... saying they were disguised as men. He's an old fellow and his mind isn't all there if you ask me. He's one from the mountain towns..."

He returned moments later with a key to her room, a piece of parchment and a quill and ink. She sat in the corner on a small table, hidden behind a booth. She finished the stew, which tasted like winter nights, and she sat with a glass of ale to write her letter:

Vivian, I am in Avenly and travelling north to you. I will hitch a boat but not sure how long the journey will take. No more than a month I should suspect, as I'll be taking a longer route past Keeper's Cove. I have a message to deliver to the Gedogin, as I do to you. I can't say any more but please wait for me, Adrienne.

She read it through, it was short and to the point, but not risking giving anything away if it fell into the wrong hands. Her aunt should be able to read between the lines enough to realise that Adrienne was alone for a reason. Her aunt worked for King Tristain, trying to establish peace in the war effort and lobbying for funds to keep the commoners fed. She was also in constant touch with Adrienne's father: if she knew more than Adrienne, which Adrienne strongly suspected she did, then this would be enough for her to piece things together for now.

She sat by the fire for a while before retiring to her room, considering her options. The temptation was to go to her aunt in Senelin straight away, and perhaps then she'd have means of safely getting word to the Gedogin by one of their Revolters. She figured there might be some sort of secret Revolter that the Gedogin used, which couldn't be accessed or hacked into. She'd certainly heard of such things, and surely if anyone had a safe network of Revolters it would be the people who'd created them? However, there was always the risk that her aunt would not be in Senelin when she arrived, or wasn't connected to the right people to get a message safely across. Then another thought struck her, whoever had taken her father would benefit very little from intercepting any message confirming his disappearance. Who was she trying to hide this information from? What if it really was the Consortium who had taken him? The men never saw her, so they thought that her father, hidden on an island, had disappeared and no one would find out until it was too late. It was then that she realised that she was not only protecting him, but she was protecting herself.

  She was the unknown survivor of an attack and the daughter of a fugitive, she had been protected all this time as well, but from what? It was as if her entire life had been based on covering up a lie. There was clearly so much that she didn't know and as a result of that she felt more alone than she could possibly have imagined. What was worse was the thought of what might happen after her journey was over, if they couldn't rescue her father. Even with her father's purse, which she'd taken from under the kitchen floorboards - nine Glames full and maybe four more worth of copper Tadalls in change (this was about a month's living for any commoner in the north) just enough to get her to Keeper's Cove, if she was smart about it.

  Then, all at once, she felt her body give in to tiredness, having permission to do so now that she was in front of a heated fireplace, cosying into the leather tavern chair with the food and drink warm in her belly. Her body would get used to these journeys perhaps, and the stress would lessen once she became more comfortable with this new way of life. For now, the worry and the panic and the physical tiredness was rinsing her dry. All this and yet a small inch of her looked forward to acclimatising to her new way of life. As much as she lamented what she'd lost, for in journeys we grow, and we discover.

In the morning she got up early, breakfasted at the inn on fruit and oatmeal provided by one of the barmaids, and walked across the road to the King's Tavern. She spoke to the owner, telling him that she was a distant cousin who had heard of the attack and had come to make sure that the old man was OK.

She was brought upstairs into a dark room, blue curtains closed to the morning sun. In here it smelt of musk and stale air. The man was lying, propped upright in his bed, an uneaten bowl of broth on his bedside table.

"Good morning," he said knowingly, "I believe you are a distant cousin."

Adrienne blushed, "I apologise, I wouldn't have gone through such measures to meet with you, only it's important that I talk to you."

The old man shrugged and gestured towards a small glass bottle on the table, "I have had few visitors because there are very few left who would visit me. I am a lone soldier now, just me with my goats in my mountain home, not that I'll be heading back there any time soon, 'said the man, 'It is nice to have company, even if you are here to kill me."

Adrienne laughed at this, "I am certainly not here to do that," as she said this the man started coughing, "Would you like me to open the window and draw some air into the room?"

"Yes please, they won't let me open it... something about safety. I am sure that whatever is left out there to take me, it won't be half as bad as what has already happened."

Adrienne pulled the curtains back and lifted the windows up as far as they would go. Fresh, sea air immediately drifted past her face and into the room. The man stretched his face forward and breathed a deep sigh, "That is what I have been dreaming of," he said, "I always find it's the simplest things that cause the greatest pleasure after a big, unwanted event."

Adrienne sat back down and looked at the man with serious eyes, "That's why I've come. I wanted to ask you about what happened."

"Well," said the man, "Where to start! I was in the middle of haggling with a southern woman over the price of my honey jars, and out of nowhere there were three creatures. I say creatures, well they looked quite human to me, only that now I know they weren't. I will say that something about their energy was off... it was like they weren't really there at all, just their bodies... and their skin was pasty and leather-like, and they felt... taller somehow. I remember one of them laughed. It was cold and empty, piercing... Their clothes were strange, and I couldn't see their faces underneath their hoods, as is the way with mysterious things, but I could swear otherwise if you'd shown me a picture of them I'd have called them some form of human."

"Did you hear anything? Before they arrived, I mean?"

The man thought for a moment, "No, 'he said, "It was all a blur."

She thanked him and stood up to leave. As she stood, she noticed the state of the man's clothes, his lack of possessions, the scratches on his face.

She placed two gold coins from her purse on the table next to him, "So you can get home to your mountains," she said.

Just as she was at the door the man spoke again, "There was a crack," he said.

Adrienne turned back to him, "A crack?"

"Just before they arrived, there was a loud crack," he was somewhere else now, his mind half remembering, half dreaming.

"Thank you," she said.

Chapter 5 - Shanaki - Old Wives Tales

"It is the most unusual thing for a person's life to change so suddenly," reflected Shanaki, "but tales are retold because of unusual things. It is because they are unusual that we marvel at them from afar. The characters make choices that you or I couldn't imagine possible, but of course, this is not *our* story."

Shanaki lifted his head to look around at his audience. Some of the workers and school children had gone back to their tasks, but the square was starting to fill with new faces who'd been called in by the stillness his story had created in a space that would usually brim and bustle.

"We all know the part of the story where Adrianna travels the world as a spy, fighting the Consortium under their noses, on a great naval ship. And we all know the story of her companions, and how one eventually slew the other. However, and I warn you, the reality of what happened is a little more... tepid than that," as Shanaki spoke directly to the audience and broke the spell, his audience stirred as if out of a dream.

"Every hero or villain's story is, to them, separate from their own legend. Our choices link together with that of those around us, like string linking the paths of our lives. Whether they are good or bad choices is simultaneously in the eye of the teller and the ears they fall on. To speak of such things reminds me: there is another player in this game whose story we must visit from time to time..."

Chapter 6 - The Player's Circle

At first, there was a struggle. He didn't remember who it was with, or for how long. It didn't really matter, as it didn't do any good. The world around him dissolved, slowly and then all at once. His heart rate sped up and his veins filled with unnatural adrenaline. He could feel his trapped arms behind him, held in place by rough, unkind hands, but he couldn't feel his feet or the ground below him, if there was any ground. Suddenly even his hands seemed to disappear and all at once the entire world was faded and blurry. Blankness came for a moment then his feet, he felt it, below him... leaves? Or was it bark? He couldn't see, it was as if he was being built back from the ground up. The wave hit his stomach and then suddenly he could feel his empty lungs. He breathed in a huge gulp and staggered as he began to feel his arms, neck, face again. His eyes squinted as they slowly adjusted to the light. It was cold, or was it just windy? Suddenly he realised the practicalities of such impure magicks and he bent down to hide his naked form in shame. He was sure that if he could just open his eyes it would be OK, but not yet. He let the weight of him drop down to the ground, realising he'd forgotten to breathe... breathe first, then think. Whatever happened he knew he had to breathe first. He felt the ground, whatever the ground was, followed by euphoria, all at once filling him to the brim in one quick wave and then...

Adrienne left the tavern and made her way from the inn down the cobbled streets of Avenly to the port. Her heart was racing. Could it have been the Seldelige who attacked their small island in the middle of nowhere? She couldn't let her childish thoughts run away with her, it was far more likely that they had been attacked by pirates, bandits, privateers even, but not Seldelige! After she rounded the corner she ducked into an empty alleyway and sat with her head between her legs trying to regain control of her breath for what felt like an age. How could her father have left her so unprepared?

She passed the crowds of sailors bidding for places on voyages down to the south, the drunken Navy men on stopovers stumbling out of brothels and taverns, ending their evenings in the bright morning sun and the unvanquished ladies of the night waving off their puffed-up friends. A child in Tamh Day best was unfazed as he passed the scene with his parents, on the way to some luncheon or other. An admiral on one of the docked ships coordinated his sailors as they loaded medical supplies onto carts, bound for his Majesty's hospital. And there were warships, also bound for the south. These strange scenes melded together with synchronicity, as if they had not been opposite after all but interweaving parts of a perfectly balanced painting. There were never any beggars in Avenly, as there was always work to be found here with all the world passing through, and it was without the harsh class structures that moulded cities like Velgrave and Senelin, that the folk here were able to stay afloat.

Street performers were looking to audition for a place on a trouper's ship, and the odd tinker on his or her way somewhere could be found selling their wares in the street. There was also the sobering sight of returning soldiers, some laced in medals and glory, and some steeped silently in trauma as they held onto railings for support on walkways, with scarred or missing limbs. Some still were lying in caskets, carried systematically by their comrades. So, it seemed, the war wasn't at a complete stalemate as she'd been told before.

She passed the crowds and made her way to a narrower side of the port, the northern terminal. This side was less busy, as most of the north bound theatre troupes had already taken the best of the hires and departed in the last couple of weeks, and the warships in the north were mainly stalemated in the northern seas. If you wanted to travel north you had to go around the Alba Islands towards Medicina cove and up over to the far north coast of Senelin. There were supply ships chartered to go straight across the sea to Senelin They were looking for joiners, but they would go west, right into the face of the 'stalemate', or what actual action was left in the war. She'd been told that there were a few naval skirmishes out at sea and that was about it, she hadn't considered what that meant for the people living through them.

Though the stewards on these ships assured Adrienne that there had been little actual fighting for many months on the northern front, she did not want to test that theory, and after all, she had a reason to go east first.

There were also passenger vehicles, which bore the neutral banner, so as not to be drawn into any scurry between the two sides. These ships would stop off at Keeper's Cove and then to Senelin, but even if Adrienne could haggle down the price, it would be, at least, everything she had. *If it s Tamh Day,* she thought back to the young boy in the street, *there may be more opportunities tomorrow.*

As she thought this, a loud thud and a clang came from a navy ship that was harboured in the corner of the port. Someone had dropped something incredibly heavy onto the deck and the crew were shouting and cursing at each other as they picked up broken bits of wood.

"For all my ancestors, what have you done?" shouted a woman from the crow's nest.

A bearded man in an admiral's frock, who had been standing facing the sea in Adrienne's direction, turned and picked up a piece of white painted wood.

"What do you expect us to do now Noah, my boy? Create a soundscape using metal tins and pans from the kitchen?"

The boy, Noah, screwed his face up like a sour grape and sucked at his teeth at these words. He was in fact less a boy and more like a man, though admittedly a little rough looking around the edges, with his short, unkept beard and leather smock. And he was one of those people whose energy, upon meeting with it for the first time, immediately gave off the impression of an unpredictable nature; a capricious spirit that told you he could likely switch moods at any given second; like a battle between benignity and an untamed nature held in place by it.

She moved closer and peered at the object he was holding, curious to see what had caused such an uproar that drew the attention of the entire dock. Once closer she saw that it wasn't wood, it was in fact an ivory key, a key that had once been attached to the large object that now lay scattered in pieces on the deck: a broken piano.

The admiral was now waving orders around the deck, gesturing dramatically to boxes that were being carried up the ramp, back to the broken pieces on the floor, and vaguely towards the sea. He had authority in his actions, yet there was something whimsical about him as well. He was indeed wearing the outward costume of a sea captain, but underneath he had what looked like jupe pantaloons, the sorts of lighter clothing that travellers wore when they ventured further south than Velgrave. His face was weathered from being outside for too long, his body more robust than you'd expect from a leader of a Navy ship. His crew collectively gave off a must of sweat and pipe, and some of them had white and red powder creases in the crevices of their weatherworn faces. It was a theatre ship and a grand one at that. It couldn't be anything other.

The captain turned back towards land and finally spotted Adrienne peering at the scene, he tipped his hat towards her and walked up to the railings, resting his arms over the side.

"And what can I do for you, miss?" he said, curiously, as he threw the ivory key back at the frustrated looking Noah, without taking a second to look where it hit him.

"My name is Adrienne, I have travelled here from the forests of Wiberia and I am seeking passage to Keeper's Cove," she said, "I was hoping you might be able to give me leave to join you until you get to the north, in exchange for work on deck."

The man eyed her, uncertainly. "Why don't you search for passage somewhere more fitting?" he asked, "We need strong workers, you might be better off trying for one of the passenger boats."

"I am of southern tongue sir, but I assure you, I've lived in Wiberia for my adult life, and I barely remember the south. I hunt my own food and I can build and mend. I know a bit of carpentry and a lot of herb lore. I used to watch companies playing in the Royal Cour..." she broke off mid-sentence, "The Velgrave town square when I was a child... I know what you'll need from me and I'm not afraid of hard work... and I could sleep on deck..." she added.

The man looked curiouser still, and a little amused, "No offence meant, miss, but we need people who can carry and haul the sets with the best of our crew, and preferably not to break the equipment before we've even left the port," he cast a shady look at Noah, who was now speaking to a civilian from land about fixing the piano, "And we need people who can think on their feet and deliver quality work. We have a reputation to protect."

Of course, all ships were proud, this was the capital port for seafarers after all. They all had reputations that they believed reached far out of the Central Lands. Adrienne stepped forward and looked the man in the eye, "I am," she said without blinking, "I am all of those things, and you will not be disappointed."

In reality, she'd said it to buy herself time, not in the least bit sure of herself that she could contribute anything to the ship at all, but she had no choice but to push those voices aside. She couldn't offer money as she would need it. She would have to prove her value some other way, and even so, she'd only need to last until Keeper's Cove.

"How about this," she said, stepping a little further up the ramp towards him, "If I can get that piano standing upright by the time you set sail, you give me a shot."

He stared at the girl incredulously, and then, after a pause, burst into laughter.

"You've got guts, missy," he said, reaching out his hand, "I'll take that offer, just for the guts you've got. You can get on with fixing that leg as soon as we get you set up in your lodgings, I have no doubt that between you and Noah something will end up standing, or *he'll* pay for it."

As the captain pulled her up on deck, something fell out of her pocket. They both looked down to see the Noch lying on the dusty ramp.

The man went silent for a moment, taken aback, "Where did you find that?"

Adrienne bent down quickly and scooped the Noch up, stuffing it back in her pocket, whilst doing her best to mask her alarm, "We found them in a pawn shop on our way back from the market town a few years ago," Adrienne improvised, "The man said it was a replica of some instruments used in the north, and that ladies wear them, " she shrugged, "I liked the pattern, and honestly, it's all I have left of..." She trailed off, aware that her story was truer than she wanted to admit to herself. For a moment it looked as if the man was changed, but instead of pressing it further, he smiled sympathetically, revealing kind eyes.

Adrienne was relieved that she didn't have to answer any questions about where she'd come from, or her family, or where they were now, which was too raw in her heart to speak of just yet, let alone make something else up to hide the truth. She'd rather not have to lie to someone who was taking a chance on her, but she must have given away some sense of sadness all the same. The man's expression upon looking at her more closely turned to pity, as if he'd just found a wounded bird on the road that had been hit by a horse cart. "I'll tell you what, you help the lads out on deck and pitch in with the cooking and the mending where it's needed, and we'll take you on. We could use a lady like you to force some manners into them," he nodded towards a woman smoking a pipe and reading a map at the helm, "Especially this one," he raised his voice so that the woman looked up and snorted playfully. He continued, "We're heading across to Medicina first, and then the mountain regions to play to the miners, have you ever been north?"

"Only Senelin sir, and Alba. I need to get to Senelin City, and I need to do it via Keeper's Cove," she answered, "I mean, I'd love to see the lights if you're going that way anyway."

He nodded with familiarity, "Of course you do. We can take you there, sure enough, if you don't mind enduring a few stop offs along the way. We go to Medicina, the mountain mines, then Keeper's Cove," he stopped, "erm, are you familiar with stagehand work at all?"

"I'm a fast learner." she replied, "and by the by, you probably want to check what kind of wood that piano is made of before you go ordering anything. I'd say it's probably Eiken wood, but that's hard to come by at short notice, maybe you could use some of the wood from that lifeboat you've got there. The one with the broken oars, at least until you can find somewhere that stocks it."

The man chuckled at her, resolved, and stretched out his hand for her to shake it, "I'm Thomas," he said, "Thomas Decanté"

Thomas led her onto the deck and past the commotion over the broken piano. They passed men and women scattered about the boat, making the finishing touches to start the voyage. Some of them hummed old shanties to themselves, some of them singing new, ruder versions of the same old tunes. He took her to the woman who'd been reading the map, "Adrienne, this is my second in command, Miss Jill Jones."

Jill looked up at this and instantly reached out her arms to embrace Adrienne into a mother bear hug, the full force of which took Adrienne by surprise.

Jill's embrace was soft and warm and she smelt like lavender. Adrienne was so small in comparison to the woman that she almost disappeared into her embrace. Jill pulled back and stood with her arms on Adrienne's shoulder, "Now let's take a look at you," she said, "I'm not going to ask what you said to Thomas to convince him to give up a place for you, if you fooled him then you'll fool me too. We're all fools on a player's ship, you'll be right at home," she winked.

Thomas raised an eyebrow, "Exactly, don't let her take you in Adrienne. Jill can conjure up the most headstrong Queen this company has ever seen, and she's not bad on the stage either," he said, dryly, "I mean... on deck she's as lovely as a peach unless you cross her. Then she goes back to being a tyrant.'

Jill rolled her eyes, "Enough now, Tom. I'm delighted to meet you, Miss Adrienne. How long are you with us?"

"Only as far as Senelin, ma'am," replied Adrienne, curtseying without thinking. She caught herself mid-curtsey and coughed her way upright, feeling awkward, "Though I hope I can make myself useful on the way."

"We'll have to get you to do a cameo in one of the plays at least," Jill said, walking along the deck with her, "Tell me, have you ever taken a turn as a chicken before?"

Thomas frowned, "Now you ease her in slowly why don't you..."

Jill was quite pleasantly pretty underneath her sailor's stance, and kind seeming while also quite intimidating. Adrienne didn't doubt for a second that she was all of those things.

They continued to walk when a snarly looking sailor did a mock curtsey at her as they passed. She raised an eyebrow and tried to look unfazed.

"They'll tease everyone who's new," said Thomas, "They don't really get a chance these days as most of them are lifers. Best to ignore it, they'll get bored soon enough."

The ship was majestic indeed, like a ship of the line - a warship belonging to the King's Navy - and would have been mistaken for no other if it wasn't for the lack of gun ports. Half of them had been boarded up with planks that had been painted with blues and greens, and the canons that did remain were out of place and unused in the corner of the gun deck, where hammocks were sprawled out across a relatively clean and tidy space. However, there were open gun ports, and they had the mark of black smog signalling that they had been used of late. She kept her eye on them as Thomas led them past and down to the galley through the cargo hold, which was filled with spare sails and rigging nestled amongst brightly coloured costumes and lavish pieces of portable stage set. A large, hooded costume was lodged awkwardly inside a castle turret, with a pot of silver paint and stilts. There was a ferocious looking mask next to it and extra arms made of cloth that had been attached to the hood with wire.

"That's Jill's attempt at keeping with the times," said Thomas, "Audiences like to be scared, and right now this is what they're scared of... the monsters of the Consortium."

"Have you ever seen one?" asked Adrienne, sombrely.

"No," shrugged Thomas, "But neither have most of the folk we play to, and when they do see them, well... terror can do strange things to a person's memory. I doubt they remember what they saw as much as they listen to the tales that pass as swiftly as rumours from one ear to the next. If the people want monsters, then that's what we'll give them."

He led them through a door and down a ladder into the galley, "New cabin girl for you Lorcan," he said as Adrienne's feet landed on the wooden floor. In front of her stood a young man, maybe a year or so older than she was. He might have been the same age as her, only for the fact that he was senior enough to run a galley, for he looked young in his face, boyish and tanned. He was sitting on a chest peeling potatoes, "Can you get one of the boys to make a hammock up for her below?" asked Thomas, turning to Adrienne, "I'll send Noah for you to help with the piano when he gets back from the town with supplies." She smiled at this.

"I'm alright sleeping on deck, I mean that," she said.

"Everyone gets a space down below, Adrienne," said Thomas, his attention already drawn upwards towards the action on deck, "You can sleep on deck if it's warm, but if a storm hits you'll be glad enough that we put a space aside for you." He gestured to Lorcan, who promptly disappeared out of the room.

"I'll leave you in Lorcan's capable hands," Thomas said, "We leave tomorrow at sunrise. Welcome aboard the Player's Circle!" And with that, he climbed back up the ladder towards the chaos up above and left Adrienne in the dark, still kitchen cabin.

She looked around the compact space that was assigned to the ship's cook. It was stocked up to the nines, filled with sacks of potatoes and carrots, barrels of apples and onions and a garden of dried herbs and spices that were left out to dry by the porthole. The floor smelt of fresh polish and in the corner of the room, a cooking vessel made of stone was brewing a stew, which steamed up through the ceiling boards. It was a well-kept space - with pots and kitchen utensils hanging from the cabin ceiling and no need for wood or coal with the forever cauldron. This addition no doubt allowed for the food to be fresher than most boats of this calibre, as well as the fact that they weren't likely to be away from the shore for more than days at a time.

Moments later, Lorcan returned with a cabin boy, who had been instructed to take Adrienne back up to the hammocks. They went deeper into the room this time and emerged from a sea of cloth into an open space at the back with a gap and then more hammocks.

"Most women in the ship are high up like..." said the cabin boy, "So they got their own cabins. There's a couple a ' girls like yerself who are still in the shared lodgings, but there ain't enough for us to give them another room."

She tucked her Noch and purse safely inside her cloak pocket and left the rest of her belongings in one of the small trunks to the side of the hammocks. Before going back to the galley, she took a moment to sit alone with her thoughts. She had done it. She'd found passage and not spent a penny. She just needed to let the chips land where they would and keep her head down until they got to Keeper's Cove.

She joined Lorcan back in the kitchen, he had already set to work peeling the rest of the potatoes for next week's stew. She sat on an unopened sack of onions and picked up a knife from the side table to join him. He looked up and watched her, and then went back to his peeling as if the two of them had been working together for so long that the silence was earned.

The social awkwardness that came from sitting alone with a complete stranger eventually took Adrienne over, and after a few minutes of tightly held breath, she made an offering: "It's a big boat..."

He laughed at her, clearly endeared, "Haven't you ever heard of the Player's Circle before?" he said, shaking his head into his work.

"No, I... sorry, I haven't. I mean... no, I haven't!"

"Well, everyone's seen sea troupes at least once in their lives, even those further inland, but I never met a northerner who hadn't heard of The Player's Circle!" he frowned.

"Well, I'm not from the north," Adrienne confessed.

He gasped, feigning horror, "You're a southerner? Well..." he smirked, looking pleased with the opportunity to introduce a newcomer to his home, "The Player's Circle is the most famous theatre troupe in all the north! Possibly one of the most famous ships an 'all. Most troupes travel around on smaller ships for the ones who do the proper touring, but all the islands of the north are so far apart that to really get any mileage out of a show you need a proper ship. That's how it started, the history of it. Back in the old days when players travelled on land or sometimes barges, out of work sailors would double up as stagehands in the back. Eventually, someone realised that if you put the troupe on the ship, you've got a ready-made crew to start taking the shows all around the Central Lands, and you can pick up odd jobs along the way, with space for cargo and privateering. The Player's Circle is so old that they were one of the first ever, though this isn't the original ship."

"Do you go south as well?" she asked, "I mean, do you go to the Velgrave courts of the southern king? Is that even possible at the moment, with the war?"

"We do, that's where we get most of our money from, the courts in Velgrave and Alba," he said, "you'd think the war would have an effect, but if anything, it's made people want us more. They want entertainment an 'that. There are a lot of places not doing so well because of the war though. Common folk are starving now, and for us, it means they can't afford to tip so much in the hat. Thomas likes us to go there anyway because it gives them hope that things will get better and that they haven't been forgotten."

"That's sad," said Adrienne, "It's not their war..."

Lorcan's eye twitched and he quickly changed the subject, "We thought the southern King would ban us travelling down there at one point, but it seems to have become such an event for his 'Courtly calendar 'that he basically begged Thomas to keep coming," he pulled open a new bag of carrots and started piling them onto the table.

"Don't you care about the amount of effort that's going into this war? I wonder if... surely if you refused to go until the war ended it might..."

He laughed, "It would be a drop in the bucket. We're good but not that good!"

"I just... I don't know," she stopped herself. Her father had taught her to sit and listen and not be noticed - to pick up things that others might miss - but she hadn't actually realised how much this had impacted her engagement with politics. On a ship like this, no one cared about what happened in locked rooms full of diplomats in foreign cities, as long as they coughed up after the final bow. Just like the commoners, all they really cared about was how much it impacted their individual lives in the moment: they couldn't see what was coming for them, like a domino effect that crushed the very bottom all that harder.

"We just don't get involved in that stuff, that's why I love this place, that and we don't play for the courts," he said, "I mean we do of course play for them, and of course, they pay our way better than the commoners that visit on the streets afterwards do... but they're not the ones we play for: we play for the people. The people of the common lands are free, they can farm for themselves, and they don't need to pay much dividends to the northern lords, those of them that are left. But the sanctions... if they're hard up, the Gedogin won't help the Consortium in looking after them, and that causes all sorts." He stopped quickly on his last word, rushing it as though another thought threatened to take him.

She changed the subject, "I bet keeping a ship and crew this size is pretty expensive?" said Adrienne, "Your patronage must be very high."

"We're the only ship that sails to all corners of the northern lands. Even Black Isle Cove, not that they need it. Them lot could travel anywhere faster than anyone on the sea. Because the ship is so big, sometimes we bring two shows at once, so one company can take a comedy up to the nobles in their houses, and the other can do a tragedy in the town square. We can do them at the same time, and we can swap the next day, or a couple of days later, depending on how much we like where we are. Double the money, half the effort you see? Plus, we're really good, some ships just rest on their laurels or just use it as a shroud to cover up the privateer work, but we do a good job of it."

"I thought privateer work was legal..."

"In a war everything's legal, and we're always at war. But what happens after both nations are at peace? Then they're just pirates, thieving from ships for no one. It's best to keep anything like that out of sight, legal or not."

"I've never been on a troupers' ship before," said Adrienne, following Lorcan's lead and wiping away the potato peels into a barrel, "I don't know much."

She held his eyes for a moment, curious to see something, because this boy who had been so silent and lacking in character before, was actually anything but. He had a strange awkwardness about him, with his crooked smile and dimples, but his eyes were different: bright and deliberate, though one was considerably brighter than the other. Elsen used to say you could tell if a person had been through something life changing by their eyes, one eye would look bright and honest, the other would look darker as if something good had been torn out of it and it was mourning its loss: she called it the evil eye.

"And you," asked Adrienne, "How long have you been at sea?"

"Four years now," he said, "My parents died in the war, back when they were properly fighting it. Stupid thing is they didn't even die fighting, they died of a sickness that took the whole village, and because of the way everything is, we didn't have supplies enough to look after them. Then I was on my own, and I had a choice: to stay and work in a small town where everything I relied on had been destroyed, where there wasn't enough to go around anyway, and no way I could help myself, let alone anyone else trapped there, or to join a ship and lessen their load. I walked for a day and a half with nothing but a skin of water and my hunting knife and the clothes on my back. When I got to the port it was late, and most of the docked ships had put their lights out, but there was one that had a candle burning. Thomas was alone on the deck, drinking and, I guess, looking out at the sky. When he addressed me and asked if I was lost I just burst into tears. I guess he had to take me on after that, after I'd told him my story. He's good like that. This ship saved my life."

Lorcan's face flushed, "Anyway, it's good to join a troupers 'ship because everyone knows what they're getting; all the cutthroat behaviour is upfront," he grinned, "and it's easier to work your way up through the ranks on a ship like this. I'm in charge of all the cabin boys, and when I get a bit more experienced I'll be able to get involved in things like the scheduling. Thomas promised me. This is all I have now and I'm in, you know? Anyway, Thomas has tasked me with looking after you, and I'm going to take that very seriously. If you need help, you can ask."

Adrienne smiled and leaned over to smell the stew in the pot. She sniffed and then grabbed a spoon to taste it, "This needs more salt," she said, "My mother died when I was thirteen," she added, "I had to move away from home too."

He smiled a vacant smile and pulled his focus away back to his vegetable peeling as if it was the most important task in the world. He moved a bit closer to her on his stool and breathed out heavily. It's no secret that shared experiences, rare ones, can bring two people together better than most things. In hindsight, you have to wonder whether their fates had been tied together all along; or whether any small coincidence like this would affect a person's decisions from then on. Coincidence linking two people's destinies together as a parody of itself, all linear, as they all contribute to a larger end.

Chapter 7 - The Toll Gate

He was back in the room with a blast and a sharp cracking noise. An overwhelming sensation crept over him, a sense that he was not meant to be there... That's right, he doesn't want to be there... Now he remembers. No, not that, it's that he doesn't belong anywhere, no one does. He didn't exactly have an opinion about this, just an indifference, but he could tell that this in itself wasn't right. Then he felt it, a flooding despair, a desperate ache where his heart used to be, where something almost whole now filled it. Unfathomable despair was all he could see or feel, except for a shadow in the corner, a figure crouching in the candlelight.

He felt around, but he wasn't connected to anything anymore. He searched for something to grasp onto but fell instead. He'd never felt this way before, but he now had the sense that what this is had always been true, an absolute darkness, lurking beneath the surface. This is my body, he thought, It has always been my body, but I don't belong in it. It's wrong, I cannot sense it where it used to be. For a brief, conscious moment he fought the feeling of emptiness, the sense that he was disconnected from a former life, This is good, the pain would be too much, and then he drifted away, somewhere between sleeping and blacking out.

The next morning they set sail on the two-week journey to Medicina Cove, northeast of Avenly and the base camp in most travellers' journeys towards Keeper's Cove. Lots of traders would embark there and do the rest of the journey by cart, up through the mountains to enter the keep through the famous golden doors. It was the traveller's way, but many who had made the pilgrimage already would opt to go around the coast on the quicker, less compelling journey, in spite of the danger of privateering that awaited them. It would be a day and night before they got there, and Adrienne spent most of her time helping Noah measure and file down pieces of wood to fix the broken piano leg. The master of music, a man they called Cal, constantly flitted over them, fussing and muttering over the missing keys.

"Do you have any idea how much it's going to cost me to get this thing properly fixed in somewhere as small as Medicina?" he huffed at Noah, "We'll no doubt have to stay at the port an extra day, and then Thomas and his boys will get pissed at the Tavern two nights in a row, and Jill'll be grouchy at him all the way up to Keeper's Cove. Honestly, boy, before we even set bloody sail."

Noah waited until Cal's back was turned and whispered to Adrienne,

"Cal is Jill's lover. That's why he's annoyed. Jill's second in command, and she says she needs to keep Thomas straight from time to time, but I know... she only gets ratty with him because she wants to be out at the Tavern as well."

Adrienne stifled a laugh as Noah went back to filing down the wood he'd brought back from the carpenter's shop in Avenly.

"You'll get to know that most of the people on this ship have their quirks, and it's very rarely anything to do with you. Some of them you can explain, like that one... and some just are." He shook his head in bemusement.

"I think I know about that."

"Really? How so."

He wasn't challenging her, he was making conversation, so why did she feel so defensive, as if he was about to ridicule her, or write her off as unworthy of his attentions? She didn't want to care.

"My father had mood spells, inexplicable ones. It was nothing bad really, but it was enough to take the energy out of a room and make you feel like it was you that had done something to him," she said, "I spent years thinking there was something wrong with me until one day, something happened that made me realise I how little I knew of the life he'd led. I didn't suddenly understand what it was that made him like that, but I understood that there was no way I could possibly know. Does that make sense?" She winced a bit, waiting for his reply, feeling wretched with herself for being so honest to a complete stranger who hours ago had seemed so unapproachable, and half expecting him to burst into laughter.

 He reached over her shoulder, picked up a sanding stone and started filing down where he'd cut the wood, "I get that. Everyone here's so busy getting by that they don't ever have the time to get to the bottom of things. I like that about this boat. To be fair, I came from the depths of nothingness in comparison to this place, I mean... we've all come from different places... except for Thomas and some of the older crew, they're all from his home island. On the whole, though, we're a bunch of misfits, 'he smiled a cheeky, nonchalant smile that deliberately showed his bottom teeth, 'And so you don't talk about it, you just let people have their moments and you move on. It sort of makes everyone equal in a weird way."

 "I like that," she said.

 A silence then fell between them, and as Adrienne observed it, it began to feel weighted somehow. As it went on - for what felt like longer than it should - Adrienne was wracking her brain for something, anything to say that would allow them to keep talking. Eventually, and to her relief, he spoke again. "What brings you out here anyway?" He asked, "Travelling on a troupers 'ship, I mean... If you don't mind me saying, you don't seem at all like the type..."

 "I am no type that you could possibly be referring to," she said.

He leaned forward in curiosity.

"I'm just travelling to see some family, or what's left of them," she continued, "There's not much left for me where I came from... not that there was much there to begin with. I mean, we didn't want for anything, but Wiberia is... kind of empty." She looked down, not allowing the intimacy of the moment to sway her into giving away too much.

Noah played with a piece of rogue wood between his thumb and finger, eventually flicking it overboard, "Maybe I'm wrong entirely," he said, getting up, "Maybe you're exactly the sort of person to join a troupers' ship... you're drifting, and you're full of secrets," he smiled, "but be warned, once you join it's very hard to leave. Jill keeps deserters in a secret cabin below the galley."

"Oh really?" She couldn't help but grin, though she tried not to as she got the sense he was fully aware of his effect on her and enjoying every moment.

"'I'll have to stay out of Jill's way when I make my escape then," she popped the new leg under the piano. "There, that should fit well until you can get it to a proper mender," she screwed the leg in place and blew away the dust shavings.

Noah observed her, pensive. "I'm sorry, some of the crew, well, we don't often meet someone with your... disposition and manners let's say... at least we don't meet someone who can also do woodwork. Some of the lads had a bet on that you were a runaway Velgrave bride."

With no answer for him that wouldn't lead to a barrel of more unwanted questions, she chose to let the mystery build instead. She shrugged, and as she stood and she dusted off her trousers, looking up to see Noah with a raised eyebrow.

"I am not a runaway bride," she smiled, flatly, as she turned to leave.

Noah stared back and cocked his head to the side as she made her way back to the galley. Sailors watched her as she went and one of them shouted something about her trousers being covered in dirt, which she tried to ignore. She couldn't help being pleased though, they were treating her like one of the crew, teasing and talking like they would any new member, and that couldn't be bad.

The next couple of weeks on board passed quickly for Adrienne, with the kitchen work taking up half her day, and the rest taken up by the laborious task of fixing the piano with Noah - which did not feel so laborious. Adrienne began to wonder if a sailor's life might perhaps be for her after all, or if it was the company, perhaps, that swayed her course. This ship, of which she knew so little, represented a place of safety in a world that had so recently become dark to her. Her recent memories were hidden so deeply inside her heart that she barely felt how heavy they really were. With all that had occurred, you can hardly blame her for wanting excitement of a different kind, can you?

"Land ahoy!" shouted a man from the other side of the deck, his face and arms hidden in an eccentric green fairy mask. Ceremoniously, each and every person on the upper deck then responded to his call, shouting and screeching "Land ahoy!", whilst running up and down the deck over and over, jumping over things and generally causing chaos. This then turned seamlessly into a strange sort of chant, which was accompanied by an unchoreographed dance, which crescendoed in a mock ritualistic slaughter of the boy at the helm. It was the same lad that had taken Adrienne to her lodgings and he didn't look best pleased about what was happening to him. When the man with the green hat pretended to throw him in the ocean, Adrienne could have sworn she saw the boy wince and tense up as the man in the green mask picked him up and pretended to throw him overboard. It didn't look fun or kind like the friendly mocking she'd received, it seemed cruel somehow. What had started off as a bit of fun had somehow taken a misdirect, and a strange tension grew in the air as the boy, who clearly had no control of the situation, looked visibly more unhappy by the second. She looked around, but only a few people had seen what she'd seen. They were mainly clapping and cheering like the schoolboys in Velgrave used to when they'd picked on a weak link in their ranks.

When she asked Lorcan why they were acting like that, he told her that the Player's Circle were reluctant tradesmen and even more reluctant actors. A great ship had been gifted to them by King Tristain, and it had provoked awestruck reactions from the land dwellers as they docked into any new harbour, so the ritual had become something of an inside joke, "One of these times, the crew decided to pretend they were Royal ambassadors, and they kept it up for as long as they could get away with before someone clocked it and they had to come clean. The tradition sort of stuck, and got weirder and weirder, I guess... I'm not sure where the slaughtering of cabin boys came from..."

She looked at the boy, who was now bleeding, and she thought she saw a tear in his eye. When he caught her looking at him with pity he became stone faced, telling her without telling her that the worst thing in the world would be for the rest of the crew to see his weakness, so she looked away and pretended to inspect the knots on the mast. Out of the corner of her eye, she saw the boy sitting by the bulwark until the man with his face hidden in the costume leant over to pick him up.

"Noah can get a bit carried away," said Lorcan.

"That's Noah?" asked Adrienne, looking at the man in the green mask.

"Didn't you know?"

"I wouldn't have expected it to be him..."

"He's done worse," said Lorcan, with a hint of bitterness, "They say Thomas is grooming him to become his second in command. I think it's a bad move..."

Adrienne scoffed, "He doesn't treat the cabin boys well even though he used to be one himself?"

Lorcan shrugged, "Most of us worked our way up from there. I think he came from a bad family: crooks and thieves in Senelin City, all down on the lower levels. People tend to make excuses for him, on account of him making good."

Adrienne folded her arms nervously as she watched Noah jump from the side of the ship back onto the decking.

"Why are you so bothered by Noah?" asked Lorcan.

"I don't know," she said, "I don't like... inconsistency." She muttered this last part to herself mainly, looking down at the dishevelled cabin boy, "Why are you so bothered by him?"

"I'm not," said Lorcan, "I mean yes, it irritates me that gets everything handed to him on a plate, and people just flock to him and he does nothing to deserve it, but honestly I'm not bothered by *him*. Just the way other people are around him."

Adrienne felt pity for her new friend, who'd worked so hard and had come from so little, "He does bother you," she said, "I guess, in a way, you're very similar."

There was something urgent on Lorcan's face, he almost looked hurt. "I saw you earlier, with him, and the day before," he said, "You barely spoke to anyone else."

Adrienne blushed and turned her face towards the back of the ship, "We were working on the piano..."

"I said I'd look out for you... I'd just be careful, that's all," he said with a strange and unexpected intensity, "Noah doesn't care about anyone but himself."

Adrienne looked up to see Noah, who was standing across the way and looking at her. She quickly flashed her eyes down to the floor, hoping that Lorcan wouldn't notice, "Perhaps," she said.

They arrived at the side of the cove, where two battleships had positioned themselves on either side of the coast about half a mile apart. The ship slowed to a stop adjacent to the one nearest where Thomas and Jill had a long exchange with one of the men on the battleship, holding up crests and answering questions until he finally let them continue into the port.

"That's Medicina's checkpoint," said Lorcan, "They need to make sure we're who we say we are. The war is in stalemate in most parts, but only because they keep it like this..."

They walked down to where the crew were preparing boats to go ashore and helped load pieces of set onto the larger ones. Eventually, Noah, who was now out of his phantom costume, announced that they'd be departing soon and to make ready.

"This," Noah made a dramatic sweeping gesture with his hand that implied he owned it, "is Medicina, our first call on the tour of the northern states, my lady..."

He put his hand out to Adrienne and pulled her up onto the upper level.

"Please make your preparations, we will be on solid land within the hour."

He seemed to sense her reluctance because he slowed and looked at her, frowning ever so slightly. Then he jumped down below deck before she could speak.

Thomas was standing a few feet away from Adrienne now, watching the men and women on the battleships. Adrienne looked out at the small, granite port, unconvinced that such a harmless keep would be of use to the war effort.

Thomas, sensing he was being watched, turned and faced Adrienne and shook his head, looking back at the ship. "It's getting tense out there, I wonder how much longer we'll be able to visit ports like this."

"I thought the war was about Senelin and Velgrave fighting over who had possession of the Wiberia Mountains? I don't see why this port would have anything to do with it."

"That's a fair observation," he said, tipping his hat to the glaring sun, "but the reason Medicina is important is the reason the mountains are important. Think about it - the mountains are the south's direct access to the Avenly Coast. There's nothing but a short piece of sea in between the two. They are part of the south's direct trade route with all of the north, and..." he added, "they're not a seafaring nation. The people of Senelin and the northern islands have to be seafarers, and they always have been. They're not as advanced in their ways as the people of Black Isle, of course, that's known without question, but their skill is greater than those in the south, who can get along just fine without ever taking to water, except for that one route. Currently, the north has control of both Wiberia and Medicina and everything in between."

"Velgrave is more powerful though."

"That's true indeed, their southern territories are far richer and more influential in the wider world. Up here we're nothing but islands and coves and peninsulas all over the ocean, but the southerners are land folk. They need that route for trade: they want the mountains, so they can take Medicina and go straight up to Keepers Cove, the home of all technology and trade in the Central Lands. That would make them invincible."

Suddenly the pieces fit together in Adrienne's mind, and something else, niggling below the surface, that she couldn't quite put her finger on yet.

"So, the war is more of an arms race? For resources?" she asked.

"Always has been, but only partly," he replied, "If the north and the south were to break ties it would break apart the Consortium - and chaos would ensue if the Consortium was left without anyone to answer for at all. That's why it's taking so long, and there's so much stalemate. All it takes is a bit of mistrust on either side for it to spiral, just a thought in one person's head to trickle into existence, and suddenly..." He trailed off, "I guess, the very fact that I'm saying this means that it has, in some form somewhere, already happened. Whoever ends up with control of Medicina has control of Keeper's Cove. And both sides need Keeper's Cove, but more importantly, the Consortium needs Keeper's Cove. I guess we'll know that the war is nearly over when the Consortium makes a bold decision on its own to take the place whilst the others are at each other's throats."

"So, it's not an arms race, it's a technology race, the race for advanced magicks?"

"The race to control the people who make it, yes, and the tor at Keeper's Cove where the Channel can be accessed. It's a shame, everyone knows that the Consortium wants to take control from under the noses of Senelin and Velgrave whilst they fight, but no one seems prepared to do anything to prevent it. The Gedogin people of Keeper's Cove don't work for anyone anymore, but they don't seem to be working for money either. That means that neither the Consortium nor either of the two kingdoms can control them, and they don't like that. Whoever has access to the industrial world of the Gedogin at Keeper's Cove has control of medicine, communication, advancements in technology, everything. If the Consortium gained total control then the ancient king's and queen's dynasties would lose all power. It would be them running things. King Tristain would be a puppet. He might be considered a bit of a dandy at times, and a supporter of the arts I might add, but to have the Consortium in control... many say that it would be right, that they'd supply the people with more magicks, help the commoners, but others say it would be a disaster."

"There must be somewhere else they can make vessels other than Keeper's Cove?"

"It's where all the world's energy comes from. It's strange, support for the Consortium and Keeper's Cove is almost evenly split these days. The people need to be given the information to make the right choices, yet all they can really judge this on is how it affects them. Either the commoners starving or the people of Keeper's Cove watching their resources dwindle and fester by the day. I guess on top of that, there's so many rumours going around these days that it's hard to figure out what the truth of the matter is. Forgive me, I can get carried away, it seems to be all I think about these days."

Adrienne thought back to the settlement on that tiny island in the middle of nowhere. She thought about how it had been destroyed by privateers, who'd been hired by the king to steal resources for the war effort; or if not them then the Seldelige, who had been discovered, or created, or something by the Consortium to wreak havoc. And if not either of them then by bandits or pirates, people who'd lost maybe even more than she had, "I used to think the war wouldn't affect me," she said, "but it affects everyone, one way or another."

"Most people don't know anything other than the simple fact that we're at war and who's in charge. We're often in the Royal courts. Courtiers like to be entertained and are quick to give troupers the information they need to make the right choices, to stay afloat so to speak, but only that. I am, after all, still just a lowly troublemaker." She smiled at that, and with that Thomas left his post and marched towards a couple of sailors who were bickering over who had to carry the castle turret ashore. Fair enough, she thought, you do meet the most unexpected people in taverns, especially the ones far out from metropolitan cities.

She went to the cabin to pack all she needed for the day on shore. Thomas's words rang in her ears, *the information needed to make the right choices, only that.* Is that what her father had done to her? Of course, she had known some of what Thomas had told her, how could she not, but there was something he'd said that shook her: that the Consortium might take control of Keeper's Cove. Suddenly the true meaning of those words sunk in like they hadn't ever before. Maybe because for the first time since she'd been old enough to understand, she could see what catastrophic consequences could come from it.

Chapter 8 - King Tristain's Players

He woke up feeling achy and strange in a new place. He was in a large room this time, and the floor was uncommonly warm, probably heated from a steel cooker somewhere below. The room was large and the smell of roasting meat met his nose as a relieving reminder that he was still whole. Before him was a large armchair stretched out towards a cavernous window that looked out into the darkness. Waves lapped against a shore somewhere in the distance, and the soundscape they created in the darkness that surrounded the building made him feel he was alone in oblivion. He sat, once again going through that same old routine: getting his bearings after they'd put him through the same ordeal night after night, a new place every time. He grappled with the idea that if this did end it would mean something awful, something that he had been trying to fight would rear its ugly head, but he couldn't remember what. When would this end? It had to end at some point?

Jill Jones took a small group of cabin crew, including Adrienne, to shore, with a few boxes on a pull-cart. They journeyed through the port, out onto the coach road and along to the main town of Medicina. It was smaller than Adrienne had expected for such a notable location, and it didn't present as prosperous, not compared to the ports of the south. Adrienne's memories of the southern beaches were of palm trees, coffee houses and wide white terraces of waterfront buildings. Even the port of Avenly had three layers of promenades leading down to the beaches surrounding it, with entertainers and night workers scattered along the streets when the sun went down, and businessmen taking lunches during the day. Medicina port was quaint, filled with smaller fishing boats, family businesses and older folk leaning out of the porches of granite houses. It was full of the smell of fish, salt and seaweed, a quiet existence in direct juxtaposition with the battleships on the horizon.

    They walked a short while down a dirt road until they were back amongst movement and brickwork, and through that they moved, with their heavy cargo of props and tools, to the town square. Most players 'companies had very little props and equipment, as the big houses usually had all the archetypal costumes and props stored safely in their halls, ready for the next visiting players. In the public shows most troupes would just do without, but the Players Circle didn't like to do one show for the commoners and something different for the nobles. Every audience got the same, which meant they had a lot to carry on days like these. The town square in Medicina was a large open space, as you'd expect with any town square, but this one had been utilised to its full potential as if the town was so small that they'd had to compact every inch of it for multi-usage. There were old men playing chess on makeshift tables and stalls set up on the floor selling weaved goods, metals and crockery. There was a cobbler's stall, a blacksmith's tent, children having school lessons in the sun, and an array of more established stores facing inwards on the accompanying roads.

    Jill immediately started talking with a representative of the mayor's office. Adrienne watched as she showed him her crest, and she saw his eyes widen as he looked at it. He made a hurried comment about being honoured to have the Player's Circle back, and then in a flurry, he started asking people to vacate the square in readiness for King Tristain's Players. There were a few objections displaying nothing more than irritation at the inconvenience. The old men were nearing the end of a very tense game of chess and the school children were halted in the middle of a lesson about the discovery of the northern islands, but within twenty minutes they had all cleared.

As she watched this scene, memories came back to her of summers in Velgrave. A summer theatre show in the great gardens below her aunt's house, and now the mutterings amongst the crowds: The Player's Circle, King Tristain's players, were here! They were indeed known far and wide! She was almost glad she hadn't known before or she might have not had the confidence to present to Thomas as she had done those few days before. There was no doubt plenty of people willing to take her place on the ship, and she suspected that she'd have to really pull her socks up if she didn't want to get ditched the moment they pulled out from Medicina.

"I thought you were the Player's Circle, not King Tristain's men? I've heard of King Tristain's men! Everyone has." gasped Adrienne to one of the cabin girls, who was evidently endeared and patted her on the back without uttering a word.

Jill laughed, "One and the same! We don't like to make a thing of it. In most places it gets us the respect and protection we need, and when you're somewhere like here, where they're traditionalists and supporters of the northern crown, they'll just name you themselves, but it's not our official title, especially at the moment," Jill started unpacking the boxes as she spoke, unloading props and set without looking at them, as if she'd done it a thousand times before, "We're being as careful as we can. Troupers don't take sides in politics, but by association can be just as harmful when we journey south, which is where most of our money comes from in the winter. Even though we have been invited to play there, well... it's best to stick with the Players Circle."

The other crew and company started arriving in dribs and drabs, some carrying bits of set, or instruments, some with food for later, and one pair of cabin boys were carrying a barrel of whisky that they'd picked up from the local brewers 'for much later'. The rest of the day was spent setting up the performance space, rehearsing entrances and exits, and running through songs and fight scenes - where the actors have to go over their fights to make sure no one gets a stick in the face mid-performance. According to Jill, the latter was still a regular occurrence, depending on how rowdy the crowd would get.

As this was their first stop on the summer tour, they needed to get the work right, and as they carried on through the north lands they could rest a little easier as they got more comfortable with the six new shows they were touring. They'd journey to Keeper's Cove, the Laten Islands, Black Isle Cove, down to Senelin, Senelin City, then down to Alba where they would visit various towns and the great schools of knowledge, ending in a night performing in the court of King Tristain. Then they'd head back to Wiberia for their mid-season break before the start of the winter tour in the southern lands.

Today's show would be *The Night of the Eight Kingdoms*, which was a tale of betrayal and treason as eight cousins fight it out for the throne of Velgrave. It was based on a true story, set only two hundred years ago when the king left no heir apparent and the bloodlines of the realm fought each other to claim sovereignty. Miss Jill Jones said it was a modern version of the story, where they poked fun at the idea that cousins and relatives would kill each other without remorse for something as inconsequential as a crown.

"What's the court of King Tristain like?" asked Adrienne, as she helped the cabin boys set up a mini stage over a rickety part of the square.

"It's full of books," said Jill, whimsically, as she sat on the grass painting her face with madder root, "Lots of tall, curvy buildings filled with gold and thousands of thousands of books, I mean I haven't counted. The libraries there are said to be the best in the world. There are six schools owned by the crown, where you can be educated in everything except magick. Of course, King Tristain's family are all educated in the south for societal reasons when they are young, and some are being sent to those god-awful new order islands where they fill your head with sand, but Alba is home to the academies and that's where everyone ends up in the end. Now if you want to learn about art and love," she said, "they say you should apprentice under the bohemian masters in Senelin City,'" she grinned at the thought, "but if you ask me, I recommend you just jump on a theatre boat the first chance you get."

"I've been to Alba, but I've always wanted to go farther north and see Senelin City," said Adrienne, "We visited a few times when I was little, but only really got to see it out of the windows. I never got to explore it. I hope I do get to see it."

"Senelin is more my kind of place," Jill mused, putting away her makeup and picking up her cue script, "The streets are narrow and twisting, there are interlinking canals, layers upon layers. There's riffraff downtown, in the lower levels, but that just adds to the colour of it all. I reckon whoever built that city was an artist and refused to allow it to become anywhere that wasn't full of art. There are so many folk from all over the place, you can buy anything you want from anywhere in the world, and there's always a lot of merriment about when night falls in the lower streets of the town. There's nothing quite like artists and players performing to one another for the love of it under a tavern roof. You can't go there and not be inspired, even if your existence is dull, and your work is filled with bureaucracy. Especially if that's the case. Send them all to Senelin, that's what I say..."

Eventually, the rest of the crew, including Lorcan and Noah, arrived at the square and the show started in the mid-afternoon. Before long, crowds of people had lined around the square and across the streets surrounding it, right up to the doors of the shops. Noah played one of the younger cousins of the king, boisterous and over-confident in a comedic sort of way. He was very watchable, and Adrienne couldn't help but follow him with her eyes when he was on stage, in spite of herself. As in all stories where your morals dictate your end, his pig-headedness got him into trouble: he ended up poisoned by his uncle in the dead of night and thrown out of a tower. Adrienne wondered if the character was written so, or if Noah had brought much of himself to the role, either way, it was weirdly satisfying to see. She revelled and cheered on Lorcan when he came on for his few scenes, the clumsy officer and then the angry villager who addressed the audience directly, telling them of what had happened in-between scenes.

The play ended up with everyone dead, except Jill, the grieving mother, who had been as much of a player in the story as anyone else, but as with many women in ancient times, her influence had to be hidden behind men who were nothing but instruments to her whim. In the story, she'd worked her way to the top and took over as Queen Regent, until her daughter was old enough to assume the crown and marry her 3rd cousin. What a life, thought Adrienne, so much power and privilege and yet no freedom whatsoever. Well, unless you're willing to take it and trample on the people you know best to get it.

This was followed by a jig, where all the actors came back on stage and played a short comedy to get everyone back into the mood for merriment. Adrienne wasn't entirely sure of the plot for this one, but it was something to do with a tailor getting in trouble with a pompous lord for not mending his suit, and then somehow tricking the lord into wearing vulgar, disgusting attire - there were polka dots involved - to a very important 'do'. The crowd clapped and cheered and screamed for more, and eventually, they ended with a dance, where all the locals joined them in the centre of the square. Players and audience joined together with the 'Maid's Attack', a dance that everyone in the northern and southern kingdoms combined had ingrained into them as much as their own name.

It had been dark for several hours before the crowds started to subside, and the cask of whisky was nearly empty. Adrienne was sitting on the curb, just off the square, holding onto the Noch and looking at the strange image of the Keeper's crest on the front. She'd seen it on vessels that were made direct from Keeper's Cove, but it was usually just the cylinder inside a circle. This one had markings in four corners and a square overlapping the circle. She'd never bothered to ask her father what the picture meant, but she'd noticed the change in Thomas 'expression when it had fallen out of her pocket and it had made her curious. She ran her fingers over the cylinder-shaped trunk and to the outer edges where the picture faded a bit.

When she spotted Noah walking up to her from the fire, carrying keys and a glass of whisky, she tried to tuck the Noch back into her pocket, but her sleeve got caught, so she kept it covered by her hand in her lap.

"We're all starting to pack up now," he said, "If you can find Lorcan, I think he's got some tasks for you to do. They always overdo it on the first night and then forget there's a whole set to carry back to the ship."

"OK, I'll find him," said Adrienne, shifting in her seat, not looking up.

"It looked like you were having a pretty intense discussion earlier?" he said.

She nodded knowingly, "We've become friends, I think he wants to be my protector," and she laughed ever so slightly at this, which made Noah relax. He sat down on a mound of grass next to her and stretched out his overworked body.

"I don't think you need a protector, Adrienne," he said, running his hands through his hair and lying back into the grass, "at least, not from us."

"Is the boy from earlier OK?" said Adrienne, "He was frightened. You should have seen his face."

Noah sighed and took off his hat, sucking air through his mouth like he had the time Thomas had scolded him about the piano.

Adrienne, "I don't know… maybe he told you he was OK, but he wasn't"

"That's just how lads are with each other…"

"…don't give me that!"

"It is," said Noah, gritting his teeth down, "You'd know that if you'd spent more than a few days here. The sea is a rough place to be these days. It's what we do to protect them when they're coming up, to train them and toughen them up."

Adrienne shuffled uncomfortably, "From the sounds of things, many of you ended up on the boat because you'd already been through something."

"Oh yeah?" He said, "You know that do you?"

She shrugged and looked up, catching his eye so that it was hard to look anywhere else and she could smell him and the whisky on his breath. Suddenly she became very aware of her breathing.

"Many of us have come from broken places, it's no secret. I'm not about to use my past as a weapon or an excuse though. Everyone's been through something, right? You've got a story too I bet or you wouldn't be here. I'm not about to play a game of who's had the worst time of it."

"I went to Senelin City once," she said, "when I was a child we went in a carriage that belonged to my godfather. I only remember pieces of it, but there was one part that stuck with me. We were heading through the middle level, and the carriage stopped at a toll gate as we were passing from the upper levels to the canal. I'd found this mouse on the road coming up from the Alba coast, it was injured but not dying. My father had let me rescue it. It escaped out of the carriage when we were sitting waiting for the inspectors to let us through - I think there was a holdup as they'd been looking for a criminal who'd smuggled himself in from the lower levels. I ran out to chase it and crashed right into a child on the canal who was probably the same age as me. He was covered in dirt, and he smelled just... and he clearly hadn't eaten in days. To top it all off I'd run straight into him! And do you know what he said?" she said, "Sorry miss! As if he was to blame, and yet I could see in his face he wasn't sorry at all, he despised me."

    Noah had started twiddling with the keys in his hand now, moving them back and forth between his fingers, *a nervous tick* she thought.

    "That sounds about right actually. If he'd reacted any other way he'd... he'd have been beaten, arrested even. Class rules in Senelin City. Everyone knows their place, that's how it functions. The great artists of the world are propped up by the labour of forgotten people ten streets below them. What they never see can't hurt them, and what they do see they choose to forget. It's almost poetic," he sighed, adding "I had a feeling I'd come down on him a bit too hard."

    "He would never admit to you that you hurt him," she said, "He looks up to you too much, they all do, even Lorcan does... although I'm not entirely sure he'd want to admit that."

    Noah rolled his eyes, laughed and then breathed heavily, "If I'm honest with you, that's sort of the problem. I don't really know if the boys on this crew like me or are just a bit scared," he said, "and if they think they like me, well they don't really... They don't know me. They think I represent something, but I don't."

"You're the captain's apprentice!" she said, incredulously, "It comes with the territory, doesn't it?"

"I don't know, does it?" he said, "Where I grew up, you made your own power and didn't trust authority. The respect of your peers was the only thing that meant anything, that was what kept you alive."

Adrienne looked into her lap for a moment, nervously. He was sitting very close to her, and the intensity she'd felt before in the silence between them was creeping back in. She eventually broke the silence by looking him in the eye, and with a decided nod said, "And what kept me alive was staying away from mine."

He laughed, "Well, aren't we a pair... Look, I'll take him aside, let him know I feel bad about it," he said, standing up, "Thank you. You're the first person to speak to me like that who isn't Thomas."

She stifled a grin, "I'll be here, anytime you need someone to insult you."

He nodded to himself, still laughing, "Thanks."

Then there was a moment that neither of them expected. A brief intensity, fleetingly filling the air around them and then gone as quickly as it came, then he suddenly jumped back, as if he'd just remembered something he needed to fix, or forgotten himself entirely.

"Well, I'd, um, I... I need to get back to the um..." He hovered, then stopped still, peering at the curious gold objects that Adrienne was fiddling with in her lap, "Thanks again," he said distractedly, eyes on her hands.

She smiled at him as he left, and as soon as he was well enough away she realised her heart rate had in fact doubled. She pitied Noah for what he'd been through and despised him for what he'd become, but she also couldn't help liking him in spite of it. He was different from anyone she'd met before, maybe because, as he rightly pointed out, she'd never seen his world, just as he'd never seen hers. Though there were other things that she was unable to process into clear thoughts, these are the things that the young will never know until it's too late, things left for the storyteller to observe and comment on, with bittersweet omnipresence. We were young once too: we know so very well, the different kinds of friendships that can appear all at once, and drift away before we've properly made them out, like a flock of boats sailing past an empty harbour on a misty night.

Chapter 9 - A New Plan

There was water in this room. He reached out to pick up the jug. He could barely lift it with his weakened hands. When was the last time he'd eaten? He drank furiously, too fast and so his empty stomach was stifled by it. His body repaid him by causing him to choke and cough out the last of it. Each time he woke he wanted to look for a way out, but every time they put him through this he would be so wiped out that he'd waste the last of his energy in searching the place to no avail. So this time he just sat, contemplating, focusing on the energy in the air, hoping to connect with it somehow, hoping that maybe this would be the way out. He didn't know where he was and even if he did he had no idea how long for. The moment of despair when he contemplated what they had taken from him came early this time, and he closed his eyes, trying to remember what it was that they'd taken from him, perhaps forever. He couldn't remember how fast it was meant to happen, but it was happening all the same.

It was a hot night aboard the Player's Circle that followed their show in Medicina Town. Many of the crew had moved onto the deck, to take advantage of any cool breeze that might work its way through the stillness. Some, unable to sleep, were playing cards by candlelight or sharing stories of sea monsters with unimpressed cabin boys.

Lorcan stayed in his hammock. He didn't much care for socialising in the midnight hour, those who did so woke tired and stayed tired for the entire tour. He was head of the galley, and he'd worked a full few years as a cabin boy to get here; he wasn't going to let himself fall behind like most of the crew on the ship did. He had ambitions, and they were plain and simple: to work his way up to quartermaster. He was going to earn it honestly, not like some other sailors did, he'd earn it fair and square and there was next to nothing that could dissuade him. He wanted to make Thomas proud: the man who had picked him up from the gutter, the man who had given him a home.

This night was full of the sort of humid heat that festered your mind as well as your body, and after lying with his eyes shut and willing to sleep to come to no avail for what felt like half the night, he got up with his pillow and blanket and wandered up ship. He was intent on finding a spot on the deck and made his way for the ladder, but as he crept along the narrow hallway he was stopped by a whisper coming from what he thought was an empty cabin.

"I'm telling you, I saw the crest, it wasn't like any other I've seen... it's got to be worth ten thousand Glames at least," came the voice of Noah, through the keyhole, "The question is, where did she get it from? It couldn't be hers. It couldn't be! Who in this world is she otherwise?"

Someone was pacing up and down inside the cabin, the light from their oil lamp shone through the crack in the door, "I wouldn't be so sure of that. It may not even be real... but then again, maybe I was too hasty in inviting her aboard," it was Thomas.

"You don't think it's real do you? Who are we dealing with here?"

"Maybe it would be a good idea to lock her in one of the brigs until we know what to do with her... "

"No," said Noah, "I mean, if you think that's what needs to happen."

"No? Really? Are you worried about scaring her away? Don't think the entire crew hasn't noticed... "

"...it's nothing," hissed Noah.

"Good," said Thomas, and his voice became a whisper and their shadows merged in the light as he moved closer to Noah, "We must be cautious, I agree. Don't let on to the girl that we know anything until we're absolutely certain, she's more likely to trust us that way. These are strange times, and we may be able to use this to our advantage if we time it right."

The sound of steps moved towards the door and Lorcan piled backwards around the corner. He heard the faint sound of Thomas's whisper as he stopped before leaving the room "And Noah... not a word to any of the crew. We want to be the ones to deal with it when the time comes."

Lorcan, frozen in mounting fear, broke free and crept, slowly out of the corridor onto the safety of the deck.

Adrienne was lying at the starboard, away from everyone, with her back to a mast, facing the bright moonlight and watching it ripple in the waves.

"I need to talk to you," Lorcan said as he sat down beside her. She sat up and looked at him, wiping her messy hair off her face as the breeze caught it.

He tried his best to hide his nerves, he was going to broach the subject subtly, but his voice was shaky and he was struggling to look her in the eye, so after a bit of fidgeting he came out with it, "Who are you?" he said.

Adrienne seemed taken aback at Lorcan's accusatory tone, but weirdly, not surprised.

She took a breath to speak and then paused for a moment, biding her time. Their eyes met and she seemed to relax somewhat:

"I... grew up on one of those New Order islands. I... escaped."

A wave sprayed Lorcan in the face and he spat over the side of the boat, "You worship the New Order?"

"No!" said Adrienne, "It's complicated. My father hated the Consortium schools, he said they were built on lies. He thought the Consortium schools and the New Order Islands were two sides of the same coin. He said they were run by the same people."

"Then what were you doing there?" asked Lorcan.

"When my mother died, and my father was sad. Looking back, I don't think he dealt with it well. My grandfather tried to take me away, he was going to send me to one of the Consortium schools, so my father chose the only other option..."

Lorcan blinked at this, his sighs dulled down by the sound of the waves, "OK. I believe you. Listen, this is a strange thing to ask... Have you got anything valuable with you? Anything you wouldn't want people to know about?"

"No," said Adrienne, and then backtracked nervously as Lorcan buried his head in his hands, "I have an old metal object that my father gave me as a gift," she said, "I have nothing else of any value. Why are you asking me this?"

" I don't know what I should say, I don't know if I should trust you."

"I'm not here to hurt anyone," she said, almost laughing, "Look at me, how could I?"

He took a deep breath and let it out as a deep sigh, "I just heard... I don't know what I heard exactly, but Noah and Thomas, they were speaking about you, about something you owned... and I wondered..."

"Thomas knows about it, he knows it's fake."

Lorcan went over her words in his head, looking more and more troubled, "How do you know what I'm referring to?"

She didn't reply but just stared helplessly at him. He waited and stepped forward so that his face was visible to hers in the moonlight, "Are you sure it's a fake?"

"Why are you asking me this?" She stepped back behind a ghillie box and then leaned forward so that they were still visible to each other.

"I'm trying to help you!" he snapped, his entire body filling with frustration as he sank down with his back against the box. She joined him facing the other way and whispered, "If you're trying to help me then you must trust me! Lorcan, if someone is planning on... robbing me, then you need to tell me."

"Why? I don't know you."

"Lorcan, make up your mind, we don't have time for this, it's too late for all that," said Adrienne, starting to visibly panic now, "You wouldn't have come straight to me if you hadn't thought it was the right thing to do... Are we going to do this the long way, or are you going to say what you came here to say?"

Lorcan was silent for what felt like minutes, until he finally resigned himself to a decision, "You don't understand. Thomas saved me. I didn't think this through," he sighed heavily, the realisation that it really was too late to turn back, finally hitting him, "I think you should leave. I'll find a way to get you off the boat and then you can escape," he said, reluctantly, "They won't know it had anything to do with me."

She raised an eyebrow, "You're telling me to leave but you're not telling me why?"

"I promised to protect you. I'm meant to be looking out for you, correct? Well, right now I think that the best way to do that is to let you leave."

She looked into his eyes. Half hidden in shadow and half lit up by moonlight, he was trying to look as sincere as he could. He heaved a sigh and leaned back against the ship's side, "It's not good Adrienne," he finally said after what felt like a long interval, "I don't know what they're planning, maybe on stealing and selling it, but they seemed willing to lock you away to get to it. I don't want to betray anyone... I would have expected it from Noah, but not Thomas, and that makes it a lot worse now I think of it. It was only ever something really bad, but I've seen crew members get treated like dirt when they've gotten on the wrong side of him."

Adrienne stared at him for a moment, processing the information, "What did they say exactly?"

Lorcan knelt down and lowered his voice so that it was almost inaudible, "They were talking about something you owned, an object... said they'd deal with you later, but not to tell the crew."

"Are you sure it was Noah?"

"And Thomas," he muttered.

"I don't understand," she said, "Why are you helping me?"

He grimaced his face and looked up into the night sky so as not to catch her eye, "I don't want any trouble for the boat," he said, "Thomas can get himself into rough situations sometimes despite himself, but thievery between crew members is a different thing altogether. That's what *he* taught *me*! That's not the sailors' code and it's not the player's code, if that sort of thing got around, it would damage us... You need to tell me, Adrienne. What is it you're carrying that's so important? Where did you get it?"

"Why are you asking?" she said suddenly, backing away from him.

"I just," he grappled with his words, "They're not petty thieves, Adrienne. It must be something... and I can't help you if you don't tell me anything."

"I'm heading to see my family. I thought people didn't ask questions like that on this boat?" she snapped.

"Well, I'm asking you."

She sat for a moment, tentatively, and watched his face for signs that this was a trick, "You're one of them."

"I am, and I'm proud to be, but the reason this ship works is because - though we can be underhanded about it - we do the right thing, and we hold each other accountable. This is the right thing. If I have to stand for it later then I will, Thomas will understand why I did it. This ship is everything... so the sheer fact that I'm..."

"Are you privateers? Is that the secret? That boat..."

"No, we're not," said Lorcan, sitting down next to her and leaning against the ghillie box, "Look, you don't understand. There hasn't been a real fight on these waters between merchant ships for years. If you're given a boat by any crown, you're expected to privateer alongside whatever else it is that you're meant to be doing. As a gesture to King Tristain, we do occasionally board smaller ships en route... but it's just that. We don't usually take anything either, Thomas usually just has a chat with them and then we're on our way. Thomas has this sort of agreement, you see, with the southern King: we only take the occasional insignificant trader's boat to signify our loyalty to King Tristain, and in return he lets us continue to perform in the south. We're not pirates, not even privateers..."

"OK," she said. "Look, I can't tell you everything because I don't know everything. That's the truth of it. I'm trying to get to Keeper's Cove because, well, there are people there who... who knew my father, and I want to see them. I do have a Noch," she added, "but it doesn't do anything" she said, "It's a vessel that Gedogin use, but it isn't special like Noah says it is, it's fake."

Lorcan listened intently, his arms folded as he ducked under the side of the deck to shelter from the waves that were now spitting over the side in the wind.

"What happened to your father, Adrienne?" he asked.

She tensed, wondering what she should divulge, how much she could even remember, and all the while knowing how much she wanted to trust him, "He was attacked by bandits in the woods, and then I was alone... I have some distant family in Senelin. I'll be safe there. So, there it is."

Lorcan nodded his head, "OK, I believe you," he said, "But... is that all there is? Is there anything else I should know before I put my neck on the line to get you off this boat? You haven't got any secret powers or strange ailments I should be aware of?"

It had been such a long time since Adrienne had had a true friend her age. Despite her better judgement, she believed he was being truthful and she didn't want to leave him: he had been the only thing that had come close to stopping her from feeling alone since she'd left Wiberia. Thomas and Jill were kind to her, and Noah was strange and interesting, but Lorcan was different, he was a friend, "Either way, I don't want to be trapped on a boat where people might betray me any minute," she said, "You're right, I should leave..."

"Tomorrow," said Lorcan, looking down into his sleeves, "When they send people out to get supplies before they get coaches to the mountain town. I'll make sure it's me, and I'll make sure you're with me."

"Thank you," she said, and he leant back against the ghillie box. The salt spray was lighter where she was, and a welcome balancer for the hot night. They passed the rest of the night in silence, staring out at the waves, cooled by the salt spray, and eventually, they both fell into a deep sleep under Lorcan's blanket.

Chapter 10 - The Dirt Road

When he awoke this time he was lying outside in a strange warm garden, humid and breezeless. He felt the earth beneath hold him steady as the world swirled above him. His hands squeezed down into the moss that caked the grass as he took his first decisive breath, the breath that said he would not give in this time either. He was still disorientated, but in spite of that, he pulled himself upright to rest against the dead trunk of an old tree. The figure was back, the one that taunted him night after night, but this time it sat opposite him on a white garden bench smoking a pipe. The man came close and handed him a skin of water, close enough to spark a memory. The figure felt familiar somehow, not just because he'd been the one who was consistently there throughout this grievous ordeal, but from his life before. He couldn't put his finger on how, so he just stared to no end.

After a long silence, the man in the chair finally spoke, "Are you now ready to tell me where they are?" He whispered to his charge's blank expression, "What form do they take?"

Of course, he doesn't give an answer, he just stares back at the figure, stoic as a corpse. His lack of feeling was somehow spurring him on to do what he was sure must be right, but he could remember very little of why it wasn't. The fact that this cold figure was causing him distress was enough to make anyone not want to do what was asked of them, but there was something else, from before. He knew he had the answers to the man's questions, that was holding something from him, but it was all so far away now. It would be back soon of course, but his mind hadn't caught up with his body just yet.

And then there it was, his whole meaning, the reason he was still alive, the reason still that he had been torn out of his life and brought here, and there was no hope in all the Channels that he would give that reason up. Did they honestly think that he would give it up after all this time? After all, he'd done to protect it, after all that others had done? Those countless perturbing sacrifices that didn't belong to him? Then there was silence, and at some point the figure left. He'd be back, and it wouldn't be as easy next time.

Getting Adrienne off the boat proved simple enough as, with no suspicions on their part, Lorcan was still the star student training up a budding carpentry apprentice in the ways of troupe life. Lorcan needed someone to accompany him into town, and Adrienne was the most likely contender to go with him. She was, simply put, the smallest. So though she'd proved useful at mending and fixing things, it was impossible to ignore that she did not possess the physical attributes needed to carry large pieces of set up a rickety ladder over water and rocks or to support the weight of a large man if he were to fall a great height whilst tightening a sail to a mast.

They set off at dawn to go into town in order to place orders at various stores, which would then be picked up in the afternoon. Lorcan had grown accustomed to his seasonal afternoons spent waiting for the shops to prepare Thomas' orders, basking in the last rays of sun before the journey into the cold north. He had a list of things for the galley that he needed to buy and another list of things for other areas of the ship. Keeper's Cove was great for vessels, but the basics - food, repairs, materials - were best bought in Medicina. After playing to the Keeper's markets, they'd travel to the Laten Islands, covering the longest stretch of sea until they journeyed back south, so this was their main chance to stock up for the journey.

The day was bright, and when they reached the town square there were already people readying themselves for a day of commerce. There were a few props and costumes that had needed mending: particularly a dress that was too small for Thomas to wear - which apparently was nothing to do with him eating or drinking too much and everything to do with the material. The dress needed expert tending from a dressmaker as the character was a countess, and the material needed for a countess's clothes was not so easy to obtain that they would have stores of it on the ship. There was also a prop that, as it turned out, was too large to fit through a crack in a fake wall and needed to be remade at the carpenter's. These were tasks that would take all day and so the pair had time on their hands to spend before Adrienne needed to think about slipping away.

Once they'd dropped off the various pieces, they were free to visit all the shops and stalls, which were within a short walking distance of the square. They made orders for meat and butter to be delivered to the ship by cart before sundown, and then visited the bakers. Adrienne took five small copper Tadhalls from her purse and bought them both two cream Damson puffs. They sat in the square drinking coffee from metal cups and watching the crowd.

The comfortable silence from their first meeting had come back, where both were too unsure of the other to name what was on their minds. Adrienne picked at a hole in her shoe and scolded herself for not making more of a fuss about it the last time she visited the market town. Lorcan picked up a couple of books, not plays, as he was sure to point out, for their journey north. He handed a third one to Adrienne, who took it from him and pressed her thumbs against the indented title, 'The Crow and the Magpie 'by Agnes Decanté.

"It's an old children's story," he said, "There was an old lady in the town I grew up in who used to read books to the children in the town square. Most of the children couldn't read, but then the Consortium set up a school. This one is about a Magpie and a Crow who work together to save a farming family from some robbers. I thought you could have it, you know..." He pulled that now familiar crooked grin, "because... I don't really know why... because you're leaving."

She smiled a sad smile and thanked him. She trailed through the pages, taking note of the faded illustrations. *Decanté,* she thought, *Isn t that Thomas s name?*

She pulled back the cover and read the forward on the first page:

Agnes Decanté is one of the most celebrated children s authors of the century. Her works include The Crow and The Magpie, The Fantastical Journey and All Along the Road.

Agnes conducted her early education in King Tristain s court school in Alba, and later with the masters of arts in Senelin Town, where she apprenticed under Elio Ferrar, academic and writer of The Histories of the North. Whilst in Senelin City she wrote her first book of stories, before moving back to Alba. She now resides in a quiet life in her family home on Black Isle, and rarely ventures out into society.

Footnotes: The Decanté Family of Black Isle Cove. The Decanté people of Black Isle Cove are one of the oldest people left in the world. They are known for being solitary people, though they still hold power in political circles. The commoners of Black Isle Island primarily function as sea traders: fishermen, merchants, occasionally as theatre troupes. Black Isle is home to one of the old-world temples, Black Isle Temple

"I didn't realise Thomas came from Black Isle? Is he nobility?" she asked.

"I don't think he knows, but probably not," said Lorcan, "Or if he is, it's a long and faded lineage. A lot of the houses are old enough to have lost touch with their original routes. The workers from the island used to take on the names of the nobles, and the workers came from all over, especially in the wars way back where prisoners became servants. Thomas was born on this boat, I don't think he sees himself as anything else."

It was nearing late afternoon, and the cart they'd hired to take Adrienne to Keeper's Cove would arrive any minute. Overhead four magpies flew in perfect unison along the sky, landing on a chimney above where they were sitting. Adrienne stared at them curiously, remembering Elsen's story and wondering if there was any truth to it.

The cart finally came into view coming along the cobbled street from the direction of the port, but there was someone else on it. It was Thomas.

She nudged Lorcan and pointed in their direction.

"How in the...?" He got up and picked up the dress and pack. They hadn't seen them yet but they would any second now, "I'll distract them. You go." He said, moving towards them without looking back.

Adrienne picked up her things and, in a bid not to draw too much attention to herself, walked casually down a short side street that had nothing but a bookshop along it. She pulled her hood up and stopped, facing away from the square into the bookshop window. When she felt she'd stayed there long enough, she picked up a fast pace and walked to the end of the street, which turned onto an uphill road leading away from the town.

Panic filled Adrienne's head as she realised how much they knew, and what might happen if that information got into the wrong hands. More panic came when she wondered if it was already in the wrong hands. If it was Thomas and Noah who she needed to protect herself from. She shouldn't even have told Lorcan what she had. She needed to be more cautious, but a lot of good it did telling herself that now.

She tensed and quickened her pace as she turned the corner, but soon she became aware of light footsteps behind her. She could barely hear them, but there was some force of knowledge telling her that what she heard was a danger, willing her to hide. She dared not turn around to look, instead ducking behind a wall at the edge of a shop. The footsteps came closer, and a shadow formed on the ground in front of her. She held her breath, but it was as if their eyes were on the back of her neck already. She pulled herself back so that her shadow disappeared behind that of a dustbin, and she crouched down as small as she could. She considered calling for help, but as she was out of sight of the main road, there was no one she could call on, no public road to prevent whatever was about to happen. She was about to start running when she heard a voice, "Adrienne."

It was Noah.

"What are you doing?" he said, pulling her up from the ground.

"I'm leaving," she replied with as much casualness as she could muster. This was a game of deception now, and they were both in on it. She placed her hands in her pocket, using her nerves to justify it, and reached for the hunting knife on the inside of her pack.

"Thanks, Noah, but it's just the sea... it isn't for me. Really, I'd rather take my chances on the road from here. I told Lorcan to let everyone know, so as not to cause a fuss. I don't want anyone to think I'm ungrateful," her voice was shaking now under her calm exterior, but she could barely tell what from.

"Don't go," he said, breathlessly, "We all want you to stay. You really impressed the troupe, and Jill has taken such a shine to you," his manner was charming and eerily cordial.

She searched his expression for any kind of giveaway, some sign that he might not be speaking earnestly, though she knew he wasn't. He flinched as she moved forward. She shook her head, her knife now poised inside her cloak pocket, "I'm flattered, I really have enjoyed my time on the ship, but I felt the Channel move and I need to move with it, as they say," she said quietly.

"'You have free will, you know Adrienne," he smiled an indecipherable, ambiguous sort of smile, "Your fate isn't determined by the movement of invisible lines in the air. We move them right? That's what they say? If you believe that stuff."

"It's just an expression," she said, looking deep into his eyes now, searching for anything that might prove her thoughts of him wrong, "I need to go with my gut. I need to be on land... I feel safer that way."

"Is it us?" asked Noah, "Is it something we've done?"

She didn't respond, though something in her wanted to speak against all her better judgement.

"Is there something you're not telling me, Adrienne? Why would you feel unsafe? Tell me. You can tell me"

He stepped forward.

"Don't," she lifted her hunting knife, "Don't come any closer, please."

He stood over her, threatening and tall. She could barely breathe as the moment seemed to go on forever, and in an overwhelming muddle of confusion, she gasped, before stepping back to guard herself with the knife. She wasn't scared to fight him, but despite all that was happening, she didn't want to. Or was it that a part of her didn't want to believe that he would hurt her? Or was it that she didn't care if he did? They both held their ground, not breaking eye contact, barely breathing, close but not close enough for anything to happen. Then Noah let his guard down for a second, his expression dropped, and all she saw under the facade was worry. *Another trick?* she wondered.

He was watching her closely, his chest was rising and falling at double speed. She wanted to reach out to him, and yet she wanted to run. She wanted to escape from her body just to get away from it. She wanted to tell Noah everything, to throw herself at his feet and beg for him to take the burden away from her. She wanted him to be good. She wanted anything other than to be here, with this impossible task that she barely comprehended.

"Come back to the boat with me," he urged her, "Adrienne, you must, don't you understand?"

Then, in a leap of blind faith, Adrienne dropped the hand holding the knife and turned her head to look at the flint road before them, then back at Noah, "I cannot," she said.

"Well then, I can't let you go. You know I can't."

So it was true. The bitter disappointment then crept through her like a hot flush.

"I know," she said, stepping back a few steps, but he didn't move. She stepped back again, but he just stood there, not looking threatening at all anymore, just a longing in his eyes that she couldn't name. He still held himself as if he meant it, stoic and unflinching, but his face gave away something else. He wasn't going to force her to do anything, and they both knew it.

With that, she turned back to the road and walked. He didn't follow.

She kept walking, and as she walked the pavement turned to dirt and the walls turned to grass and underbrush, and after about fifteen minutes she finally felt safe enough to rest. At the top of the hill was an old, ancient fort. She sat on a stone slab and looked out over the trees to the port down below. The Player's Circle was still there, and the port was much busier than it had been when they arrived. Yesterday there were two ships and now she counted six. The season was starting. Not just troupers 'ships but merchants, travelling salesmen, healers and tinkers, they would all start their journeys across the Central Lands over the coming months, all in boats or ships made for travelling from island to island.

A sailor covered in a travelling cloak was walking directly up the hill towards her. She readied herself to run until she saw his face and dimples: it was Lorcan.

"I spoke to Thomas, told him you'd run off and I couldn't find you," he said when he reached the top of the hill, "He's sent out a search party. You need to hurry," he pushed a large, rolled up piece of paper into her hands and looked down towards the town nervously, "I should go."

"Will you be OK?" asked Adrienne, looking at the lost boy in front of her. He looked so conflicted, his face forcing a fake smile so that his dimples showed through a weathered expression.

He lifted the hood of his cloak and turned back nervously to face the town, "Thomas won't hurt me," he said, "I'll be fine. It's what I know. I have to go back," he considered his words, "I want to."

Chapter 11 - Shanaki, Storm's End

The sound of rain had dissipated from the glass walls of the menagerie, and its sulphurous smell had overtaken the fading aroma of the now closed up coffee cart. Taps of metal upon metal echoed through the square as the shops closed up for the day, and the last hour of bird song harmonised into the distance.

Shanaki stood up to address his listeners, "And that is where we'll leave it for today. The rest of the tale I have not heard for so long that I will need to go back over it tonight. I will have to consult some texts and piece the rest of the story together as truthfully as I can. It is a long story and it may take a few sittings to tell." He might as well break it up and make as much as he can of this.

"Good sir?"

Shanaki almost let out a groan in front of his entire audience, almost.

"Pray forgive me," said the man from earlier in his most fastidious tone, "I do not understand why you have to consult such texts. The reason being that this is not a true story. The reason for me knowing this is that the timings don't work. They say Adrianna lived a full thousand years ago. There are yet stories of Adrianna's children fighting in the great wars two hundred years ago. It is not a true story, and there has been no attempt to make it even appear as such, sir, with respect. Is this not part of a web of lies told for entertainment and the collective understanding of morals and what not? You do not need to pretend there is anything more..."

Shanaki solemnly stood and began to pick up his things, without looking at the man, "I suppose that, even if there's no way I can convince you that the story is true, would you not want to hear a story that is the closest to the one that was originally told?"

The man thought for a moment, "I supposed you'd be right... but this story is so different from what I 'eard... .er..." having exposed himself by letting what he thought was a perfect gentlemanly accent slip, he took a moment to compose himself, "I have come to know well upon many a visiting..."

There was muttering amongst the crowd now, Shanaki was in danger of losing them, he braced himself for what he was about to say.

"What if I was to tell you that I know just that bit more than any of the storytellers and that I have a personal hand in this tale?"

"That's impossible! You'd have to be a thousand years old for that to be true!"

"Are there not other ways?" he said. The crowd went silent.

Shanaki had lost control of himself. This man, this derelict, had poked and prodded and inadvertently brought something out of him. Was it pride? He wasn't sure. But now that it was out, he could not turn back. He would have to continue this saga until its very end.

He looked around at the crowd. Even if half of them came back he'd still do better than he had in months, "I will see you all, tomorrow."

As he spoke he stood and hovered with a capricious turn that years of leaving stories on a cliffhanger had learnt him to do so well, and then he exited.

"And I!" shouted the drunk man after him, "And I will not, I repeat, will not be wearing this disposition in the morrow. My daughter was married this afternoon you see, and though I am merry as a Midmoon baby I cannot stand her mother. She and her new husband have made their exit from the wedding." He winked, and carried on although Shanaki was now well out of earshot, "I have taken myself off to find some joy someplace else. I do promise, I will be sober and respectful tomorrow. If you will oblige, tell us the tale."

He proceeded to wander back outside in his own time, whilst reciting (in perfect verse) the tale of Old Charles Halomey.

"Oh when I was easy under the apple balms, did the strange scent of spring bring me life, life…"

The story had been on Shanaki's mind. Not the details of it, for that was simple enough. And besides, not one storyteller got through a telling without tweaking or exaggerating with dramatic licence. It was rare that the entire, objective truth made its way to an audience, large or small. After all, how useful would a story be if we all discovered the same things every time we heard it? But this was different. He needed to do this, and it would most likely be the end of him to tell it.

There was, of course, the other more immediate issue: the Senelin City parliament had recently decreed wide scale censorship for anyone speaking ill of the state, and he didn't want anything he said to be, well, misinterpreted by the wrong people. Many stories had been banned for a number of years during the Great Modernisation two hundred years ago, and though they were no longer banned, it was considered uncouth to retell stories such as Adrienne or The Queen of Keeper's Cove in the ways of old. The song was an exception to this rule because it was so well known and impossible to audit. Other than that, it was only in private tellings inside of homes, or occasionally at the end of a heavy night of drinking in some tavern that was far, far away from the eyes of the law, that the tale would be told out loud.

He peered down at an antique Stairs Book from his display case. It was, of course, no longer performing the function of a Stairs Book. Everyone knew they no longer harnessed any energy and hadn't done so for hundreds of years. And that's if they believed any vessels ever did.

In spite of that, something compelled him to take the dusty key from the overmantel, unlock the cabinet and take out the book. He opened it to see old, dateless notes from forgotten times: tracking of embargoed ships from the north to the south during the great Consortium wars, messages to loved ones, or the smuggling of cargo into poorer areas of Senelin. The book was full of them until halfway through, where the writing stopped dead and there was nothing but a blank page following it. Still so crisp as it had been left all those years ago.

Shanaki ran his wrinkled hands over the pages and let out a sigh. He sat with the book for what felt like a lot longer than it was, his trance only broken by the wind picking up and knocking the window, which had been left ajar, ever so gently shut.

Then, as if it was the most natural thing in the world, he picked up a gold pen that had been lying next to it and began to write. He didn't write for the sake of anything, of anyone, he simply wrote for his own sake. For the sake of that moment and nothing more. He wrote:

"I do not know who I speak to. Sometimes it's important to believe that something is there, for your own sake if no one else's.

I have decided that now is the time, before I forget my own altogether, to tell the story that is true to very few. Then I will make my final journey into the woods, and this time I will not return."

He put the pen down, blew gently on the ink and left it to dry on his desk. There was an emotion brewing under the surface, which he hadn't known was there, or at least hadn't truly acknowledged was there, until now. It was like the intense feeling of returning home from a long journey. The closer one gets to their destination, the more urgent it feels and the truth of their homesickness surfaces. Shanaki observed in himself the beginnings of the end of his own homesickness. He felt it in his heart with reluctance, for there was no home to return to. But in spite of it all, he found the strength to ease it out, like poison from a snake bite. It was loneliness. He had been alone for so long, and he had stored it up inside of him because there was nowhere else to put it, but perhaps now he could start to let it flow out of him into the world, into the air, and let the energy of it be turned into something new, something better.

He lit a fire to warm up the room as the storm outside took hold. He pulled out some Trikken cake from his cupboards, placed a piece of it onto a small plate and put a kettle of water over the wood burner and brewed some tea. He then sat under a blanket, in a chair beside it.

He woke the next morning, unable to remember dozing off at all. He had, after all, spent the best part of a day speaking in an animated fashion to a group of strangers. That was nearly double the amount of time he usually would spend working, and he was a little wiped out. He rubbed his eyes and made his way across the hall to the study. It was a small room with shelves lining every wall, some shelves were overflowing with books stacked on top of each other and some flowing out onto the floor. On the side by the window was a large leather-bound atlas, too big to fit in any case or unit. At the very back, behind his desk, was a glass cabinet.

He picked up a key from behind *The Ballads of The Northern Isles* and opened the cabinet. Inside were more books, a couple of trinkets, a compass, some precious stones and a photograph of an old couple on a boat.

Today had a gloriously clear sky. The storm had ended in the early hours of the morning, and Shanaki stared out of his lodging window at the pink, grey spectacle that you only see after heavy rainfall. Something had been building up in the atmosphere, desperate to release itself, and after it had, the world was calm for a brief moment before the endless cycle started once again.

At the very back, he pulled out a large, tattered old book with gold-rimmed pages and a seal at the front. There was an emblem on it, faded so much that you could barely notice it had ever been there unless you were super close. It was the shape of a tree trunk that landed on a circular base, with lines coming out of them in circle-like routes at all sides.

As he left his room, he didn't notice the markings that had appeared in the open Stair Book; under the line he had written moments before was a new line, three words: "We are here."

Shanaki made his way to the square, book in hand. He felt his heartbeat; he felt calm but he could feel the nerves had spread throughout his body. As long as it doesn't show in my voice, he thought. He collected himself and looked around. The man from yesterday was there, looking slightly dishevelled but upright, perched on the ancient tree root that had driven back out of the ground to form seating that circled around the square. The man gave Shanaki a knowing nod as he passed him and followed him round to take his place on the edge of the tree root bench. The students too had returned, and new crowds began to slow their pace at his arrival.

Unlike the old days, storytellers, street entertainers and musicians worked alone in this town, and Shanaki knew he was lucky to have the best spot. They were too far inland to get a huge number of theatre boats in Senelin City these days, as all the traditional patronages had died out, and most of the artists had moved south with the masters, where the festivals were in the summer. Most troops had decided to stay put, and working a festival season in the summer would set them up to write new plays and play the Christmas balls in the winter. Shanaki thought they were lazy, that real troupers stayed on the road, and wanted adventure, but who was he to judge? He'd seen enough adventure for a lifetime, and here he was, living out the end of his days walking one long street from his rooms to his playhouse.

    He walked through the glass doors of the greenhouse, sat himself down in the square and looked out again at the man from yesterday. The man nodded as if to say, 'begin.' Shanaki pulled out his dusty reference book from his pocket, opened it out, placed it on the floor, and began to speak.

Chapter 12 - The Lonely Man

When Lorcan arrived back in the square without Adrienne, Thomas was waiting for him on the bench they'd been sitting on. He had an expression of quiet rage on his face, and he was armed with a sword.

"You let her go."

"As opposed to what?" said Lorcan defiantly.

"I wasn't talking to you."

Behind Lorcan, Noah was drifting up to the bench, looking shaken. Lorcan scowled at him, disgusted by his involvement. Jealous, even.

"She got away," Noah whispered.

"We've lost it, and her. What am I meant to do with this?" hissed Thomas.

"What is going on?" shouted Lorcan.

"Take this cargo back to the ship," Thomas ordered Noah before turning his attention to Lorcan.

Even after what he'd heard on the boat, he hadn't been expecting any of this. All for a Noch? A shiny metal ornament that makes fairy noises when the Channel is busy? The Channel is always busy! He must have missed something. He now realised that he had no idea what value the object had to Thomas or what any of it might have meant. *But focus,* he thought. Thomas was staring him down, silently waiting for him to make a move. If one of them drew, the other had to as well. On a bad day, Lorcan had heard of fights breaking out on boats over a lot less: over gin and women, oversleeping spaces, over respect. It was the inevitable result of being in close quarters with the same people for such a long time, like fighting with family. This was in public though, and the reputation of the troupe was on the line. Surely Thomas wouldn't risk that over this? Their reputation had taken lifetimes to build and could be broken the second that blood was drawn. Suddenly though, Lorcan realised that two men standing on either side of the square were members of the crew as well - it was a trap.

"With me," said Thomas.

Thomas and two men led Lorcan around a corner into a secluded area of grass and woodland just off the town. He tried to slow down the pace of his walking to buy himself time but the sailors kicked at his heels. Thomas stopped on the road by an old oak tree that sheltered them from the hill.

This was it. Lorcan had nothing. He was lucky to be alive, and after finding the Player's Circle he did everything in his power to get to a place where he felt secure and valued. He'd just thrown that all away for a pretty face. *Wait* he thought *I'm not the one in the wrong here. I did the right thing!* Surely Thomas wouldn't have him murdered for that? Thomas wasn't evil. So few people were really evil. broken maybe, or ill, but not evil. Thomas had a temper and sometimes he did compromising things, bad things, which he could justify at the time. But not this? Lorcan thought back to the time just before he'd been forced to leave his village. He remembered the shocking things that the villagers had been driven to do, the justified things, the things that humans can be driven to when desperation took hold. How much of a difference in impact was there between the fear of poverty and the power of greed?

Thomas faced Lorcan with intent, but would he speak or attack? The two men were heading for either side of the tree, and the thistle and hedges to the other side were so thick that they blocked his way. There was no way out of this that wasn't through Thomas. Lorcan had exactly six seconds before he had to make a decision.

What happened next happened all at once, Lorcan stuck his foot out as one of the unsuspecting sailors failed to stop in time, tripping him up. Lorcan then drew his sword fast enough to get a slight advantage over the other two. The standing man crashed his sword into Lorcan's, and the blow knocked him back into a tree. He rolled out of the way just in time as the sailor thug struck the trunk, leaving a gash in the bark.

He dodged another blow from the other sailor who had managed to get to his feet but he felt Thomas's sword pierce his arm in between blows. He fell back and the sailors grabbed him and held him down.

"Come on boy," said Thomas, "Throw everything away over a stranger? Everything you've worked for? You haven't even the faintest idea what you're getting yourself mixed up in."

"Not a stranger, a crew member! I didn't think I was throwing anything away. It wasn't right, Thomas, you know it wasn't! You told me to look out for her so I did. Ain't worth stealing..." he croaked through the tightly gripped hands on his chest.

Thomas laughed, throwing Lorcan to the floor, "Steal? That object never belonged to her in the first place," he said, "We were just going to take it back to its rightful owner. Did she tell you what she was planning on doing with it?"

Lorcan didn't answer.

"I thought so," Thomas gestured for the men to let Lorcan go, "Go. You're no use to me now."

A flicker of what looked like regret lingered in Thomas 'eyes, and Lorcan opened his mouth to protest but it was to no avail.

"I'm done with you," said Thomas callously, and turned away.

Lorcan froze in confusion; all of a sudden he was free of restraint and free to go, and just like that, it was done. The last four years of his life were over in a split second, over what? Thomas was using logic he didn't understand and perhaps he should have gone to him first before Adrienne - perhaps. Regardless, the ship was his home, his place of security. He needed it. It was too much to process, but he didn't seem to have a choice in the matter, so without any other idea of what to do, he began to walk north.

Adrienne came off the dirt road just by the path leading to the mountain towns. A sign in the other direction said Keeper's Forest, and another, in the middle, led to the Medicina Mountain route. The walk into Medicina town hadn't seemed so far away from the coast when she was with Lorcan, but on her own, not knowing her way, she realised it must have taken them a good half of the morning to get there. She tried to get her bearings to make the safest journey to Keeper's Cove that she could. If she journeyed on the forest route, which matched up with the coast much further north of where the Player's Circle was docked, she could get to the coast by sundown without a port in sight. She might even be in with a chance of finding somewhere to stop for the night, and in the morning could try her luck at hitching a lift on a trade cart all the way up to the Keeper's gates.

After a few hours of walking, she was down to her last few sips of water and was starting to think about resting in the shade for a time. Perhaps she could stick the metal of her water bottle into a birch tree for a bit of sustenance - a trick taught to her by Elsen. Or maybe she would walk onwards in the hopes of finding a coast road tavern to bunk up in for the night. What she really wanted was to get to Keeper's Cove as quickly as she could, but the heat and dust were too much without a cart, so she needed to rest.

In the distance in front of her, the horizon was clear as far as she could see, just a path and a few gulls flying in the early evening dusk. But as she dropped her things, she realised that something or someone was blocking her view. She couldn't make out if the figure had been there the entire time, but it must have been - there was nowhere it could have come from. It was a body, facing away from her, and she was sure she saw it turn in her direction, then in a blink, it was gone.

She stood for a while, fear creeping over her. Aware that the last moments of sunlight were moving further and further away from her and that there was something out there, and it had seen her. She pulled out the Noch and looked at it. It looked different; the normal faint white light was as bright as she'd ever seen it. She closed her eyes and listened. A faint sound buzzed from it, like a crackling whisper. It was in her head and all around her, like nothing she'd heard before. There was someone nearby manipulating magick from the Channel.

A cracking sound came from behind her and she turned. A man was crumpled up on the floor behind her. She backed away until she realised he was starved, stripped naked and on the floor only because he was unable to stand. Shivering and drooling, his expression filled with fear and torment. He smiled strangely, his hands shielding his eyes from the glare of the setting sun. His smile turned to an ugly cry of despair, and took a breath as if to speak but couldn't get the air out. Then he cowered back into himself, mumbling something to himself.

"What did you say?" whispered Adrienne, "I can't hear you."

"Who are you? What are you doing to me!" he yelled, "I will never..." His speech fizzled out. She stared in horror at this broken, piteous man on the side of a dirt road. Not knowing what to do, she dug in her pack for something to give him: water, a cloak, anything, but as she looked up he had disappeared again as if he'd never been there at all. He'd vanished into thin air.

She sat next to the pack and took the final sip of the water herself. She pulled the Noch out from her pocket. There was a fading orange glow now, ever so slight. She took another sip of water, ready to walk some more, but as she did the Noch lit up again, brightly this time. She stood holding it. There was another crack.

In the same spot that the broken figure had appeared stood a huge man in a dark cloak, with chalky skin and long fingernails, his mouth just visible under his hood. She had heard of these men in stories, she'd heard of the real ones from the man in the tavern in Avenly, but nothing could have prepared her for the sight of it. This strange being in the flesh was so alien, so void of humanity, that her body froze in fear, like game caught in the path of an arrow. His expression turned to a cruel grimace, and he took a step towards her, towering over her like a base god. The thought of running seemed pointless.

Then something else happened. An arrow struck him in the shoulder and an axe landed low on the ground towards Adrienne's feet. She wasted no time in surprise and picked up the axe, swinging it at the surprised man's face. He ducked back and pulled the arrow out of his shoulder. He then took a swing at Adrienne with his staff, which she avoided by leaning back and swinging the axe to his right side. He had his sword now though and blocked her blow, using the force to push back and knock her clean off her feet. His body sunk under the weight of its wounds, but he didn't cry out or show any signs of pain.

Lorcan stood with his bow pointing at the man's head. The man limped forwards, pulling arrows out of him as he did, unfazed by the blood spurting out of his shoulder and leg. Lorcan inched forwards and grabbed Adrienne's arm. She picked up the axe and they ran.

The trouble with running in a wide clearing is that there's nowhere to hide. After a fast and desperate sprint,

Lorcan started to clutch his chest. Adrienne stopped and turned, pulling out her dagger to throw in the stranger's direction. But when she turned, she saw nothing. The man who had been unable to walk was gone from sight.

"What was that?" asked Lorcan, breathlessly.

Adrienne had found shade, and was leaning against the foot of a tree on the side of the road.

"Seldelige," said Adrienne, "They were saying in Avenly that they are out of control" she trailed off, perplexed, "but I didn't believe it. That's the first time I've seen one up close."

"I didn't mean that," he said, "I meant the man."

"I know," said Adrienne, "I don't know. Are you OK? You're sweating?"

His arm was bandaged up with a piece of cloth.

"What happened?" she said, wasting no time as she hunted through the weeds on the side of the road to find something to rub on it.

Lorcan paced back and forth a while before stopping still in front of her, resolved, "I just left my troupe."

She tried to speak but she couldn't find the words. She pulled a root out of the ground and used her knife to crush it onto a nearby stone, "Put this inside the cloth for now, it should help clean it."

"Adrienne," he said, forcefully, "You need to tell me why we're here."

Chapter 13 - Shanaki, The Intruder

"He's a spy!" shouted the previously drunk man from the tree stalls.

Shanaki paused, unfazed by the interruption, "Ah good to hear from you. I was beginning to wonder if you'd fallen asleep," he tilted his head to the man, "Might you regale us with your name before it becomes socially unacceptable for me to ask?"

The man drifted to the front of the space and sat next to Shanaki by the tree, now fully part of the act, "Goodrum Bernder," said the man, "and everyone knows that Lorcan betrayed Adrienne, just when she least expected it. It was his plan all along! It's right there in the song in the fifth verse:

> There never was a time of such
> When she had been misplayed
> Than all the while her company
> Had been the one who stayed
> The boy beneath the banner
> The boy who gave away
> The trust that he had earned
> And the trust that he betrayed
> OOOOHHH..."

This time, he didn't bellow the verse across the building like a drunken soldier, so the storyteller was able to exercise some thin-wavering patience.

"What makes you think he had a plan?" interrupted Shanaki.

"They've always got a plan!" said Goodrum.

Shanaki chuckled and raised his hand to his head to block the mid-afternoon glare of the sun from his eyes. He wanted to look Goodrum straight in the eye, "Does Adrienne have a plan?"

The man looked bemused at this, "Well no, but she's the main character in the story..."

"People aren't that simple," said Shanaki, "in stories, there is always a plan, because we are looking at what happened in hindsight, but I am telling you the real story, and in real life people are messy; we only see the symmetry in the aftermath..."

"No," said Goodrum, "I do not accept that. Lorcan made a mistake and he's in the story so we can learn not to trust people like him!"

"Lorcan was a well-meaning man!" Shanaki belted in a rare outburst of genuine emotion, "Flawed, but well meaning."

Goodrum sniffed his nose at this, "And by your reaction, I would presume that you knew him."

"And how do you know I didn't?" said Shanaki, and at this, he actually heard the crowd collectively gasp. "If you want to hear the story as it was, as it happened, then I suggest you listen. It will not always make sense or fit in with your ideas of what it *should* be, but trust that it will unfold in the way that it did unfold. We will not skip ahead."

He was now genuinely irritated for the first time since meeting the man. Shanaki had to consider finishing his tale for the day then and there, but after a moment, he persisted:

"A story," he said, more calmly, "is reflective only of the time it is told; it is always passed on by someone who has already taken it into themselves, do you see?"

Goodrum stared back at him, blankly.

"Every person wants to believe they are good, Lorcan and Adrienne, the men who commit their lives to the Consortium, the Gedogin Keepers... but with so much conflict in the world, we find ourselves both monster and hero. We are a muddle of beauty and vulgarity, in direct contradiction with ourselves, right to the very route of our souls. It is only with retelling our tales that we see the black and white of it: we seek out the beginning, middle and end, to tie ourselves up in meaning and purpose. It's what makes us human. But whilst our stories are happening, we are nothing but a muddle of actions, decisions and reactions: a lone soldier in a sea of armour, unable to see the shape of their own war."

"Right," said Goodrum.

"So, may I continue?"

Goodrum reacted strangely. He smiled knowingly, though knowing what was not clear to Shanaki or the crowd. He gestured to the crowd, and to Shanaki, and he walked back to his seat, "Carry on" he said, picking up his gin bottle with a dramatic gesture and sipping it daintily.

Shanaki obliged, "Well..."

Chapter 14 - Between Sea and Land

    They carried along the road in silence for another hour, and as they walked they felt the presence of the coast; the smell of salty water; the faint hint of sand in the breeze. After a while, the dirt road became sand dunes and the gulls were more constant in breaking up the skyline. Just before sundown they saw a sign to an Inn and followed it off the track to the coast. Adrienne's eyes were sore and she had to stop at one point to cough out the dust from the road. It was an uncommonly hot day. One of the first of summer, but it was the humid kind, and the sea breeze was comforting and familiar.

    The Inn was closed off by a wooden wall, and behind it was a stone garden with candles lighting the way all along the path to the front door. It was a small Inn, full of chatter from the public areas and clanking from the kitchens, and a mixture of travellers scattered around the main room. The Inns in Avenly were dark places, with log fires and leather sunken chairs, but this place, at the edge of the track, with nothing but sea stretched out before it and mountains and forest behind it, felt like a bright haven amidst the darkness. Behind the bar on the back wall, Adrienne saw a solid wooden crest, with the same tree trunk-shaped circles that melded into each other as the markings on her Noch. The only difference was that this one was clearer, as it was carved deeply into thick wood instead of faint curved markings on metal.

    At the bar was a tall woman draped in red floaty robes chatting to some of the locals. She had frizzy hair, full lips and a crisp, soothing voice. She smiled warmly at both of them, her eyes going directly to the player's crest on Lorcan's shirt.

"What brings two sea players onto land so far away from a port?" she asked, looking at the crest on Lorcan's shirt.

Lorcan tucked the badge inside his pocket, embarrassed that he had been so foolish as not to hide it before they'd entered, "We had to take a detour," he said. She nodded, not wanting to scare any customers away by prying for information that was of no use to her.

"I'm on the way to visit my family in the north and he's escorting me before he goes back to his boat," Adrienne said, only half lying.

The bartender nodded her head again, "I used to live on the sea too. I know what keeps people there but I also know what makes them leave. Families can be tricky, and so can politics. I'll ask no more about it, shall I," she smiled.

Another woman with golden hair and an apron over a blue dress walked out with some fish and placed it in front of two gentlemen by the window sill.

Adrienne pulled out her purse, "What's the food today, Miss?"

"Fish and potato cobbler," said the woman, "caught this morning."

"Can we have two of them to go with our ales, and have you got a room with two beds for the night?" she asked, pushing a Glame towards the first bartender on the countertop.

The woman from the kitchen, whose name was Siggi, showed them up to a small room at the back of the Tavern. It wasn't much, but it had a fireplace, two beds with a curtain in between, a dresser and some old books nestled on the windowsill. The branch of a willow tree, full of blossom, blocked the view to the left of the window, which otherwise faced the sea, and you could just about hear it as the waves hit the shore. Directly below them was the public garden, starting to fill with travellers and their pipes around an open fire pit. One of the travellers had a dog sitting on his lap, and it gave Adrienne a pang for a home that was no longer there.

They put their packs down and went back downstairs, seating themselves on a bench in the corner of the garden with a hearty cobbler and ale. The saltwater fish tasted different to river fish, or the heavily seasoned delicacies one might be fed at a dinner party either side of Wiberia. The only thing Adrienne had tried that came even close to this, was the traditional fish and bread dishes in the Laten Islands, where they lived off fish and grain for most of the year. It was exactly what they needed, and almost enough to completely distract them from what they'd left behind and what lay ahead, for a short while at least.

"I don't know if the Noch is fake or not," said Adrienne eventually, breaking another one of Lorcan's uncomfortable silences.

Lorcan listened, slowly sipping his ale and watching the crowd on the other side of the garden, "Why couldn't you just have said that to me before?"

She bit her lip and sat up straight, her head tangling with the overgrown honeysuckle that sheltered the bench. She brushed it away, "I didn't know who I could trust," she said, hesitantly, "You might have just wanted information from me..."

"...I left my crew," he interrupted.

She searched his face: it had a look of vulnerability, of genuine hurt, of fear. If he wasn't telling the truth now, then she didn't know who ever had.

"I had no way of knowing what you'd do in that situation, but I know now..." she said, "I'm sorry it came to that..."

"It was the right thing to do," he said, "It was either that or turn you in, and I dunno what they'd have done to you. I've never seen that side of Thomas, people said it was there, but I never saw it, so I didn't believe it. He has that effect on people, they said that as well. If Noah or the others had found you first you'd have been..."

"...you don't know that," she said, without thinking, and turned her face to the shore, "He was following orders, the same as you."

"Me and him have been through so much of the same. He's no good. He's the one who turned you in!" snapped Lorcan, a faint glimmer of jealousy simmering under the surface.

"I just mean that... maybe he didn't know what he was doing," she said.

Lorcan let out a long sigh and took another sip of his beer, "You are naive if you think that everyone has good intentions, Adrienne."

"I don't think everyone is good, but I do think everyone believes they have good intentions," she said, "There's a difference."

"So someone betrays you, or puts you in danger, and you let them keep your trust because you know they didn't exactly mean it like that?" Lorcan laughed at the thought, "That's not the way the world works."

"I didn't say I trusted him."

Later, in the evening the Inn had grown quiet. It was just the overnighters left, who were either sleeping or still downstairs making the most of the proper fireplace and the landlady's ales.

Lorcan and Adrienne were invited to join Siggi and Helena in a quiet corner, as they took in some peace and quiet after a busy shift. They shared stories of their time on the sea. The women were both ex-pirates who made good and joined a theatre troupe, fell in love and decided to settle on land.

"I lived on the wrong side of the Consortium for years," Helena said, "They've had the contract for state security since before I was born. Tolling taxes from both north and south have been heavy with the Consortium in charge. Their privateers would often stop and search ships for no reason, confiscating what they wanted. Many independent merchants and traders were forced into privateering themselves, if they could get sponsorship from either kingdom, or worse piracy. All that does is it gives the Consortium more leverage to keep the measures up. It's a vicious cycle."

"What kind of... pirate were you?" asked Adrienne, not sure how to phrase the question.

"Smuggling mainly," said Helena, "My father was a privateer, and when I went out on my own I refused to work for anyone. Siggi worked her way up and was a 1st mate on a legitimate trading ship before she turned her back on the northern crown. We still refused to board northern ships, but when the war started, that's when it got complicated. In a war, the wage goes up to disrupt the opposition's trade, but a war has to end. Truces happen, and then they turn back to the pirates as if they've caused it in the first place. When I joined a theatre troupe it was better. Less fights, less hangings, but there's a way with seafarers that seems to stick: they're fully loyal until they're not. We all come from the same end you see, without anyone to answer to except ourselves. We're all seeking a place to belong and we settle into ship family so quickly, but we can walk away from it just as easily... and that's how people end up selling each other out..."

Lorcan was leaning back in his chair, fidgeting, his eyes cast downwards. He opened his mouth to protest but Helena continued, "I know, I bet yours was different right? But did they turn out to be in the end? Does it matter who it was? Everyone can turn on someone, every place in the world has its merits and its faults. Sea folk are wonderful people, they're passionate and honest and raw, but the bad always catches up with the good."

"That's why we decided we wanted something more sustainable," said Siggi, "We met on a ship going south and fell for each other instantly," the two women had reached across their chairs towards each other, "I looked around the ship one day, watching the sailors on the deck in the evening after all the work was done. That was the bit I enjoyed the most: the evenings, the people you meet when you're travelling, from all walks of life. They eat and drink together, sharing stories of other worlds, singing shanties. That's when I realised that working in an inn was what I wanted. The connection and safety and warmth. The work is just as hard, but it's ours and it's solid."

"And if anyone causes trouble," said Helena, "You can kick them out without drowning them... and if it's on the road then you likely won't see them again. Now we have a home and no one can take it away from us. People come and go but willingly. So many people pass through, I feel like I've met every kind of person in the Central Islands."

Lorcan held in her words for a moment, looked around at the beautiful surroundings, at the sturdy willow tree that grounded the tavern to the shore in comparison with the vast space of sea that stretched out before them, "Bad can catch up with you wherever you are, even here."

She smiled at this, "That it can, Lorcan. You're not planning on bringing us any are you?"

Adrienne had enough money in her purse to pay for the room and board and had at least seven Glames left after that, so given that they were very unlikely to come across anyone else on the road up north, it was hopefully enough to get her to Senelin from Keeper's Cove. It did feel like a longer journey than she'd expected. In fact, she wasn't sure what she'd expected. Perhaps she'd imagined that the journey would pass her by, that she'd arrive in Keeper's Cove without anything to tell of it. Perhaps it was more frustrating that she'd had no time to grieve, and perhaps at some point soon that grief might turn to anger, but despite all this, she carried on.

That evening she chatted with a farmer, who was on his way back south from Keeper's Cove, where he had travelled to bulk buy Nesters for his farm without having to pay the huge taxations to the Consortium. He told her about his small freehold in the southern farmlands, and how most of the small farmers were struggling to get enough produce to the north due to sanctions from the war. He said there was talk of the Consortium experimenting with Nesters to see if they could recreate them, but that nothing quite worked as well as the ones from Keeper's Cove, as their prototypes often broke or malfunctioned before long. He explained that the reason everything was taxed so high wasn't because of the Consortium but because those in Keeper's Cove were so miserly with the distribution of their resources. He was kind and told her she reminded him of his daughter back home.

Elsewhere, after not so many pints of ale, Lorcan was full of energy and deep in conversation with some locals around a table.

"Bandits? In the forests?" he asked, "That's what they say on the sea, that they're everywhere, waiting to attack traders travelling down to the bigger port in Avenly."

"Desperate folk," said a woman with fiery red hair, who had arrived earlier on her way to visit her husband in the mining town, "Folk who have been banished from society for one reason or another, but they're far and few. A few generations ago the northern crown started banishing whoever they wanted to the woods below Keeper's Cove, probably to signal sovereignty over the Gedogin as no one wants a forest full of bandits right outside their doors. Anyway, these banished people were understandably angry, so they went out into the deepest parts of the forests and found its inhabitants. They slaughtered them, stealing their houses and homes for themselves," she said matter-of-factly. "Now they prey on the ones coming up and down on the trade route, like normal bandits."

"Some say that evil Danaan witches joined forces with them, that they use wild magicks, which they can produce from summoning energy from the sky instead of using vessels like everyone else."

Half listening to this, Adrienne was sitting in the corner by the fire, looking at the map up to Keeper's Cove. There wasn't anyone else in that corner of the bar, except for Suki, who was cleaning a nearby table. Adrienne pointed at the wooden crest behind the bar, "What is that?"

"That's the Gedogin crest. It doesn't mean much being there. It's mainly for the traders, people like to see it as it signals that they're nearing Keeper's Cove."

"I've seen it on pendants."

Siggi looked back at Adrienne curiously, "The Gedogin Alliance are said to have all sorts of jewellery with the crest on. In the south, people like to claim that they have originals, made in Keeper's Cove and once owned by Gedogin Alliance fighters back in the day. They are collector's items. But most of them are fakes."

"Why would they fake them?" asked Adrienne.

"They say that certain items of jewellery in the crest provide the wearer with certain powers. Some say they can make you read other people's thoughts or that it contains energy directly from the Inner Channel. Again, I don't think this is true."

"But what if it was on a Noch?" asked Adrienne.

"I don't know," Sukki shrugged, "Nochs are meant to amplify the sound of the Channel, but they never work..."

"Do people around here even believe in the Inner Channel?" asked Adrienne, "In the south, it's generally considered pseudo magick, I mean to believe it's anything more than harnessable energy."

Sukki sat next to Adrienne, cloth in hand, "Some folk in the more isolated islands are still superstitious, but even the Consortium only sees it as a natural phenomenon. The lights at Keeper's Cove are really beautiful, I've seen them myself, but the Gedogin do have a magickal explanation for them," she shrugged "The most likely thing is that the crests on the jewellery and the Nochs, they just act as an identity badge for other members of the Gedogin Alliance."

She glanced around the tavern at the free talking travellers mixing with the few locals that lived out this way, "Do the common people up here like the Gedogin?" she asked, "In the south, they tend to side with the Consortium."

"And if I was a struggling farmer who couldn't access the right equipment to support my family then I'd have a bone to pick with the Gedogin too," said Siggi, "There are some folk up north who say that the Gedogin should be the powerful force in the Central Lands, not the Consortium, but with the north and south getting into further debt with the Consortium as long as this war goes on, it doesn't look likely," said Siggi.

Adrienne changed the subject as two men sat down on a table near them,

"Is it true what they say, that there are dwarves and bandits in the woods?"

Siggi chuckled, "They say all sorts of things. I heard that there are giants too, but I've met a giant before and he wasn't taller than eight feet. Things pass from lips to lips and suddenly you're looking at a ten-foot-tall monster who wants to eat your children for a Midmoon feast. The Consortium tends to leave the bandit area alone, and to be honest with you it's very rare that someone comes in here claiming they've been attacked by anything other than chancers on the road."

Later, when the business of the tavern had calmed down, Lorcan looked worse for wear, evidently because of the ale he'd drunk. Adrienne took him outside and they sat in a dark spot at the edge of the garden, so as not to be heard.

"I think whatever comes next for me isn't going to be easy, and you've already done so much..." she said, tentatively, "you don't need to come with me. I never got a chance to tell you how sorry I was about your ship, it's my fault you got kicked out."

"It's OK," he said, unconvincingly, "Sailors get close pretty quickly, you spend every waking moment together, you can't help it. People get used to moving around from ship to ship. The fact that I haven't moved yet is a miracle. I can find another family on another ship, but I should come with you, at least until we get you to the Gedogin. I started this, I'll finish it."

She shuffled uncomfortably in her seat, "Should?"

"Yes, should."

"Because I'm defenceless?"

"You're clearly not that, but two people travelling are much safer than one, that's all. Anyway, most of the ships have left Avenly, so it's more likely I'll find a new ship at Keeper's Cove, and it wouldn't make sense for us to go separately now, would it?"

She nodded, though she was unsure and nervous about bringing anyone else into her business, he was right. Two was indeed safer than one.

Lorcan fell to sleep early that night, saying he was tired from the journey, but Adrienne could see that he wasn't well, maybe even disturbed by their talk with Siggi and Helena. His foundations had been shaken, just like hers, and she knew the feeling of events out of your control forcing you to question everything you thought you knew. She knew that feeling all too well.

Chapter 15 - The Crack in the Darkness

Adrienne woke up with a start, but it took her a moment to remember where she was. There was a faint noise coming from the tavern garden as the leftover revellers from the evening's frivolities smoked from pipes, and sang folk songs into the night that the darkness absorbed up like oil on slate. She looked up to see Lorcan, who was sitting in the corner of the room, clutching his arm and shivering in the pale moonlight that cast over him from the window ledge.

"What is it, Lorcan?" she whispered.

"Nothing," he assured her, "Just when Thomas 'sword got me in my damn arm... I don't know, I think he hit a nerve. I was changing the bandages."

She got up and lit a candle, and as she did so he carried on talking in his half delirious state, "I didn't think he would do it, actually hurt me I mean, but his face was so cold when he let me loose, that hurt. It's been fine, just, it's been hurting..."

She lit a candle and knelt down beside him. She slowly unpeeled the makeshift bandaging on his left arm. The wound was deep, and he was still bleeding. How was it infected so soon?

"Why didn't you say something before?" she whispered, as she threw the dirty bandages into the smouldering embers in the fireplace.

"Put your arm flat on the table," she pulled out fresh bandages from her satchel, a bottle of healing oil and a cloth. She soaked the cloth in some water from her satchel and got to work.

She managed to clean the wound and put a layer of healing ointment on it, but he was still sweating, and feverish. She took up a night cloak from the wardrobe in the room, and the candle, and made for Helena and Siggi's lodgings down the narrow corridor. She noticed, in all the midst of her panic, that the tavern itself reminded her of a ship's innings, the narrow corridors and rickety floorboards seemed to sway in the nighttime.

"You did the right thing calling on us, Adrienne. What did you put on it?" asked Helena.

"Healing ointment, but it's homemade, so I don't know that it will have done much. And it needs to be washed properly."

"But what's in it?"

"Two parts lavender, three parts bottle weed, and Miara to soothe the skin," whispered Adrienne.

"Any alcohol?" asked Helena, holding her candle to Lorcan's arm.

"A little."

Lorcan's shirt was ripped and stuck to the drips of blood on his arm. Noticing this, Helena went to fetch another from their costume wardrobe. Apparently, you can take the person out of the troupe but the trouper will bring their spoils with them. "Good," she said, examining what was underneath the shirt, "It's not a deep wound but it needed cleaning. You should have told Adrienne before Lorcan, you would have been in safe hands."

"I used Arnite oil" he protested.

"Useless stuff, diluted from the source, and can often poison you if it's not made right. I don't know why the apothecaries insist on selling it," tutted Helena, and looking back at him with a kindlier bedside manner, she said, "Rest now."

She had now deeply soaked the wound in spirit and rubbed more of Adrienne's oil on the outer edges. She then took a needle, burnt it on the fire and sewed up the wound. Adrienne then dressed the wound with the bandage, whilst Siggi came in with an extra blanket from the wardrobe and left the rest of the whisky on Lorcan's bedside table with a tumbler.

"Make sure he sleeps," she said to Adrienne, and bid her goodnight.

Adrienne was alone again, with Lorcan's heavy breathing and a bright pink moon. Even the singing below had stopped, and she could see nothing but the fire timbers slowly fading in the dark.

I will not sleep, she said to herself, *I must think. I must figure out what to do. I cannot just take Lorcan with me on a journey without telling him... I can t keep putting him in danger. I must find out where my fath...*

The last thing she saw was the log burner, bright red embers to reflect the fire outside, nestling down into the time of night where none would see it.

That night she dreamt about her mother, her soft raven hair, olive skin and warm neck. She had wrapped Adrienne in a blanket and was cradling her by the fire the way she did when she was a baby.

And then she turned to Adrienne and whispered, "This time the chain will be broken." Suddenly there was darkness all around, and her mother was ghostly pale, and dark spirits were emerging from the trees. Adrienne knew in this moment that the entire weight of the world rested on her shoulders, and if she could only keep it up all would be fine. But it was heavy and she was growing weak. If she could just rest for one moment, but no. She had been going a long time, and forever was a very long time still, and her heart was growing weak. She finally let it all go, her mother, the spirits, the fire and all around it disappeared to blackness, and she felt - relief.

The next morning Adrienne sat outside of the tavern by the shore and scrolled over her map. The forest was dense, and there was a severe lack of detail on the east side of it on the route up towards Keeper's Cove. The road was clear, but the rest was uncharted and owned by no one, like home. Lorcan had slept in. Adrienne had worried he still hadn't passed the fever, so she left him to rest. She was eager to move on though, as she'd lost a huge amount of time by jumping ship - for all she knew the Player's Circle was already at Keeper's Cove - and every minute she lost was another minute towards losing her father for good.

Lorcan walked out, dishevelled but much better. The fever was gone, but his arm was still hurting and he had had to wrap it in a sling.

"Last chance," she said, "are you sure you don't want to turn back and try your luck in Medicina?"

Lorcan looked out at the waves and took a deep breath of salty air, grabbed some stones from under his knees and let out a breath.

"A few days on land?" He said, "I can handle that, you know. The sea isn't going anywhere. If the life of a sailor is anything, it's that we can come and go as we want. Other people are different from you and me, they know who they are, they've got roots."

"I've got roots," she protested.

"Not ones that make any sense to you right now. That's why you're out here isn't it - trying to piece them together? That's what I mean: we've been unlucky but we're also lucky. There's no clear path for us, so we've got nothing to lose, and it means we get to look for something else. To travel and meet people. I've met so many people, Adrienne. If I hadn't taken a chance on that first boat, I wouldn't have learnt all the things I learnt, and I wouldn't have met you. Now we have a purpose for a bit... I like having a purpose."

"Lorcan, you were nearly killed! And look, I really do need to get to Keeper's Cove as soon as possible, and I'm worried that..."

"That I'll hold you back? What do you think would have happened if I hadn't gotten you off that boat?"

"I know," she said, "I'm sorry, I can't explain it, I'm just... running out of time..."

"I'm sure you can imagine, that's not the first time I've been in a scrape," he shrugged, "Although, I'd rather next time there weren't so many swords pointed in my direction at one time. It's over now, I'm free to go wherever I go, that's what I mean... I'm with you for this."

She grabbed at the pebbles on the ground as if trying to mimic him for that sense of clarity that she was apparently missing, "I'm not built for this, I'm in way over my head."

"I wouldn't be so sure," he said, "I know the sea, but I wouldn't have survived last night if it wasn't for you. I'm too stubborn, it'll be my downfall. And don't forget you bargained your way onto a prime-time touring ship, do you realise how difficult that is?"

She didn't look at him, and instead stared at the floor, fiddling with the chain around her neck, "I didn't know what I was doing. Inside I was panicking the entire time. I'm not like those heroes in storybooks who just know what to do," she said.

"But you did what you did instinctually, and the people in the storybooks, they don't know the ending of their story either. People living adventures, they're all just making it up as they go along, probably having a meltdown inside, just like us..."

"You as well?"

He shook his head, folded his arms and leaned back into his chair, "Oh my ancestors, yes, I've got no bloody idea what I'm doing from one moment to the next. I just know I'll get found out any minute."

They set out that afternoon for the well-trodden path that all merchants took through the woods to the Keeper's

Cove, and both were sorry to leave the tavern. Suki met them at the gate and wished Adrienne well on her journey. She took Lorcan's arm, "How's it feeling?"

"Sore," he said, "But better. I've thrown that ointment out, you'll be happy to hear."

"Good," she said, "next time, a bottle of whisky will clean it just fine."

Adrienne started picking up their packs to load onto the cart, as more travellers started to emerge from the caverns all bound for further afield.

"If you ever grow tired of the sea, Lorcan," said Suki, "There's a place for you here. We sailors have to look out for each other, but more importantly, we'd be happy to have you."

"Thanks," he said, with an awkward smile "I'll keep that in mind."

For Adrienne, the unconditional openness by which the landladies had invited them into their home, stirred something in her that had been sound asleep in these past few weeks. It was as if she ceased to believe that there could be lightness or joy in the world. Coming into someone else's space, where both existed in bounty, had forced her to face up to the fact that at some point - if she allowed for it - things would be OK again. It filled her with melancholy too, that she was able to visit this space, but unable to bring it with her. This place was a transient state between journeys; a resting haven for those who had no other place to go; a spot between sleeping and waking.

Adrienne looked back at the tavern as the cart trudged forwards. Helena and Siggy were still outside the tavern, chatting together as they worked. She turned to face the road in front of them: the uncertain, inconstant, jagged road that twisted and turned so that there was no way of seeing what was beyond the horizon, other than a bright space of sky and a collective woodland of muddled trees.

The cart was travelling up to the crossroads at the foot of the woods, where Adrienne and Lorcan would have to alight and take the rest of the journey by foot. They'd hitched a ride with a few travellers who were heading to the mining towns, including the red-haired lady from the evening before. Before they left, she handed them a bag of shortbread to take on their journey. Adrienne tucked the bag away, along with what was left of her food stores: a block of cheese, some apples and some sweet wine in a flask that Helena and Siggi had sold them.

The road was dry and the day was bright. The cart dropped them off at the foot of a flat hill and then drove off, scattering the remainder of mud and puddles from the night before in its wake. They journeyed on foot for a few hours, stopping at the view behind them every now and then to take it all in, until the trees became thicker and all they could see was the road behind them and the birds flying overhead.

By nightfall, Lorcan's wound had started to bother him again. His arm, he said, ached, but only because it was healing and nothing more. They decided to look for somewhere to sleep and pitch their tent. In the past, the tent had only been used for shelter from the rain when fishing in the Wiberian forests. In those times it had worked just fine, but it was colder in the north, more prone to rain and frost, even in the wake of summer.

That night it did rain. It was nothing too violent or unbearable, but enough for the droplets to leak into their tent, dampening their belongings and soaking half of their remaining food. They spent that night and the night after sleeping side by side for warmth, taking turns to keep watch through a flap in the tent.

On the third night, when they were within half a day's walk of Keeper's Cove, they pitched the tent by a stream and caught some fish with sticks over a rocky patch of water. By sundown they had a fire going, and allowed themselves to enjoy their spoils as well as the last of the sweet wine. They decided to save what was left of the bread and cheese for the next day but helped themselves to the shortbreads.

That night the forest was quiet. Owls hooted and bats leapt, flying from tree to tree, visible in the bright moonlight that shone over the stream. Adrienne lay awake on her back, worrying and wondering. She had so many questions. What if all this didn't lead to the answers she wanted? The Gedogin were powerful, if they were able to rescue her father, would it even matter what she knew as long as he was safe? A shade of bitterness crept over her. She'd been forced to take on this responsibility and yet her lack of knowing left her feeling so much still like a child. She looked over at Lorcan, suddenly so grateful for his presence. Her tired mind was unable to concentrate, her eyes were stinging and longing for sleep. She had been so busy trying to keep on track, trying to stay safe, that none of these thoughts had really surfaced properly until now. She sat up and peered outside of the tent, taking in the night. A raindrop landed on her cheek and she noticed there was already a solitary tear making its way down her face.

Suddenly she was lying down and Lorcan's arm was on her shoulder, "Wake up," he whispered. Perhaps he'd heard her crying in the night, she couldn't know. The silence of the woods was still present, silent but full of life, and then a crack.

"That's two," he said.

Another crack came. She put her hand in her pocket to check the Noch was still in place. She felt her pulse race and her senses heighten. She nudged Lorcan and pointed towards the sound. Two men in great cloaks were standing, searching for something, just out of sight of the tent. They were carrying spears. Lorcan silently handed her her hunting bow and reached for the axe. She shook her head at him, she knew what he was thinking. He could fight them, and she was a hunter - there was no difference between shooting a deer and shooting a man - but Adrienne had seen what these men could do, and probably only half of what they were capable of. They'd barely escaped one in daylight, they couldn't fight two in the dark.

Without speaking, they both grabbed their travel sacks and hid a few trees away from the tent. Then they sat in silence and watched as the men ransacked their camp. There was only a matter of time before they'd start searching the surrounding trees. They needed an escape. Adrienne felt Lorcan's hand tensely gripping her shoulder. She put her finger on her lips and he nodded. She held her breath, leaned back against the trunk of the tree and breathed into the night.

The strangest sequence of events then took place. First Adrienne's vision changed. Suddenly she saw the forest as it was without darkness. Every bug and every leaf was vivid as if it were right in front of her, and then everything went grey. She started to make out tiny, transparent threads of light just visible through the grey. Some were still and some were moving, and she was unable to make out where either began or ended. They were endless, stretching for miles, connecting and reconnecting. There was a light buzzing coming from within her. *Help us*, she thought, *send help*, and a faint white light grew out of her and moved through the air towards one of the longer lines. It then trickled out of sight like a stack of dominos.

She blinked and all was dark again. Lorcan was looking at her, terrified. Then there was another series of cracks and the men were there again, right in front of them.

"Run!" shouted Lorcan.

They ran through the thickets without looking behind them, ducking under trees, the forest a blur in their peripheral vision as it whizzed past them. Adrienne kept running until the noise behind her seemed to have passed, "I think we lost them," she gasped through her breathlessness. There was no reply.

She turned to see nothing. All was silent, and there was no sight or sound of the men or Lorcan. She was alone in a dark, wet, cavern of a forest.

"Lorcan!" she whispered as loudly as she could.

A figure appeared out of the darkness. Without thinking, she shot at it with her bow. She watched as the man brushed the arrow aside as if it was nothing. It was hard to tell in the dark but she could have sworn he moved it. He lunged forwards and pushed her back; the force of his strength was so unexpected and overwhelming that she lost her balance and tripped on a tree trunk, thudding to the floor. The sky then went very dark. She lifted her hand to her head and felt something warm and wet. The man leant over her and reached for her coat pocket. Droplets of sweat fell from his hood and landed on her face. Through her dizziness she could smell his breath, foul and stale. Her vision was blurry now, there were two of him, and the sounds of shouting in the distance were echoey and dull. Her head started to feel numb. *This is it,* she thought, *this is what death feels like.* She could hear Lorcan's voice somewhere in the depths of the trees, the faint howl of a wolf in the distance, and behind all of this, a new voice, faint but clear, "Show me where you are."

Chapter 16 - The Banished

Adrienne woke up at the beginnings of dawn by a dying campfire. Upon the fire was a cauldron of boiling water. Lorcan was sitting up next to her, drinking from a tin cup, and behind him, a woman.

She had dark raven hair and pale skin, and she was wearing the most beautiful velvet cloak. It was more beautiful even than those worn in the grand parties of the south, but there was something different about the fabric, almost as if it was living or filled with light. There was too, something about her countenance - as if she could see inside of you and right out the other side into the ether. Her eyes were soft and youthful, yet full of darkness in their core. It was something Adrienne remembered from somewhere, but she couldn't put her finger on where. It was as if one eye stored the wisdom of the world within it, broken by the weight of the world and the other was pure innocent light. The woman's hair was shaved at one side, revealing a familiar blue emblem tattooed behind her ear.

"You're awake," said the stranger, "Do you feel unwell? Can you understand me?"

"A little," said Adrienne, "And yes, I can."

She handed Adrienne a mug of hot water, which had been brewed with fresh herbs, "Drink this," she said. Adrienne looked at the contents of the cup, and recognised it to be Arnica and Reviving Wart, for shock. She took a sip.

"Thank you," she said, looking at the woman curiously, "What happened?"

"You'd hit your head rather badly by the time I'd gotten to you. Thank goodness that your friend was still calling your name. I lost my connection when you passed out."

Adrienne looked around in bewilderment, "But who are you? And where are we?"

"We cannot speak here," said the woman, "You'll need to recover your senses, but I'm afraid we don't have long. We must get clear of this place."

Lorcan took Adrienne's arm as she gained some semblance of balance, "It's OK," he said, "I think she's safe."

The hour was late but the first offerings of sunlight were starting to creep their way through the cracks in the sky. They set off soon after down a hilly path towards the east, without a word, but making sure they were close behind as they glided along the mossy deepness of the woods. An hour or so passed until they came to a slow running stream. As they edged further along the bridge path they saw more and more interconnecting streams all breaking away from each other and joining up at different points. Through the misty morning haze, they could just make out a larger, deeper stream in the distance, the width of a canal, with another bridge that took them into a clearing. As their eyes adjusted to the light, they saw the clearing in all its wonder, with more streams that circled back around on themselves and into deep pools covered in mist. The pools glistened with a peculiar blue light that seemed to be coming from somewhere within and not from the dim sunlight. On the water's surface were giant butterflies, dragonflies and strange plants that floated like islands.

"If fairies exist" she whispered to Lorcan, "this is indeed where they live."

The woman stopped them in the middle of the clearing, "My name is Astair," she said softly, "and I am a woman of the Encampment..."

"The Encampment?" said Adrienne, "Is that where the bandits live? Are you taking us to the Dark Woods?"

"Once you see it, you will decide what to call it," said the woman, "But I can promise you that you will be safe there..."

The pair gave each other sceptical looks.

"Or you can stay here and take your chances on your own, though I do not think you'll get far when one of you is potentially concussed, you appear to have left behind your tent and food and you are - I suspect - lost."

"You make a good point," said Lorcan, quickening his pace to catch up with their rescuer.

" ...how did you find us?" said Adrienne.

"You called me, did you not? You are headed for the Gedogin are you not? Unless there are others still out there in the woods, seeking help from anyone who will listen, and who I have inadvertently left to their deaths?" questioned Astair, as both her audience tensed. "I am your friend," she said calmly.

Lorcan nudged Adrienne, his expression full of wonderment and confusion. Adrienne thought about what had happened when they were by the tree. She had acted on instinct, but she didn't really believe anyone could hear her thoughts. She remembered what her father had told her, *above all else, do not doubt it, even in your darkest moments.*

"Those men had no reason to be so close to the Gedogin keep, in fact, they were far too close to our home for comfort. We will have to send word to Keeper's Cove," said Astair.

"*Your* home? Were they bandits?" asked Lorcan.

"No, not bandits," she replied and turned back to their path.

Lorcan shivered, "Why are they always hooded?"

"Because," said Adrienne matter of factly, without looking back, "to know is to demystify, and there is power in the space in between."

They were deep into the woods now, far into the centre of the empty space on the map that Adrienne had been looking over back at the tavern. Once they reached the other side of the clearing and were covered again by the protection of the trees, they saw what was the front of a curved wooden building. A glimmer of sunlight from the rising sun to the east was shining through the windows. Outside the hut was a fence, in front of which were tiny clay pots, with more of the same plants that had been floating on the pool's surface. This time they had been manipulated into growing patterns, the same way that Elsen had worked with plants that she was growing for remedies and potions.

"You will have heard of us, of course. The dangerous peoples of the Medicina woods: bandits, evil witches, changelings, giants and cursed dwarf-halflings who were torn from their mothers in the dead of night and banished to the ends of the earth. All of us together will trick you out of your pack and clothes without your noticing, or sell you into slavery to eastern traders on the far shore, or sacrifice you to the Channel gods just for the sake of a slightly better harvest and a few good bottles of nectar wine," she trailed off, "Well, I think that last one depends on the day."

They both stared at her blankly, "Oh, I apologise. Am I not allowed to make merry?" she said, blank-faced.

"We've had an interesting journey, to say the least," said Adrienne, "Thank you," she added, "for saving us."

Lorcan was bewildered, "I'm sorry, I still don't get it. We didn't have a Revolter or anything to…"

"Our power is much stronger than the pull of your vessels," said Astair, "Gedogin vessels are no use to us, they tend to break when we're near them," she gave a stern look to Lorcan, who had been preparing to laugh, "I'm not joking now, it's a definite problem trying to go unnoticed in the outer world…" she shrugged playfully, "It is also objectively funny."

She walked them further into the centre of the keep and sat them down by an open fire pit so they could warm themselves. In the light, she could see that Lorcan was covered in mud on one side from where he'd crouched on the ground, and both were damp and weary. Adrienne's shoes were fraying at the edges and there was a hole in one at the back. Adrienne followed her eyes and looked embarrassed, realising she'd forgotten to change into her huntsman shoes before leaving Wiberia. No wonder they were falling apart. The Velgrave shoes had been her mother's and she liked to wear them on summer days when she had nothing to do, but they were not made for journeys.

Astair looked at the two friends and frowned, "Enough for now," she said, "I will fetch someone to ready your rooms for you, and to bring you ointment for your wound, and a hot drink to help you sleep," she stood up and bowed a small bow, "We can talk more in the morning when you are feeling better."

They woke later that day to the sound of ferocious birdsong. The night before, a woman with the same shaved hair and blue markings as Astair had led them to a small building behind the back of the camp. There were a couple more of these huts, all in a circle facing each other. From the outside, they looked like simple creations, but on the inside, they were white and clean and spacious. The door of their hut was directly opposite the door of the larger building, and they could just about see inside to a grand looking hall held up by beams. Adrienne was still a little shaky from knocking her head, but whatever the women had brought her the night before - a strange ointment that Adrienne did not recognise - it had wiped out any delirium she was falling into. She now had a headache, and a bandaged up wound on the side of her head, but she was healing.

When they were ready, they left the rooms together and went back out into the clearing. It was only in the midday light that they realised exactly what they'd walked into the night before, which now felt very far away indeed. There were more huts spread around the settlement, nestled around stand-alone pools that held the same blue light as the ones they'd passed in the early morning. And there were the people. Some of the folk had the same dark hair and deep eyes as Astair, wearing the same glimmering cloaks and covered in strange silver and blue tattoos. A few of the people were much smaller, half the size of any human, like the dwarf peoples of the Laten Islands but less polished in appearance. The neat uniforms and tidied faces of the island's court were replaced with wild-grown beards and hair, sun-weathered faces and clothes that mimicked that of Astair's people. Nestled into rows of vegetables, two of the dwarves, a couple, were bickering and chastising each other over some trivial domestic matter. Adrienne felt a pang of longing in watching them.

    At the centre of the settlement was a clearing with a communal fire and a stone monument of a woman who appeared to be piously reaching out to something in front of her.
    A group of people were building a treehouse to the side of this clearing, and a well-built man, at least nine feet tall, was handing items from an outdoor blacksmith's stand to a person standing on a ledge. Next to the blacksmith's was a stone community oven, and barrels of drink that were stacked all in a row. In another corner, a school of about six or seven young girls giggled and danced around one another, whilst their teacher, holding a large maroon book, urged them to settle.
    "This," said Lorcan, "is the dark woods?" he ignored Adrienne, who was eyeing him curiously, "I feel like we've been had," he whispered.

"Lorcan, I think these people could be more than they're letting on... the ointment she gave me, and she fought off those men..."

They were interrupted when a tall woman who had been standing at the door of the larger building approached them, introducing herself as Rainou. Her skin was not as pale as Astair's, yet she had the exact same tell-tale, mesmerising eyes. She was wearing hunting gear and green robes, and her demeanour was strict and stoic, "I've been told to take you to Astair, as soon as you are ready."

Rainou took them inside the large hall. It had a stoked fire that lay at the end of the room and a large, flat table which barely came higher than the floor around it. The table was seated with animal skins and cushions. Astair called for some wine, which arrived shortly, along with bread and cheese and a spicy relish made out of fruits that neither of them recognised.

Astair was not like what one would imagine a priestess of any calibre to be. She sat cross legged on the floor, her bare feet tickling the sheepskin rug like a child. She was looking intently at Adrienne as if seeing her for the first time in the light had revealed something.

"You're from the south?" she said, "your accent..."

"...yes, my father is from the north, but my mother was Velgrave born," said Adrienne.

"Do you know much of his ancestry?"

"I'm afraid not, only that my grandfather didn't exactly approve of the match at first."

Astair nodded as she poured them all a clear herbal tea out of a glass jug.

"Last night," said Adrienne, "In the woods, how did you..."

"Your thoughts have substance," said Astair, "they are so small that we cannot see them, but they are there. The minute you chose to let them out of your mind they were able to affect the world around you, and they worked their way through the forest to us. We all feel these things pass us but few can interpret them."

Adrienne nodded, pensive, remembering the colours she'd seen in the grey, and the muffled silence that surrounded her when she'd slid further into the Channel's abyss. Behind Astair, Adrienne spotted a white table, which had a number of Nochs displayed on it. Each was different in size and design, but they all had a distinct shell-like quality and a drawing or design on their round base.

"You look as if you have something to ask me, Adrienne," said the woman.
"It couldn't be," said Adrienne, to herself.
"Go on."
She looked back at the table, holding so many of these valuable objects that she'd thought were so rare, which she'd been chased off a boat for. Something didn't add up.
"...you have a full table full of Nochs?"
"Yes."
"I've been told that they're invaluable, that it's almost impossible to get hold of one," said Adrienne.
"They are only valuable because of the people who can use them," said Astair, "Nochs are not widely known, and they cannot be used by just anyone: they say you must either have Danaan blood or be trained by the Gedogin Alliance, preferably both if you want to really put it to good use."
"But you," said Adrienne, "You are not Gedogin."
"I am not."
"Then why do you have their mark on your neck?" Adrienne was incredulous, it was so hard to decipher what was true and what was just the leftovers of her delirium; her foggy head; her fancifulness.

Lorcan was looking out of the window at the village, his expression stoic, "You're Danaan," he said, without looking around for a response.

"I am," said Astaire, "We are."

"Danaan exist," he said, "It's easy to believe that now that I've seen men appearing out of thin air on dirt roads and women in white cloaks battling monsters in the woods," said Lorcan, "She was so fast, Adrienne, no wonder the men disappeared."

"You aren't all Danaan," said Adrienne.

Astair nodded, "Some dwarves prefer to be here with us than in the corrupt Laten Islands, where frankly generations of oppression have led to a rupture within their own government. A hundred years ago, if you were born a giant - which really only means you are taller than most as it is not passed through bloodlines - in the Central Lands you could live pretty much unnoticed, but the Consortium is so corrupt now that they will go after anything that's perceived different from them, any difference was called a deformity. They used the fear of the unknown to control the common folk," she shook her head, "Because with corruption comes distrust, and with distrust comes fears. There are many now who aren't permitted to live in society. Anyone with an abnormality or strong abilities connecting them to the powers of the Inner Channel, the Consortium do not trust so they must control them. Many of these people would rather be outlawed than courted to join the ranks of the Consortium. Or worse, held against their will."

"If you're so hidden, why are you so ready to take in strangers?" said Adrienne.

Astair fixed Adrienne with a penetrating stare, "We have circulated enough stories of this place that no one would dare enter our territories willingly. You are the first visitors from the outside that we've had in a very long time, and if you did try to share our whereabouts, it would be so mixed with tales of ogres, bandits, ghosts and witchcraft that you would be hard pressed to find someone that would believe you. We are cautious about who we bring into our fortress, and I would not have taken you here if you hadn't been able to call me."

Adrienne held her words on her tongue, scared to let them leave her mouth for what they might mean for her, "I didn't know what I was doing."

Chapter 17 - The Old Allies

They were to stay until the healers were certain Adrienne was not in any danger after her fall. That evening they were invited to partake in a meal in the clearing by the pools, consisting of broth made out of sweet vegetables and rabbit stock, and many glasses of the liquid that had been brewed in the barrels by the oven. This was, as far as they could make out, a sort of honeysuckle liqueur, not alcohol, but with a light sort of melancholy high.

It was a simple meal, but it felt like a feast after the night they'd had. As there were guests, which was a rare occasion for the Danaan and their kind, they had some entertainment in the square. People sat in rows dotted around the centre of the clearing, where pollen freely flowed through the breeze, filling the air like snow. Three dancers moved to the sound of a drum, their movements flowed like a strange machine, elegant and cog-like. Lorcan's face was aghast as he watched them move. It was as if they were bending the air around them to their will, and their bodies seemed to be moved by it, not in spite of it. Adrienne's experience of performance was wildly limited in comparison to Lorcan's, yet she could see that this was like nothing you'd experience in the great cities or ports.

Rainou explained to them that the dance was a sort of ritual or prayer. The Danaan knew their access to the Channel was not unconditional, their abilities were not theirs to squander as they pleased, and they were part of a delicate balance between the elements. If they strayed from the path of connection or took too much, the balance would be upset and they would lose their gift. To remind themselves of this they gave thanks by training in this form of dance, which in turn acted as a sort of meditative act that allowed their minds to tune better to the world around them. A woman stood in the centre of the space and spoke in an ancient language that neither of the two understood. Rainou interpreted with a whisper in their ears:

> "There were once four clans
> A long time ago when the world was different.
> Those who saw and felt all
> Those who used the world to heal
> Those who protected the world
> Those who travelled and spread the word
> These clans guarded the spirit of man
> Until its final turn."

"The story of the four clans, the protectors of man," whispered Lorcan, "So the Danaan aren't beyond telling old folk tales to each other on a dark night. They're not so all knowing as we thought. And they have the Gedogin crest," he said to Adrienne, "Isn't that weird?"

Rainou scoffed at this from the seat behind Lorcan, "You might want to ask why the Gedogin have the Danaan crest. The sign of the Keepers is much older than the Gedogin people: it's derived from ancient folklore."

"Oh," he said, embarrassed that he'd been heard, "My mistake."

A woman got up next and sang a beautiful ballad, which brought Lorcan to tears, and another group of Dwarvish men and women performed a traditional Laten Island short play without words, about a lost princess. Lorcan and Adrienne were invited to join them for part of it. They were, of course, used as comic relief to make the main characters look utterly foolish. Adrienne was given a bowl to hold and instructed to tap on the bowl using a sharp wooden instrument. Curiously, whichever way you tapped the bowl, it seemed to hum at some standard tuning that blended with the echoes in the valley. She got very excited about this and tapped it a lot, before realising that every time she tapped it the performers had to stop the scene and replay it.

After what felt like only a short while the ceremony ended, but when they turned to look at the sun, which swiftly headed for the horizon, it had been longer than they'd thought. Suddenly the sweet, sweet heaviness that had overcome Adrienne for the last few hours turned to panic.

"We need to leave," she said to Lorcan, "We've already lost so much time. Before it gets dark. We're so close to Keeper's Cove."

"Why are you so desperate to pass through Keeper's Cove?," said Lorcan. "Besides, I'd have thought you might want to stay here a bit longer," whispered Lorcan.

"Why?"

"Well, I mean," he leant into her and whispered in her ear, "You can do what they do."

"What? Where did you get that idea from?" she said, incredulously.

"In the forest," he said, "You went so strange, your eyes... and she said you called for her..."

Adrienne felt her heartbeat speed up at this ridiculous accusation, and laughed it off, "...I think she was complimenting me on how much I've picked up from my lessons with my father..."

"...though I'd be careful," he interrupted, "If the Danaan are hunted by the Consortium," said Lorcan, scathingly.

"Why," asked Adrienne, "because it would be dangerous?"

"Yes, dangerous for you, but also, I'm saying there must be a reason that the Consortium are hunting them... a reason they've stayed hidden for so long."

"Yes, there's a reason!" said Adrienne, "If they were dangerous, surely they'd make themselves known and do as they please? The Consortium are ruthless, and can't see the damage they are doing."

"The Consortium didn't cause the war that killed my family," he snapped. "That was on the Gedogin. Maybe it's them who can't see the damage they've done!"

His reaction shook her. She didn't know what to say because she didn't know where this had come from. She remembered her conversation with Noah, how he'd mused that everyone on that boat had their demons to bear, even if they weren't immediately obvious.

"Remember where we're headed Lorcan," she quietly cautioned.

"Right," he muttered, "I understand what they're trying to do. I'm not saying I agree with their methods..."

"Look," she said, "I'm not going to join up with the Danaan. That's ridiculous, there's nothing for me to even join up with."

"OK," he said.

An awkward silence followed and eventually they both resolved to drop the subject, but the damage was done. After a while she moved away from him, using the pond as an excuse to move forward. She lifted herself and edged closer to it, kneeling so that her hair was almost touching the water's edge.

A woman approached them, "Miss Adrienne, Astair has asked that you join her in her rooms."

Both Adrienne and Lorcan stood up at this.

"Sorry no," said the woman, "just the girl."

When Adrienne got to Astair's rooms, the woman was looking at a map that had been laid out on another of the white tables dotted around the edge of the room. It was a map of the Central Lands and had a selection of black marks on it: one on Black Isle Cove, one in Wiberia, one at Keeper's Cove and another exactly where they were in the forests. There was also a dark blue dot on the Laten Islands.

"Have you had a chance to think about what has happened here, Adrienne?" asked Astair, before Adrienne could enquire about the map.

"What do you mean?" asked Adrienne.

"You have natural abilities, and for your own safety, they mustn't remain unchecked. If you want the chance to find out the extent of your abilities, then perhaps you might think about seeking out training with the Gedogin. The Danaan are powerfully connected to the Channel, we can do things that others can't. You might not be able to do what we do, but you could pick up a lot with the Gedogin."

"So I could train as a diplomat? Like my parents?"

"Gedogin aren't just diplomats any more than they are purely Danaan," said Astair, "Having a connection to the Channel like you do can be very advantageous, but Gedogin is an umbrella term for many routes: diplomats, warriors, historians, magicians who invent new uses of magick, scholars and storytellers... I'm telling you because I think you should seek it out, but I am not in control of whether it finds you or not."

"That's kind of you to say," said Adrienne, "but I don't think that's what my path is."

Astair nodded, and Adrienne couldn't make out anything from her expression. She seemed neither disappointed nor in need to press her point any further.

"Wait," interrupted Adrienne, "I thought the Danaan disagreed with the use of magicks for creating new vessels? That's what the stories say: the Danaan are all powerful and they wanted to see our vessels destroyed so that only they can access the Channel"

"We do disagree to an extent, not for the reasons widely spread, but because we wish to preserve the Channel itself. We would rather - if it is to be done - that the work is done by those who also seek to protect the balance of things. The only place where magickians can charge vessels is

Keepers Cove, which is somewhere we can have a semblance of control," said Astair, "I do not think that anyone Danaan born would have an interest in developing more vessels. There are endless numbers of perfectly functioning vessels that have been discarded in this world. Danaan are silently part of the alliance. It is the best of several options. Resources will be needed somehow, the world is too full of people now for any other path."

Before Adrienne could even ask, Astair added, "The Danaan and Gedogin are tied by an older alliance than modern arguments over ethics and resources, and it would take a lot to break that bond."

Astair also asked Adrienne to show her the Noch in her pocket, and pointed out a slight alteration in the picture engraved into the front.

"Do you see that curve in the line of the Tor? It is very slight, but this is what to look for. It means that this was forged by a learned maker in Keeper's Cove, and is not a fake. Whoever it was that made this, they made it for an important member of the Gedogin alliance - one of the Keepers."

"That's funny," said Adrienne as she gazed into the centre of the object, "I could have sworn it had changed colour, or maybe it's brighter."

Astair's eyes widened and then she frowned, "Make sure you show this to Lady Tosia when she sees you."

Astair looked like she wanted to say more, but instead just smiled absentmindedly, and went back to looking at her map.

"Astair, those men in the forest, they looked like normal men, not monsters," said Adrienne, changing the subject, "They were the same men who I saw in Wiberia when my father's house was attacked, when they took him and killed my... they appeared out of nowhere, as if..."

"As if by Revolter?" asked Astair, "The Seldelige have been known to do so."

"So they really are everything they say? Great monsters with unimaginable power?"

"Not exactly," said Astair, "Everything has an explanation, everything has a price. It is possible to send a body across the world in such a way, but... they will lose their humanity, so to speak."

Adrienne suddenly felt quite sick, remembering her father's reaction when she'd stuck her head inside the revolter in his study.

"So," continued Astair, "In order to achieve this, you would have to transfer the information it recreates to another location, and every part of the human that they recreate will be exactly the same: the same body, same scars, same thoughts and memories, but the essence of the person, is gone. The person believes it is them, but their original body is destroyed in the process, and a new one recreated. Anyone who has tried, who was able to access the Channel before, has not been able to afterwards. The Seldelige have the power that their body was manipulated by - the ability to move between spaces."

"So what happens to them when they die?" Asked Adrienne.

"No one is quite sure what happens to it as the technology is so new, but many have guessed it destroys the very soul of the subject. It's not a completely blind guess either. It seems as though they don't join the Inner Channel with our ancestors, those few that have died have not been found within it."

"Why would someone choose to do that to themselves?" asked Adrienne.

"It is believed that originally, the Consortium was experimenting with their soldiers in labs, to see if there was a formula of magick that they could use to teleport with the

Revolters. By the time they'd realised the side effects it was too late for the many Seldelige who had already been created. The process is excruciatingly painful and heartbreaking to go through, I am told. The Gedogin aren't sure how many times you have to go through it before the full transformation, but the captured Danaan have been gone for months before resurfacing, and once they're finally out in the world again they feel no pain, physical or emotional, and it is easy for a creature like that to persuade a complex human to join them. For some, it is a route to freedom."

Adrienne looked down at her shoes, worried she might push the conversation too far, "Why do I keep seeing them? There was no revolter in the forest for anyone to use when we were attacked, and on the journey from Medicina. A man appeared right in front of me, out of nowhere. He was so broken. He looked half starved, he was muttering things to himself, and then he disappeared and this other figure appeared, with a cold, fearsome presence," she held her breath, nervous to hear the answer that she already knew.

"They often keep an eye out for people who are deeply connected to the Channel. They can feel the energy. It is what they crave the most... because it's what they have lost. It may be that there was some significance behind your first meeting, and that because of this, they have their eye on you. But I suspect it will not last long. It's us who they are hunting really: the Consortium secretly created the Seldelige, and in turn, the Seldelige's main purpose is to find more Danaan, to lock us up, experiment on us and find out how our powers work..." said Astair.

"I didn't think they'd seen me the first time," Adrienne said, to herself more than Astair.

It was a strange sight to see Astair in this moment, the urgency in her eyes, the concern for a stranger. She was no longer the barefooted woman from the woods. She was still, powerful and enigmatic, as the moment called for: a priestess who had experienced great pain and built up a thick skin that she could wear when she needed, and discard when wanted. It was something about the way she held her body, and though her figure and face told you she was no older than forty, she seemed much older indeed, as if she really was carrying generations of interlinking stories on her shoulders.

"Thank you so much for your help," said Adrienne, "Lorcan and I must get to Keeper's Cove. I fear I may have already left it too late."

"It is not long now, I will make sure a map is given to you. There is a shortcut through the east side of the woods," the intensity had disappeared from Astair's eyes and she was back to the calm, aloof woman from that morning.

"Thank you," said Adrienne, and she turned to leave.

"I would be careful who else I share my thoughts with if I were you," said Astair as Adrienne reached the door, "No matter how good our intentions, this world is not linear in terms of right and wrong. There are dangerous people, like the Seldelige, but there are rarely real villains. You cannot spot them in a crowd from their gait or crest. There are different ways of seeing the world, and different maxims to act on. Until you or the boy know which side of things your souls are tied to, secrets must remain secrets. At least they must until we know what they mean ourselves. Do you understand me?" To this, Adrienne nodded.

The sun was yet to disappear behind the trees, so before going back to Lorcan, Adrienne decided to wander the camp and collect her thoughts. She walked further past the barrels and cooking stations to a large, barn-shaped building at the very edge of the camp. The tall doors were wide open on one side, and inside were two dwarf women standing by great, lengthy tables, stacked paces apart across the room. They were washing and mending some fine material, the same that the Danaan wore as cloaks. The women didn't seem to know a lot of common tongue, and instead spoke to her in Latenian, with the occasional piece of common tongue thrown in.

"Algapiyce, den on aman..." said the woman, gesturing to the long robe that was soaked in water and a wooden stick that was placed by it. Adrienne picked up the stick automatically and started stirring the water. It wasn't the consistency of water. It felt like she was pushing thick, heavy steam through the cloak. After a few attempts, she put the stick down in exhaustion. Both women laughed, "It's not like your clothes," said the one who was yet to speak, "Sticky," she laughed again, "Mystery!"

Adrienne laughed as well, "I can build objects," she said, "Wooden things... how do you say? Horroch?" The woman nodded and then handed the stick to Adrienne again, this time holding it with her. She swirled the waters with her, in a peculiar pattern, upwards and around, upwards and back, and this time the waters moved with ease as if the woman had found a path through. The material seemed to absorb the mists that came off the water and it swirled with the tide, "Now you can build Danaan cloak," said the woman.

Adrienne joined Lorcan, who was talking to Rainou by the pool. She had come to bring them a map to take them the rest of the way. Their packs were lying beside him on a wooden bench.

"What if someone is born in the outside world with Danaan blood? Do they lose their abilities too?" He was asking Rainou.

"Sometimes," said Rainou, "Sometimes not. If you see someone seemingly working without objects as a vessel for their power, they are probably Danaan," she picked up a large candle that had been placed to the side of the pond but blown out by the breeze. She pinched the wick with her finger. It lit up.

"I always thought they had something hidden under their cloak when that happened! I thought that it was some sort of trouper's trick," pounded Lorcan as he swung his body around clumsily, but with a good amount of strength, the complete opposite of Rainou's controlled, sublime movements, "Bloody depths! There was a man from the Player's Circle who worked magicks without any gadgets, but he claimed it was stage tricks. I always thought it was great showmanship..."

"It may well have been," said Rainou, "You'd be surprised what people will tell themselves after seeing something they believe to be impossible, but there are many who would allow others to wonder such things about them, it gives them illusionary power."

The map had clear directions to take them off road to the gates of the castle, along with a note from Astair. She had, of course, asked them not to speak of the Danaan to anyone, not even those who claimed to know of their existence. They read over the note by the pool with Rainou, and Lorcan revelled in the task set by Astair: to drop whichever elaborate rumour they wished to deter travellers from straying from the path. There may have been a mention of war gods, for, as Lorcan put it, "Bandits are never the main character in an epic story".

But there was something else occupying Adrienne's mind. It was something she had never even thought about before. It's like questioning the origin of words for the first time, words that have become so much a part of our everyday language that when we finally look at them, it's as if we are hearing them for the first time. This thought, however, had no clear answer to it, none that her present company could or would relay:

"What are they keeping?"

Chapter 18 - Shanaki - The Final Straw

"Wait a second," interjected Goodrum, "I thought you said you'd be telling the true story? Everyone knows the Danaan are old wives' tales made up to scare children from going into the woods alone... and," he struggled to finish his sentence, "other unbearable things..."

Shanaki, now fully in control of his emotions and audience, was unfazed by this man's interjection. Coolly, he looked up from where he was nestled into his Shanaki-shaped crevice in the green trunk.

"In the future, I will give you a signal to leave the room before I bring any more of these unlikely characters into it, but I would urge you to keep an open mind. Each storybook character stems from an item of truth. The giants that we imagine today, that Adrienne and Lorcan imagined, turned out to be just uncommonly tall men. The dwarves, persecuted and campaigned against by the kings for possession of resources, were no less human than you or I. Is mystery still sorcery when someone explains it to us? It is only strange until we are assured that there is a magickal explanation for how it works. Once the mystery is gone, there is nothing left to disbelieve, or to fear for that matter."

The man cocked his leg up onto one of the unearthed tree roots and raised his hand to his chin to consider this for a moment, "If you told me you'd seen a flying chariot or had visited a magickal kingdom in the sky and then explained to me how the magick works..." he suggested, "I would believe it magickally possible, but I still might not believe it until I saw it. If the Danaan existed, then they ain't here no longer. The legend says that they disappeared into the mountains."

Shanaki relaxed somewhat at this, "they say the Danaan disappeared because of the many invaders to the Central Lands that came after Adrianna's time. It is another long and complex tale, as is this one. You are free to own them and understand them as they form."

"But, good sir, no disrespect meant, but I don't understand how you know all of this and why we're meant to believe you. Is it the truth?"

Shanaki stood up, enraged, his weathered frame cloaked in unnatural energy, which flew through his arms as he overpowered his charge, "I have been here for fifty years and I have searched long and far, travelled and worked to know things that you could not even imagine from your tiny place in the world. I know of the Danaan. You can believe me, or you can take my words with as much salt as you wish, but for the love of my ancestors, the great Channel of life and your good health, do NOT interrupt me again!"

There was a split second of silence followed by an eruption from the crowd, who gleefully jeered and clapped simultaneously at the two-hander that had reached its eleventh hour: a story within a story; the tale of the pretentious, pseudo-sceptic and the seasoned narrator. Goodrum had been silenced, for now, and the crowd's elation at his public takedown had set the scene for today's final act: Keeper's Cove.

The working day was slowing to a halt, and the rain was now a faint drizzle tapping on the glass dome that surrounded them. More punters started to enter and fill Shanaki's space, some looking around for space, some immediately throwing copper change into his pot before taking a seat. The school children remained transfixed in place beneath the treetop. One of the travellers who had disappeared to the back minutes before returned with a cup of coffee and a Trikken cake, which he handed to Shanaki. It was, evidently, not time to finish his tale for the day just yet.

Chapter 19 - The Lights

The journey up to Keeper's Cove was a lot quicker and a lot less eventful than the one from the tavern to the woods, but it felt longer. They remained in silence for most of the journey, mainly monosyllabic and only talking when it was otherwise unavoidable. Neither wanted it to be this way, but they were both in need of a break from each other. Both were frustrated with spending all their energy trying not to quarrel, and had none left for conversation.

The only real thing of consequence that actually happened on this journey was the slow realisation of Adrienne's that her shoes were now falling to pieces. They had seen a lot of wear over the past few weeks and it wasn't something she could fix herself. She'd made a hole in the sole and the side of the shoe and threaded some string though as a temporary fix, but it was already starting to come loose with the rain and constant scraping on the forest floor. They stopped by a stream so she could wash her feet in the cool water and put ointment on her blisters, all in silence. She tightened the string, all the while scolding herself for not going to a proper mender whilst they'd been in Medicina, and even further for not changing the damn shoes when she'd been able to.

"I'm sorry about before," she said eventually. "It must have been horrible losing your family and I know that you really believe that the Gedogin played a part in it all."

Lorcan refused to look at her but instead busied himself by filling up the water skins. "For the record," she said, "that was the only time I've ever reached the Channel properly... and when I did, it was muddled and confusing. It was like I was actually inside of it, if that makes sense. I didn't know what was happening and I couldn't do much... I just thought... and I don't know how but it caused something to happen... they say that happens to normal people sometimes as well, and they just think they're asleep."

She hesitated for a moment, not sure if he was even listening. He passed her a full up water skin and sat down to rest on a fallen log.

"It almost happened once when I was very little, and I didn't really understand what to do with it," she said, "there was this buzzing out of nowhere, the same noise you hear when listening to a Noch. I could sort of feel it in my body, if that makes sense? Then my vision went funny, and I guess I got scared after that because it stopped."

He wiped his brow and sighed a bit, peeking at her from the corner of his eye.

"I get why you didn't tell me," he said, staring out into the hill. "People are scared of the unfamiliar. I think if something like that happened to me, I'd try to destroy it... I wouldn't want to be associated with them."

He then ripped off half of his ruined shirt from his pack and wrapped it around her shoes to secure them for the remainder of the journey, sealing it tight using a sailor's knot. He picked her up and brushed her hair away from her face, forcing a smile.

She could tell that he was still angry, but she let it go. So cutting were his words, and yet his actions contradicted them. Elsen had always told her that nothing is ever black and white, but it is much easier for folk to think so. It was always much harder to choose to see the complexity of each moment than to pick a side. So, you see, she couldn't be completely distrusting of him, because she saw where his pain had come from. She vowed then never to look back on a situation and demonise or sugarcoat it to her fancy. So many people turn away from empathy because it requires them to accept that someone somewhere sees *them* as the monster too, but the real monsters are made through years of torment and pain; real monsters live amongst us and will not be reasoned with.

They arrived at the gate, sweaty and dusty from the road, Adrienne's feet were sopping and soggy from the rainfall of the afternoon. She had tried to tie the knot herself when it had come undone, but it hadn't gone as planned. Lorcan assured her, however, that in spite of her lack of experience, she had picked up the skills pretty damn quickly, especially given the laziness of Noah's teaching.

The gates were wide and made out of a light looking metal. Not gold or copper, but something nestled in the middle of the two. The patterns on each piece, each part of the grate, were so intricate, like something you'd expect from a small trinket in a ladies shop. It was crafted in a way that was so often avoided for large pieces of work, but the gates were covered in it: picture after picture, like a tapestry of old, so small, as if you could fit a saga on each bar. This was truly the land of makers: the place where artists and craftsmen, scientists and philosophers came to create great things.

They were greeted by a tall man with the Gedogin crest on his neck, one of the Gedogin Alliance: maybe even a Keeper from the way he held himself, and the grand looking crest on his shirt. The day was late, so the town was in recess as they walked through the keep up to the castle. Later the stalls would open for the evening, as pilgrims and tradesmen who had taken rooms in one of the three inns would reemerge - having settled any larger dealings during the day - to browse the stalls and see the famous lights for themselves. There, on the far side of the town, in the opposite direction, they could see the road that led down to the sea, and Adrienne felt a jolt of excitement in her stomach: down that road lay Keeper's Cove, another mirage from stories of old.

The guards escorted them up to the castle and they entered through wide, open doors that towered over them. At the centre of the main entrance hall was a large glass panel; the glass was like frost, but it also appeared to be floating, like the surface of a Danaan cloak. They were led down a long corridor, with gold painted clay profiles of previous lords and ladies of the castle displayed on either side, weapons on the walls, and a grand green carpet leading to a large golden door that resembled the gates. The entire space was not what either of them had imagined in the stories of Keeper's Castle: a place of men and women would train to take the oath to join the Gedogin alliance; where scholars came from Alba to continue their work after completing their studies; and where modern magicks were developed.

The grand doors swung wide open, seemingly by themselves, and inside was a great room of books. Each wall was covered in them, except for a large section of wall in the middle, which contained a mural. It pictured a figure holding out a key, a great beam of light shooting out of a cylinder-shaped tower, and on each corner of the piece was a figure. On one corner was a figure holding a book, decorated with the same gold patterns as the gate to the castle, the second showed a dark figure surrounded by a whirlpool of water, the third was a shadow of a figure draped in leaves and the fourth was holding a tincture. Adrienne took a step back from the picture and squinted. The shape of it, with the tower and the beams of light - it was the Gedogin crest, the sign of the Keepers. She breathed a heavy sigh of relief at the sight of it, they'd made it.

The lady Tosia was sitting in her chair at the end of the room behind a desk, and she stood as they entered. She was a serious looking woman, with glasses and a diplomat's dress: sharp, angular, practical attire that could easily be suited up with armour, and her hair was dreaded and beaded with white gold.

"Lady Tosia, thank you for seeing us. I travelled from the forests of Wiberia to see you. I have a message for you from a woman. I was in her charge, and she asked me to contact you..." said Adrienne.

"Elsen?" asked Lady Tosia, "Does she live? I have not felt her presence for some time now."

Adrienne wanted to swallow the words down, realising that this was the first time she had uttered them since that fateful day, "she died," she said, quietly, "she was attacked."

Tosia took a heavy breath and gestured for them to sit, "and the man she was with?"

"Missing, taken by the Seldelige"

"The Seldelige?" said Tosia, incredulously, "in Wiberia?"

Adrienne nodded, almost feeling responsible for her mistress's reaction, "They came out of nowhere, ma'am."

The woman in the chair looked pensive but didn't speak. Lorcan looked horror-stricken as he silently pieced events together in his own chair, "That's really who they were?"

Adrienne looked at Lorcan helplessly, she would have to explain later.

"Please... um... ma'am..." she stuttered, "Elsen said you would be able to help to get him back. It's why I've come."

"You were sent here?'" asked Tosia.

"Yes, I suspect Elsen had very little time to think, but she was very clear that I must seek out the Gedogin," Adrienne hesitated, "The man, you see, he was my father."

Tosia turned now, looking Adrienne up and down, "So it's true," she said.

"She told me to keep this with me, and some people tried to take it, more than once actually. I understand it was made here," she handed the Noch to Tosia, and as she did she realised that the sunken part of the engravings had changed colour again, they were now glowing a light orange.

Tosia checked the Noch back to front, looked at the glow coming from within it, and handed it back to Adrienne, "This is as I suspected," she said, "keep this safe for now. There are many who would seek to take something like that from you, even within the walls of the castle. I presume you got this from your father?"

Adrienne nodded.

"They are rare objects and very dangerous if they land in the wrong hands, let no one know you have it. There are plenty of counterfeits, but the right person will know the difference if you let them see it. Above all, you must promise me that if the light changes colour again you will tell me," she gestured for them to sit, "It's imperative that you do. I need to monitor the disruptions in the Channel, we have Nochs here, but they are not quite as powerful... it uses up a huge amount of energy to create new ones, but yours was made long ago when our people understood less of the balance, and therefore it is far more powerful."

"Of course," said Adrienne.

"You must understand, if there are disruptions coming from other parts of our world that don't fit with the harmony of the Channel, it can only mean one thing: that a new Seldelige is being created."

Adrienne and Lorcan looked at each other and then back at Tosia, both weary of her words, both unsure of what she meant by them. The woman softened ever so briefly as she looked at both her guests, so young.

"You must have endured unimaginable suffering," said Tosia, "I am sure that the manner in which these events were conducted was not pleasant."

"Yes ma'am, I had to send Elsen to the Channels myself," said Adrienne. Lorcan put his hand on her shoulder, knowing it meant that she'd had to burn Elsen's body to the skies.

"I knew your parents," said Tosia, "They were good people, always willing to change their minds, always willing to listen. That alone takes bravery in the face of such extreme conditioning. To leave the grips of Velgrave and the Consortium takes great strength. You are safe here, for as long as you need it."

"Thank you," said Adrienne, pushing down a lump in the back of her throat.

Tosia turned to face the wall of her library, ostensibly to think, and looked at the great mosaic that stretched across the walls in between the hundreds of thousands of books that lined all the way up to the ceiling. Even so, in the corner of one of the glass cases, Adrienne thought she could make out the look on Tosia's face: sorrow. Or was it fear?

Lady Tosia remained silent for a few more moments, turning thoughts over in her mind, until she eventually looked back at them, resolved. "This is grave news indeed. Forgive me. I have urgent matters to attend to."

"But please," begged Adrienne, "My father..."

"I have heard your plea. You must trust me to do what is right now. I will send for you later and we shall talk more, the guards will take you to your rooms and you will be looked after," she walked two paces towards the door, stopped, turned back to them and addressed one of the guards, "And please can it be made sure that they both have a bath."

Adrienne stood in silence outside of Tosia's rooms, dumbfounded. She had travelled across the world to find this place and to speak to its leader. Now she was here there was not a word of explanation, no words of hope other than to trust it was being dealt with. Did Tosia not understand how hard it had been for her to not know? Panic and fear gripped her. She began to feel incredibly conscious of the sound of her breathing. The sharp pain in her chest pulled her breath back so that she could only take in half the air in shallow swipes. She gripped her chest above where her overpowered heart was. Perhaps the only reason she hadn't felt this pain before was that she'd been holding it down so tightly? Well, now that she had made it to her destination maybe it was time to let it breathe? She laughed through the panic at the irony of it.

Lorcan stopped her thoughts in their tracks by holding onto both shoulders and looking her straight in the eye, "Breath," he said, "and tell me how many heroes from stories you can recognise on that tapestry in front of us."

She concentrated on her breathing and turned her eyes to the tapestry. There was the great leader of the warriors, who had once led a hundred wolves into battle against the men from the west who had once invaded the Central Islands and threatened to take the tor. There was the great sorceress, Darla, who had inhabited the middle islands where the pirates now ran their republic, and who had possessed great magickal skills, which no man had been able to learn since. There was the great ancestor, Orinth, father of all humanity, who had first chosen to enter the Inner Channel and live forever in the collective energy of all man. There was... she realised all of a sudden that the tightness in her chest had loosened, and her breathing was close to normal. She heaved in a huge breath and felt the air reach the back of her lungs, "Thank you," she said, forcing a smile.

They were to be taken to accommodation in the north west tower, and Lorcan, who was not a stickler for social norms, spent the walk coaxing the guards into telling him as much as possible. The guards told him that the castle and the tor had once been owned by one of the greatest families in all of the Central Lands, back when the northern and southern crown still had significant influence and power. A long time ago, the lord of this family, who had no heirs, had bequeathed the keep to the Gedogin, to be a place for the development of modern magicks, using the tor to power its work. His niece, who was a member of the Gedogin alliance, oversaw the conversion and inherited his title. This title still remained but was passed on as a matter of merit from one Gedogin head to the next, as were her wishes. For years Keeper's Castle stood as a beacon of light for the modern world, but then other factions grew, with different ideas as to how the Central Lands should be run, and that's where they now found themselves, in the midst of a stalemate between lands and corporations.

They walked up some winding stairs and across a great skywalk that stretched from one tower to the next, with windows looking out into the town below the castle. As everyone knew, this was the centre of commerce, with old craft families who were experts at creating vessels, and artists who moved there to contribute their skills to the craftsmanship of such things. The Revolter, Nesters and Stair Journals were their main export, as well as Keeper's lanterns and Fire Staffs for warriors.

Adrienne asked them where the term 'Keepers' came from, but the guards just stared at her blankly before responding, "It's just called that, madam. A name is a name."

But a name is never just a name, she thought.

Chapter 20 - The Letter

Their rooms consisted of one spacious parlour room, with two adjoining staircases that connected to bedrooms on either side. There was a brass writing desk, a well-stocked fireplace, and scattered around the place were stylish looking sofas and chairs. In keeping with the style of the castle, there was also a wide selection of artwork covering every inch of the walls, fitting together like a makeshift puzzle.

An old Stair book lay open in a glass cabinet, with a leather casing, possibly one of the original pieces from when it was invented in Keeper's castle. It was made of the finest parchments, in a beautifully engraved cover made out of precious stones and metals.

"I've never seen one of these up close," said Lorcan, as he leant over the cabinet, "They sent one of the later models to the village where I grew up, and it was kept in the square in case anyone needed to summon the doctor in the neighbouring village. The pages have dots on the left-hand side, like a list? That's weird."

"I think they were originally invented to help out in the castle kitchens," said Adrienne, "You would write your request in the book and then it would appear in ink on the same page in the book in the kitchen. It was a long way to go otherwise."

This was the first household where Adrienne had seen similar books, for sending servants or guards on errands, outside of Velgrave, though she decided not to mention that part.

"It's just so opulent, isn't it?" said Lorcan, "I mean all these vessels, they were created as things you could make in bulk for cheap to help commoners, that was the point, right? That's why they were given the castle in the first place, but it doesn't seem... It seems that it's about money and trade here, like everywhere else. I can't help thinking that's why the

Consortium broke with them in the first place, because they keep the tor's energy to themselves, and that's not what this place was for."

Adrienne thought for a moment and then shrugged, "I'd say that the Consortium is more about money and trade, and it doesn't care what damage it does to the world or the inner Channel in the process."

Lorcan looked as if he wanted to keep talking, but he bit his lip and turned away from her instead. A worrying realisation came over Adrienne and a flicker of doubt and mistrust entered her mind. She made her excuses and went to her room. They had a while before Lady Tosia was likely to call for them, so she did as she had been asked and called for a bath to be brought in for her to wash.

She lay in the soapy water, considering her situation. They were being looked after, that much was true, but why had Tosia disappeared like that? And what was she expected to do now? Lounge around and enjoy the sights indefinitely until someone decides to tell her more? And there was Lorcan, he might try to hide it but it was clear as day to her now, he was a supporter of the Consortium. How had she managed to miss the signs? And if he knew the real reasons behind the war, as Thomas did, then why had he agreed to come here to the Gedogin with her? The very people the Consortium are working against. If he had wanted to find his way to the inner circle of the castle, to spy or maybe worse, then befriending her was a brilliant way of going about it. But this was ridiculous, just because he had sympathies towards the Consortium didn't mean he was involved in their dirty work! Not every person who has opinions that differ from the ones she'd been led to believe were true was a radical war criminal! And besides, how could any of them have known where she was headed, or who she sought? But then, the Noch; the item that had led her into harm's way more than once already; the very thing she'd been told to protect above all else.

When she emerged from her room for dinner, she saw that a spread had been brought up to them from the kitchens. Much to their surprise, they were sent a selection of meats, breads, oils and roasted vegetables that tasted so good that their taste buds tingled with every bite. The wine sent up had a hint of the delicious nectar drink from the forest, but it was more refined as if it had been bottled up and stored in a dusty wine cellar for a decade instead of being brewed in barrels in the forest. With all this, they were able to relax, and Adrienne felt at least that they were starting to warm to each other again.

A while later a messenger entered, carrying a pair of shoes and a Revolter message. He placed the shoes by the entrance and inserted the message into the small Revolter in the corner of the room. She watched him switch the dials to play the message, expecting that they would be summoned back to Lady Tosia. The voice, however, was not Lady Tosia's. A faint image appeared within the box of a woman in a silk shaw:

"Hello Adrienne," said the shadow, "I received your letter upon returning home, after a long visit to Velgrave, sorting out some unfortunate business with the war effort. Apologies if this gets to you later than expected, I hope it hasn't caused you any worry. If you are listening to this then you have safely arrived in Keeper's Cove, and I am grateful. I cannot say much, and apologies that I cannot send you a more personal message, but when you are ready you can come here. Lady Tosia will make sure to let me know when you have left. I will wait for you here."

The letter Adrienne had written to her aunt seemed so long ago, and her memories of that time already felt so far away. She felt a little tug of pain at it, as the idea of being near someone who loved her might open a door she needed to keep shut right now. It hurt too that the one person who could truly console her was in front of her, yet so far away. She tucked the letter into her inside pocket and thanked the messenger with a copper Tadall. She was starting to run low now, so chose not to write anything back and spend any more coin.

The Revolter in the corner then started glowing green again and Adrienne herself switched the dials. This time it was Lady Tosia, just as she had been standing in her office a few hours before, only her form was dark and faded as Adrienne's aunt had been.

"Hello, Adrienne and Lorcan. Please make sure you rest and recuperate, there is much to do and you will need your strength. I have been called away for a day or so. You will be safe here until I return, and we will talk then."

The figure disappeared and the Revolter went dark, only to light up again with another message immediately afterwards:

"Also, please give your shoes to one of the servants, they will get them fixed for you in town tomorrow. I have sent along a pair of shoes for you to wear in the meantime."

"A day or so!" said Adrienne, trying to look calm and measured, "I travelled all this way only to be met with 'A day or so!'"

Her blood boiled at the thought of it. Hadn't she earned answers by now? Didn't she deserve to know what was being done?

"What's wrong?" asked Lorcan.

"How can I trust a woman I've never met when that woman can't trust me?" She was pacing the room now, not angered but despairing, trying to find somewhere to focus her energy.

"Probably the same reason you couldn't trust me," said Lorcan, "Oh, and whilst we're on the subject, the Seldelige took your father?"

Adrienne's stomach jump started at this when she realised she'd completely forgotten how little she'd told Lorcan, "I'm sorry," she said, "I was being safe, and honestly I didn't think you'd believe me, but you've seen it now... twice."

"I have to say, I sort of suspected there was a connection, or I'd have been pretty annoyed to find out then and there. You were just sharing what was necessary to share, I guess. That is what Tosia is doing as well - just doing what needs to be done."

"It's not enough!"

She stopped pacing and sat down on the sofa, "I just want to help," she said, more softly.

"You've done your bit, Adrienne. You made it, let the Gedogin take it from here."

She didn't say another word at this and instead, resigned, lay back on the sofa with her eyes shut, just for a moment. Their long journey had knocked the energy out of her in every way, and as much as she had tried to stay awake to think about all she'd encountered, she couldn't. She lay in a state of limbo, dreaming of being asleep, with flashes of the Seldelige, the Danaan, Tosia's message and Elsen's empty eyes in the flames. She wrestled with these intrusive thoughts until finally, she dozed off by the fire only to wake with a start two hours later. The sun had fully set and there was noise coming from the town as it busied for the night's revels.

Lorcan twitched as she put a blanket over him, but didn't wake.

Adrienne packed up her purse, compass and a pen, threw on her cloak and tried on the shoes that Tosia had kindly sent. They were worker's shoes, not at all delicate, but sturdy.

She pulled out a piece of paper from the Stair book by the door that was connected to the kitchen, ripped it in half and pressed it together. The paper felt uncommonly warm between her fingers as she pressed, and she knew it had worked. She placed one half of the rebounded paper on the table in front of Lorcan, dipped her pen in ink and scrolled, "Going to see the lights, will be back soon." The ink immediately dried and appeared exactly as she had written it on the paper next to Lorcan on the table. Satisfied, she placed her half in her cloak pocket and left the room.

    The energy in the town was electric, many would say that the area had healing energy, because they were so close to the Tor, and though she didn't necessarily believe that, she felt it. She was still achy and her feet were still a little sore, but the butterflies in her stomach soon overpowered those feelings. She browsed the night stalls, taking in every moment. Every new and fascinating object, every face. She stopped at a stall where a man was explaining the magic behind the Revolter, just in simple traveller terms, of the energy being copied into another place with the same stone article to hold it and using particles in the air to move it across the world, and then the original message deleted to replace the energy. She tried to apply this to what she now knew: that the Danaan were real, that by principle, the very act of thinking with a trained Danaan mind could pass to another person, no matter how far away, if they too were tapped into the same energy frequencies. The onlookers stood in awe, nodding, most likely feigning comprehension. The magicks were complicated and most people just accepted that modern technology worked without any further inquiry.

    She stopped at a stall that was selling Stair books and purchased a pair for three Glames, and she spent another penny on a glass of warm, spiced cocoa from a food seller. She remembered that she had vowed not to spend anything more until she'd found her aunt, but it was too late. Besides, she was starting to trust Tosia's words, that she was safe for the time being.

    Eventually, the stalls and displays started to thin out, and she found herself walking down the cobbled path towards Keeper's Cove. It lay to the side of her as she entered the port, and through a walkway of two adjoining caves that led her to a separate beach. She walked out into a large clearing and looked up at the towering cliff face of the cove. It was covered in giant vines that stretched all the way up to the top and around the cove. A few travellers were already assembled for the night's events, and there were mutterings that there wouldn't be much longer to wait. One of them had brought along what seemed to be a picnic and offered her a glass of nectar wine in a wooden goblet.

    For a while, they stood in the darkness. The silence was a tense one, only broken by occasion chatter brought on by anticipation. The travellers with the wine hushed and teased each other at intervals and chuckled at themselves in doing so. Then, out of nowhere, it happened, as soon as there was no hint of light in the sky other than the bright moon and stars, another light appeared: the giant vines that were growing out of the cliff face from the caves, were suddenly and all at once lit up. They didn't appear in a way that allowed you to pinpoint exactly when or how they'd appeared, instead, they were suddenly there as if they had always been and it was their eyesight that had missed it. Lashings of magnificent pale green light radiated from within; otherworldly in the purest way. And there was a noise, faint at first, perhaps not even a noise but a vibration, which felt like a million voices in one and yet too faint to make out. Adrienne concentrated and listened, and the noise grew louder and louder, until it ascended to an overwhelming climax, countless voices and vibrations all in unison, to the point that she wasn't even in her body anymore, and then, as soon as it had come, it left. Adrienne stood once more on the beach, with nothing but the waves and the voices of a few onlookers to hear.

"How is this place not cornered off?" Adrienne asked, turning to one of the castle guards who was standing a little way off. He told her it was pretty safe, that everyone knew that you couldn't harness the energy of the Tor by the roots, and even if you could, few knew how. He said that this was just the light energy and only a spectacle. He showed her, "As soon as you chop off the root," he did so with a small piece and held it in his hand. It immediately went dark, "It loses its value. Only the Gedogin in the castle know how to harness it. And it's a plant, so we can afford to have the occasional onlooker trying to test the theory. It'll grow back within the week." He handed her the root. It was now, as he had said, a plain old tree root.

"And the noise? What's that?" she asked.

"What noise?" said the guard. She stared at him in confusion for a moment and then shrugged her shoulders, turning back to the spectacle, watching the hypnotic lights drift in and out of her vision in time with the soft waves on the empty shore. She was the only one who could hear it.

Lorcan woke alone in their rooms. He pushed himself up, groggy from the sleep, and looked around. On the table across from him was a sheet of torn paper from the Stair book that said, "On my way back from the keep now".

He sat up to view the horizon from the window. The entire place made him grimace, its splendour brought out an anger in him that had been deeply hidden for an age. The Gedogin were given this place to develop new magicks that would help the struggling commoners, who the crown had left to starve, and yet in his lifetime, they had kept their new developments to themselves, hoarding them for some higher purpose. So what if the Channel was weakening? What was the point in having a Channel if there were no people alive to use it? Did they have any idea how most people lived? His family hadn't been poor: in their village they'd been one of the better-off families, but even before the war things were looking bleak. One time when he was young, the families were struggling from a particularly hot harvest season, and Consortium missionaries had arrived with Nesters for the cattle and young children: machines that heated you, restored energy and allowed you to sleep for days if you were sick. The Nesters were made as copies by the Consortium though, and without proper access to the Channel, they soon broke. His father had cursed the Gedogin for not making their resources more available to the masses. That's what everyone said, that the Gedogin were to blame, and there was nothing here that he could see that would disprove that.

 When Adrienne arrived, Lorcan was wound up and ready to lash out. He perhaps would have done so if Rainou hadn't called on them minutes later. She'd arrived just a few hours after them but had been conferring via Revolter with one of the Laten diplomats before she came to check in on them.

 Rainou looked around the room and sat down on one of the chairs. Adrienne noticed for the first time that Rainou wasn't older than them as she'd originally assumed. In fact, she couldn't be more than four or five years older than Adrienne or Lorcan. She stayed with them for an hour, and they played a game of Sailor's Squares together as Lorcan recited some of his favourite stories from his days as a sailor. Rainou had never played before, but once she got the hang of it she was, unsurprisingly, pretty competitive. Adrienne won three rounds but was a little rusty. Sailor's Squares is all about speed, and she kept forgetting which square did what.

Lorcan, a well practised hand, won the first six rounds by a landslide, though he was given a run for his money when Rainou and Adrienne realised they could play tactically to get him out.

When the game was finished, Rainou stood, "Thank you, this was... diverting," she smiled, "I have business with the Alliance in the east wing of the castle, some of the Gedogin have been hired by King Tristain to help settle another dispute in the Laten Islands, and I may need to travel there. I will be back to see you before I leave," and she gave a faint smile.

After she left Lorcan had calmed himself, but despite that, Adrienne could see that he was distressed. She tried to fill the silence with the story of her visit to the keep and the bay until she finally caved in and faced the conflict, "What's wrong?"

There was something in his eyes that looked like pain, but she couldn't be sure, "I don't like it here," he said. "These aren't my people. I feel like this is the exact place I shouldn't be... they took everything from me."

Adrienne tried to be patient with him as he had been with her, but it was hard when he was attacking her father's people, "The Gedogin didn't kill your parents, Lorcan," she said, "The war did. Everyone knows the Consortium does terrible things, they created the Seldelige! And everyone knows the Consortium spreads propaganda about the Gedogin. I think power is fickle, and you can manipulate it. I mean, I think there's a lot of factors that we don't understand."

"You're so wrapped up in your bubble that you can't even see. Adrienne, the world isn't just Keepers Cove and Velgrave... and the upper layers of Senelin. Everyone knows that the Gedogin are so high and mighty that they don't share their resources with the people who need it most!"

"That's just not true Lorcan, or have you not been in the same conversations I've been in?" she was shouting now, and she couldn't control it.

"The only really important thing is looking after the people who actually need help," he yelled back, not being able to help it, "Instead of flouncing around in the depths of nowhere tutting and fretting over what will happen to some useless tree roots if they become less shiny! You don't get it..."

"No, you don't get it..."

"No you don't, you've never been poor," he said harshly, and a tense silence fell between them.

"I have seen it," she said, "I tried to understand... when I spoke to Noah about it..."

"I don't care about Noah!" he snapped, "I don't belong here, I'm sorry I came. I left my ship. I had something there, it wasn't a lot, but it was mine. I thought that I couldn't be somewhere where people weren't honest, but I let myself forget that everywhere you go there's something wrong with it. Everyone thinks they're right because they can justify what they do, but everyone's rotten really."

He went still for a moment, and Adrienne thought she saw a glimmer of sadness in his eyes, but it went as he rubbed his face with his hands. She sat down next to him and put her hand on his shoulder; she felt him lean into it ever so slightly.

"Everyone's rotten, yes, probably," she said, "but if that's true then there's goodness in everyone too."

He looked up at her and shook his head, "I'm sorry, I just didn't think it would be this hard... maybe I should go to the harbour now. I'm in your way."

All she had to do at that moment was speak. She only needed to say something else, that she wanted to understand, that she wanted him to stay, but she didn't. Maybe because she was overwhelmed, maybe because she didn't think she could change his mind or didn't want to, but it wasn't about her this time. She'd hurt him, and probably more than he cared to admit. Not knowing what else to do, he picked up his satchel and the paper from the table, and left.

Chapter 21 - The Invisible Room

A man arrived to take him to a larger room today, three flights of stairs above him in a turret of the castle he was now in. Around him were Seldelige flags mounted on the brick walls, and in the centre of a room was a shallow stone circle surrounded by red paint markings on the floor. Against his will, he was fed and watered, and given a cloth to wipe his face. Eventually, a man brought him new clothes and a casket of wine for his glass.

A man in Seldelige robes entered the room and walked towards him. He shook his hand, I apologise for the way you have been treated thus far. My friends aren't used to dealing with the civilised. I've arranged for your rooms to be moved to a more appropriate standard for a man of your station."

The captive man was stone faced, unmoved by the glassy tactics of his oppressor, who seeing as much got up to leave.

You do have a choice in this," said the stranger, We will not simply force the information out of you, in the end, you will give it freely. I promise you this, if I promise you anything at all."

Adrienne found herself with very little to do in her rooms as she waited for Tosia to return. The town itself had kept her occupied, but all the while she waited it seemed like a fruitless activity to make use of it; time was not on her side. She hadn't seen her father in weeks now, and she'd finally made it to Keeper's Cove, the one place where they might be able to help him, and for what? He was a friend of the Gedogin, Tosia had known of him if not known him, and nothing was happening. If she was in charge, she would have every Gedogin within reach of her searching for him. But of course, *she* would.

She tried to distract herself, but her interest in taking on the same pursuits again and again was wavering. There had been some books sent to her rooms the previous night, but all that she'd received was an old copy of *All Along The Road,* written in the modern eastern tongue, and a history book about Velgrave. She skimmed the pages of the Agnes Decanté book, looking at the pictures and trying to remember anything from her lessons with Elsen, which wasn't a huge amount. She had a working knowledge of the ancient languages, but had always refused to put any extra energy into her lessons, because what good was it when no one used them anymore?

She then turned to the Velgrave book, which told her nothing she didn't already know: the land was all owned by the rich, farmers currently making good and buying land from their masters; a new class was emerging.

She had enjoyed reading the book that Lorcan had given her and considered reading it again. She picked it up and flicked through the pages like a picture book without taking anything in.

She moved to a chair by the window and watched the streets below, wondering where Lorcan was and trying to stop herself from writing to him on the torn paper she still kept in her pocket.

The next morning, Adrienne received a message to her rooms from Lady Tosia, authorising her to visit the Omphalos at once, and that someone would be sent before noon to take her there. There was a postscript informing her that Rainou was to leave the castle in a few days. Apparently, there had been further skirmishes at sea, and the northern ambassador in the Laten Islands had been attacked by protestors. It was agreed that Rainou's mission would be pushed forward and that she was to travel north to the Laten territories two sleeps from now.

To Adrienne's surprise, it was Rainou who arrived to collect her. She was wearing an official Gedogin diplomat uniform, a dark green cloak and shirt, and she had a pendant with the Keeper's crest around her neck. The Danaan tattoo was still standing out as much as ever on her neck, which made Adrienne grin. Rainou looked like the people in the old photos of the Gedogin Alliance that you'd sometimes see in books. The people walking around the castle tended not to have the markings, but Adrienne guessed the people working in the castle were mainly scholars, or Magickists, not Keepers.

"I spoke with Tosia this morning," said Rainou, "My trip has been put on hold just a little longer, as I wanted to be the one to show you what has been built here."

Adrienne felt awkward, "I haven't... I mean I'm not here to join the Gedogin. I'm here for one thing only," she said.

"That's not the intention," said Rainou, "whether you want to be or not, you may well have to be part of this fight at some point soon. If we can give you a bit of training, and a bit of knowledge, whilst we wait to make our move, then that's what we'll do. Besides, your father was one of us, aren't you just a little bit curious to find out what he did here?"

"Of course," said Adrienne, "I don't want to seem ungrateful. Thank you."

Rainou said nothing but started to walk and gestured for Adrienne to follow,

"It's still so soon for you to leave, though, in two days..." said Adrienne, "What exactly are they sending you to do?"

"Remember that you aren't yet part of the alliance, Adrienne. What we know now we'd only be able to tell you in half-truths, it would just lead to more questions. They'll tell you when the time is right," said Rainou, "For now, I am to guide you to somewhere you can seek out a greater sense of where you come from, where your parents come from. I understand there is little time, but we will make the most of the time we have."

The Omphalos was right in the centre of the castle, but it couldn't be reached directly. To get there you had to go past the kitchens, then the workshop areas - where they created new vessels and instruments - and then you had to pass out of the castle and back in through the training ground to back into the centre. Above them to the east lay guest quarters for important visitors to the keep - ambassadors and officials as well as affiliates of the Alliance - and directly opposite them was a window into a clerk's room, full of letters and post.

As they passed through the courtyard, Adrienne saw a younger looking Gedogin girl training with vessel weapons amongst the pristine gardens. She'd never seen them used before, it was a remarkable thing: they were exactly like normal weapons - a crossbow, a sword, a fire staff - but they were stronger looking, and glowed lightly. They seemed to have an energy of their own. The girl looked picturesque as she guided them through the air, with the vastly wild northern climate stretched out of the castle behind her.

Rainou then led them back inside via a new flight of winding, stone stairs, then down a corridor, into a wide, cave-like basement. It was empty, filled with cold-looking marble seats under large tables, and dusty shelves with ladders and balconies stretched right across the walls. If you looked up, you could see they had come full circle, as a skylight came through the clear ceiling. It was the glass mirage that Adrienne had walked over on her first entrance to the castle, in the entrance hall. An occasional shadow of a person walking across the glass gave a small sense of being to the otherwise unplaceable surroundings. They stood at the top of the great stone steps looking down at the cavernous, empty room. The pattern on the stone floor of the library showed vines leading all the way to a central circle with the Keeper's Crest faintly marked, *the Channel,* Adrienne thought.

Rainou pulled a chord by the side of the doorway, and then suddenly, all at once, the room was awash with movement and colour. Not hundreds, but hundreds of thousands of books now covered the shelves that had been so dusty and barren a moment before. There were ladders leading up to numerous balconies all the way up to the ceiling, with reading areas on each of them. All the way around the room were atlases, charts and displays presenting the well-known magicks of the Inner Channel, and on the marble stools surrounding the tables were about thirty scholars, scattered around the space, reading, writing, talking in hushed library tones.

"It is a little dramatic," said Rainou, "But we have to keep things strictly hidden so as not to entice any outsiders to... invite themselves in."

"Every recruit who learns the way of the Gedogin starts here. It's where they retrain," said Rainou.

"What do you mean, retrain?" asked Adrienne.

"I mean that a child has a pure connection to the Channel," said Rainou, "If we can catch them early, then the training can be as easy as teaching a dog to fetch. It's our world that conditions the child out of their understanding. That's why we at least try to start the Danaan young. When we recruit someone later on it is harder to reconnect. For non-Danaan it matters less, as they have less to gain."

To start with, Adrienne wandered around the library, browsing for pleasure and taking it all in. She looked through the displays, making note of where the sections were for each genre of book, though there were so many she hardly expected to remember.

A glass case with a book, *The History of The Consortium*, was open and it was displaying two pages. It read:

Recruits would originally train in all disciplines: history, combat, the technology of magick and the creation of modern vessels, and diplomacy. If a member of the alliance excelled in all disciplines they would become a Keeper, and learn the ways of the Channel. Those who had demonstrated strength and natural skill in one of the divisions, but did not display a natural connection to the Channel (usually non-Danaan) would be trained in just one, remaining a member of the Gedogin Alliance and not progressing to becoming a Keeper.

The Consortium was originally formed within the Gedogin, in order to create a partnership between its advancing technologies and the needs of the outside world. However, it soon became clear that modern thinkers did not wish to keep the natural balance of order that the Inner Channel required to be sustainable, and so the division broke from its original creators. The Gedogin and Consortium split, of twenty years ago, was not the end of the relationship between the two superpowers. They carried on working together for a while longer, cooperating with trade despite conflicting ideology.

She stopped reading, remembering her fight with Lorcan and how complex the entire thing had felt to him, but she was distracted by a conversation that was brewing in the main part of the room and moved towards it with curiosity.

There appeared to be a lesson going on: an old man, wearing brightly coloured scholar's robes, which signified his oneness with the Channel, was lecturing to six young Gedogin students, who were a few years younger than Adrienne. One of the boys had the crest marks already tattooed behind his ear, and Adrienne assumed he must have grown up with Danaan. She stopped behind them and listened:

"...music changing our mood is an example of this!" said a girl enthusiastically, "I mean, if everything is energy and I'm altering the energy around me by simply thinking my thoughts then..."

"...go on," said the teacher.

"Well, the music must be the same," she said, unsure.

The teacher smiled at her, encouragingly, "and why is that?"

"Because it makes me feel things," she shrugged, helplessly.

"That's certainly a good indicator that more research into that area is necessary," said the teacher.

"What about the source of the energy," said a blond, freckled boy who was sitting at the front of the group clasping an old looking, leather bound book, "Is it truly the spirits of our ancestors?"

Some of the other students laughed at this. The boy read from the book, "When we die, some of the energy we leave behind goes to the worms, but some of it rises up and joins the great Channels of the world."

There were now scoffs coming from some of the recruits, protestations that this was an old wives 'tale made up to confuse commoners and stop them from prying into the Alliance's secrets.

The teacher waited for the noise to die down before they took a serious tone with the boy, "You are reading from the ancient manuscripts laid down by those who still worship the four earth gods."

"Yes," said the boy.

"Do you believe in those gods?" the teacher asked.

"Where I come from," said the boy, "That's what people believe."

"But do you?" asked the teacher.

"It's what people believed for hundreds of years, that the progress made by those who are no longer with us still lives in the air, that we can draw from it if we follow our intuition. It's like the Danaan and those who have a connection..."

"And... what is it that guides *your* intuition?"

The boy thought hard about this, "the Channel."

"Exactly," he said, turning back to the group, "There are plenty of ways of interpreting things. What Hara speaks of has been around since the beginning of recorded history, first known as fact, then as religion, and now as an old story steeped in myth. But think on this: a child needs its mother to learn to speak, to look after itself, correct? About two hundred years ago, a woman named Lethena experimented on Water Doves from the Alba Isle, who were taken away from their mothers at birth and kept in cages for their entire lives. The doves were named after their habit of sitting next to the sea and singing their peculiar song, which sounded in fresh air as if they were cooing underwater. They were also recognisable by the nests that they built, which were oddly shaped, like a circular wave. The birds she took had no contact with the outside world or any of their kind, and yet after being bred to adulthood, they learned to sing the very song that all birds of that kind sang, and, when they were eventually given sticks and mud, they built the same wave shaped nests that their ancestors had built. How did they know? They had access to the Channel, to their own intuition, and the knowledge of their forefathers. There are many kinds of energy in this world, and they all live behind the same tale."

Adrienne started to leave and as she did she caught the teacher's eye. He nodded at her and smiled, so she smiled back. He looked vaguely familiar, but she couldn't put her finger on where she might have known him from. Then one of his students, hands raised, pulled back his attention towards them and the moment passed.

Chapter 22 - Old Lessons

For the next couple of days, Adrienne's routine allowed for as much distraction as was possible under the circumstances. She spent the mornings in her rooms, the afternoons browsing the Omphalos, and she was also brought in on basic sword skills lessons with the other warrior recruits. The opportunity to work with Keeper Vessels was a silver lining indeed, but she couldn't help thinking that she was being tested more than taught.

The unarmed combat and sword fighting were not her strong suit, and she was already starting to grow blisters on her hands from the constant drilling she was receiving from the fight masters. Her crossbow skills were already at a rather decent standard as she'd often been allowed to hunt in the woods on the island, but a Keeper's crossbow was something else entirely.

They started training in the woods to the west of the castle, where any mishandling of weapons or targets would only result in a damaged tree trunk or started game. Rainou set up a black spot on the parchment as a target, on a tree a little way off from them. She picked up the crossbow and delicately aimed it at the mark, letting loose without making even the slightest noise. Somehow, without even moving her hands, she managed to shoot the arrow clean into the bullseye. She then handed Adrienne the crossbow, who took it from her with deep scepticism. It was heavier than normal, but once Adrienne had it in place, she felt a strange connection with it, as if its energy had joined with her own. She lifted the weapon and pointed it at the target.

"The trick is to think it," said Rainou, "The crossbow is connected to you now, so you decide what happens. Try to concentrate, like you would do using any other elements of the Channel, but remember the basics: breathe out before you shoot."

Adrienne focused on the bullseye and imagined the arrow hitting it straight through the middle, and then waited, but nothing happened. She looked at Rainou, quizzically.

"You need to think about it, and then will it," said Rainou.

Adrienne looked back at the target and shrugged. She lifted the arrow for the second try, but again nothing happened, except that this time the arrow released and landed limply two meters away from them. Adrienne looked at Rain again, expectantly.

"It won't work straight away," said Rainou, "Don't give up."

Again and again, Adrienne tried, but nothing was happening. She bent down to pick up the arrow from her feet and studied it with an air of disappointment.

"Try something for me," said Rainou, "Do it with your eyes shut."

Adrienne laughed, "Surely if I can't see the target it's just going to be..." but she stopped when saw Rainou's frank expression.

Adrienne closed her eyes and focused. She couldn't allow herself to fall into the Channel and not be able to perceive the tree at all, instead, she needed to find a way of perceiving both places at once. It seemed impossible.

At least with her eyes shut she felt calmer, and with all of the outside world gone, she was able to actually feel something. She felt the breeze pass her ears, and perceived the tree, keeping her crossbow pointed in the same place as before. She thought she could also see glimmers and flashes of empty grey space and lines of colour or was she imagining them there? It didn't really matter, as long as she knew they were there somewhere. *If this doesn't work,* she thought, *nothing will.*

She let loose, commanding the damn arrow to go into the tree, and this time she felt something release. She opened her eyes. The arrow was in the middle of the black spot bullseye and had actually scraped wood shavings off of Rainou's.

As Rainou and Adrienne were leaving the courtyard on the second day, they both turned back to the training grounds when they heard a large thud. A Danaan girl had been thrown across the grass and skidded into the wall by the flower beds, the suspicious thing being that it looked like she had somehow done it herself. The teacher walked over to her, and instead of picking her up, berated her, "What made you think you had enough control of your own powers to use them in unarmed combat against another student?" he was yelling, "We tell you when you're ready, it's that way for your own protection. Foolish girl."

When it was evident that she was, at worst, a little bruised, the teacher left her sitting on the ground, and forbade anyone to offer her comfort.

"So cruel," whispered Adrienne, but Rainou looked utterly unmoved by the situation.

"She needs to learn," said Rainou, starting to walk again.

"Does she?" said Adrienne, refusing to move.

Rainou stopped and turned again, looking entirely emotionless, "You know nothing of what can be done to a Danaan. If you choose to be out in the world, then you need the thickest skin possible."

"Is that why I can't leave here?" said Adrienne, "You don't know what I went through to get here."

Rainou sighed, "It's not that way with you. They are looking for your father. They are! They have people all over tracking him, but you can't help. You can't leave Keeper's Cove as a spy! The Seldelige know who you are now, Adrienne. They are hunting you as much as we are searching for him."

"But I want to help," cried Adrienne, "I need to! I can help them strategise! I know things about him, important things..."

"Tosia is assembling a team to rescue Kernavin, and if she can use you, you will be asked. We don't know where he is but we know where he will be..."

"How do you know where he'll be?" Adrienne jumped on this new information, so desperate to learn something new, so sure her friend would give her something, anything. With that, Rainou turned and walked, alone, back to the castle.

Rainou departed on her journey to the islands later that evening, but not for as long as she had expected. She sent a Revolter message to Adrienne that night, saying that she needed to collect something and then return, though she had not said what. She also told Adrienne not to worry, and that she would see her shortly when she returned. Though it wasn't the answer she had wanted, Adrienne felt the welcome relief that she hadn't pushed away yet another friend.

She had come down early to the Omphalos the next morning to make use of the empty chairs. The other two afternoons that she'd been there, she'd arrived after lunch, and it had been full to the brim: the entire space was filled with Gedogin and she couldn't find anywhere to settle. This morning the teacher that she'd seen on her first visit was also there, sitting by one of the stone tables and making notes in a book. Adrienne was half way through *Basic Keeper's Theory* when he raised his hand and called her over to the table.

"Miss Adrienne, my name is Alexia," he said as she approached, "I am an old friend of your father. Tosia has instructed me to make myself known to you. I hear you are on your way to Senelin," he said to her as she approached the table. That was where she'd seen him before - in one of the meetings with her father in Senelin!

"I am," said Adrienne, "But where I'll go after that, I do not know yet."

"Your father was a prospective Alliance member too once," said Alexia, "I actually taught him before he became a diplomat."

Adrienne's heart raced at this, "I didn't know... I mean, I suspected..."

"...your father was part of the faction who traded with the Consortium before our links were completely severed," said Alexia, "It was a sad day when he was forced to leave us. Anyway, if you should wish for it, I am happy to carve out some time for you..."

Adrienne wasn't sure what to say to this. She was curious though, and if he'd known her father then maybe he'd know why what had happened to him had happened.

"I would like to know more about my parents," she said.

A few students started to enter the Omphalos and gathered around the table in the centre. Alexia started towards his students, but hesitated and spoke again to Adrienne, "Very well. This afternoon I will send for you. It was a pleasure to meet you, Miss Adrienne," he said.

As she was leaving the Omphalos but an hour later, Adrienne passed over to where the blue Gedogin circle lay on the floor. As she did she felt a strange vibration. This time was different from the times with the Noch, it was so overwhelming that she had to step away. She looked and watched as some of the scholars avoided the circle as one would skirt around a sculpture, and how some, the lesser few, seemed to go far out of their way to avoid it.

Chapter 23 - A Familiar Port

Lorcan looked around him at the familiar upper side port of Keeper's Cove. This was the way he knew to the port, directly north of Keeper's Castle, where most trade made its way to the islands beyond and the Players Circle visited before heading west.

He was not sure exactly why he'd left, it was more that he was no longer sure why he'd come in the first place. He couldn't look at Adrienne the same way anymore, even though he wanted to. Maybe it was his fault for not telling her before, but being there had stirred up feelings he'd long since forgotten, and he simply couldn't continue like that anymore.

It was evening by the time he'd made it to the port hub, and he'd stopped to sit on the walkway that was lit up by Keeper's Lamps. He gazed at the docked ships, wondering for a moment if one of them might be a smaller player's ship that he could gain passage on or even join up with. When he realised it was too late in the day for direct enquiries, however, he made his way to the nearest tavern to enquire about rooms and hovered near the sailors at the bar.

He ordered a glass of mead, and sat himself down in earshot of the men, in a tall armchair facing away from the bar. Most of what he heard was the usual gossip about the safest trade routes, the latest sanctions and embargoes in place, and what places were short on what. He eventually approached the man who seemed to be the most vocal and in the know, who was sitting on a stool wearing a logger ship's uniform.

"Sorry to trouble you, but do you know of any ships looking for cabin workers nearby?" he asked the man.

"Nothin 'right now," he replied, "A few just took off a couple a 'weeks back. It's been quieter and quieter these last few... on account of the Laten Islands ports being closed. There's trouble up that way, you can be sure of it."

"Thank you," said Lorcan, not bothering to hide his disappointment and turning to leave.

"Wait," said the man, "No openings bein 'advertised, but there's been a great ship in the eastern dock for about a week, looks like a warship but I'm told it's one of the grand troopers ships. You could try your luck I guess," the man tipped his hat and Lorcan bowed slightly in gratitude.

As soon as Lorcan left the tavern he immediately sped up his pace back along the harbour. How, he thought, had they been there a whole week and no word of them in the town? Why was their sail down? Was it even them? He donned his hood and walked as stealthily as he could down to the east side of the port.

In front of him was the outline of a large king's merchant ship, marks hidden with canvas and the sails down. He sat on a bench on the other side of the walk, he needed to see the mainstay but he couldn't get close enough without seeming suspicious. Damn these bright Gedogin lights, he thought. He stood up from the bench after a while and started to walk, as slowly as he could without drawing attention, to the end of the port where rails marked a dead end to the sea. He would be in view of the ship's watchmen but if he only stood there for a moment he could fake being lost and turn around immediately. He placed his hands on the railings, looking out at the dark green waters, breathing in the salty, dense scent of the harbour. He looked, just for a moment, directly over the mainstay, and there it was: the damaged lifeboat with the missing oar that Adrienne had used to fix the piano. Then, something heavy hit him in the back of the head and the world went dark.

He woke up on the wooden floor of a cabin. His ear was bleeding. He knew this because, from the way he'd been lying there, the blood had dripped down his face into his eyes. He wiped his face. His nose was dripping blood and snot onto the wooden floor and the rickety motion of the room made him feel sick.

"Morning, sunshine," said a voice from above, but he couldn't make out the face through the blood that had caked in his eyes.

Someone handed him a handkerchief and he wiped his face. He pulled himself up and readied himself, and with a sweeping blow knocked his capturer, who was taken by surprise and fell back against a desk. Without losing a second of his advantage he jumped around and grabbed the man's arm, smacking him in the face again whilst he pinned him onto the floor.Lorcan's

"Stop it will you!" yelled the man, pushing Lorcan's hands away, "Just stop!"

Lorcan stopped. He removed one hand from the man's wrist and wiped his eyes again.

"Noah?"

Chapter 24 – Alexia

His eyes opened in the dark and below him he felt a cold damp floor. There was a chair with clothes underneath the windowsill, just visible in the moonlight. There was a drip coming from the corner of the room, of course, there was, it echoed in the empty space, whilst the rain outside overlapped in an offbeat counter rhythm. He tried to sit up but the walls were so clammy that he had nothing to hold onto. Or was it his hands that were damp? The world was so foggy now, foggier still, and once he regained his sense his link to Channel was coming back a little weaker every time. This must mean it was working, he thought, it won't be long now.

The east wing of the castle was a singular long corridor with rooms on either side. Adrienne had been in the first room you came to in that corridor, on the night she'd arrived at the castle, but she hadn't noticed a turning to the side that led into another small corridor. The walls were wooden, and the doors were round and oversized, making Adrienne feel as small as a cat. Even the door handles were twice the size of normal ones, and the doors themselves were marked with the names of Gedogin leaders. They read 'Lady Tosia of Keeper's Cove', 'Professor Alexia 'and 'Gazia, of the Merchants.' The rest of the doors had names on them, each as unusually large and round as each other. There's something that was almost too perfect about them. There was another door with one more name, which looked new as if the entire room had recently been added. Just to the end was one more door. The engraving was smaller than the others but clear as day: 'Rainou, Head of Mission.'

She knocked and entered Alexia's room, it was smaller than she'd expected but felt bigger, with a huge window at the back and a door leading out into a garden. An Atticus lay on the side ledge, and scattered to the sides of the room was a selection of tinctures, herbs and potions. The other side of the room was covered in shelves containing red books with numbers on them, all dated.

"Let me see," said Alexia in his thin and jovial sounding voice, sifting through the shelves, "Your father would have been here about thirty years ago now, but your mother..."

He pulled out a book from one of the middle shelves, flipped through it and started searching with his finger for a name, "There," he said, triumphantly. They were pointing at a name, Meredith, daughter of Tevelawn.

"My mother?" said Adrienne, as astonished as she would have been if her own name was read out from one of the papers.

"Well," said Alexia, "Kernavin and Meredith met here. But Meredith left, rather abruptly I might add. She went back to Velgrave before she'd chosen a path here, though the records do not tell us why."

"I know why," said Adrienne, "She joined the Consortium. My grandfather asked her to, and so that's what she did."

"And she fell in love with a northerner," said Alexia, knowingly.

"She did," said Adrienne, "Alexia, do you know if my mother ever came into contact with the Seldelige?"

At this, he stopped reading and looked up from the papers, "I do not know the answer to that. But why do you ask such questions?"

"I never saw them when they came to the house. But I've seen them twice since, they sort of just appeared," said Adrienne, "I thought for a moment that they might be following me, because of something about me... but I was told it could be my Noch that attracted them."

"Like a moth to a flame," he said, "Nasty creatures, the Seldelige, and a reminder of the cruelty of the Consortium that they're allowed to exist at all. Do you know what Seldelige means in old Senelin?" He asked, "Sel-da-Lige".

"Those without souls," said Adrienne. There was a momentary silence.

"Why did my father leave here?" asked Adrienne.

"I would guess," grinned Alexia, "To be with your mother."

"That can't be all there is," she said, "He left here and my mother had me, and when she died he disappeared to the ends of the world. I want to know why the Seldelige were after him. I mean, why they were *really* after him. I think the answer to all my questions is the same, but I have no idea what that answer is and I feel so helpless just waiting! My father said that he spoke his mind too much in the south, and he spoke up against the Consortium, and that most of the families there are rich because of them. He spoke up so much that he was unsafe to be there once my mother died. My grandfather wanted to take me in, but he wouldn't have that. But the Seldelige wanted him. They searched for him, they must have. No one knew where we were! Why did they take him? And poor Elsen, she fought back and they killed her."

"My dear, do you really think it was the Seldelige who killed Elsen?"

Adrienne looked back, perplexed.

"Let me ask you a question," said Alexia, "You clearly have a knack for magick, that much is clear from what Astair has told us. And we would be very willing to work with you, and help you get to the point where you can at least control what you already have," he said, "Astair has told us that you were able to call a Danaan from the other side of the forest?"

"Yes, but I keep telling everyone, I don't know how I did it!"

"I would expect not," he said delicately, "And do you know what other powers are gifted to the Danaan?"

Adrienne thought back to the old bedtime stories she'd heard, "There's healing... and telepathy. You can sense the Channel's lines and take energy from them. You can influence the way of things by disrupting the flow of the Channel. There's also access to the ancestors of the Inner Channel, so a strong intuition and foresight, and magic without vessels; you can light fires using the wind, change the weather, help things grow... oh! And you can talk to animals."

"That last one is, I'm afraid, an old wives tale," said Alexia.

"And the cloaks only work on them. I think they store energy," she finished.

"Very good," said Alexia, "Now, I must ask you, did Elsen do any of these things?"

"No," she said, "I mean she knew the ways of the wood, but she always had a vessel, I'm sure of it."

She tried to remain still, but the reality of the situation was simmering somewhere below the surface, she could feel it. Every fibre of her being was fighting it, unable to accept it. It couldn't be true. Alexia sat down on one of the chairs and Adrienne lent back against the dark wooden wall behind her, keeping her eyes firmly fixed on the ground and focusing only on her breath. She sifted through the memories hidden inside her subconscious, fitting them together like a dusted off puzzle.

"Am I..."

"My Ancestors, Adrienne, have you not had a good look at yourself in a mirror lately?"

She gazed at the glass in the window, at the reflection of her dark features on her heavily freckled, pale face framed by her raven black hair.

"When my mother disappeared, Elsen brought me up," she muttered, "And when she was gone I was so alone. After I'd sent her to the Channels I tried to listen out to hear her there, like my father had taught me... but nothing came. Nothing! I couldn't do it! She's gone and I can't find her. I can't be Danaan!" She realised that her voice had crumbled, and the red hot tears that had been building in her mind since the moment all this had happened; the ones she'd held back to protect herself, for fear that if she fell down she would not be able to get back up; those tears were now pouring down her face.

"I didn't feel anything, I just burnt her. I burnt her body as if I was tidying up, and I hated myself." She was weeping now, she slid down the wall she'd been standing against as her body gave in to the weight of it.

"And yet," said Alexia, "You somehow felt the strength to get here anyway, and you did what needed to be done. The Inner Channel comes to us in many ways, Adrienne, and not always in such obvious ways that we can feel it there. It's always there, under the surface, sometimes we don't notice it, but sometimes, when we need it most, we are so entirely in it that we don't notice it lifting us up and charging us forward. Sometimes, what we need more than anything is to simply get from one moment to the next."

"Well I certainly did that," she said, flippantly, "I'm not strong enough to be Danaan. All I feel is anger and numbness and..."

The old teacher handed her a handkerchief and knelt down next to her on the floor.

"You don't look numb to me, you look alive."

"I'm sorry for... crying..." she said.

"Do you think," he asked softly, "That your body is weeping for another reason?"

"...she loved my mother," Adrienne interjected, "She loved her and she wanted me to know they did their best..."

"Yes."

"But that's not right," she said.

"And why is that?"

"Because Elsen was my mother."

She said it as if it was an absolute; as if she'd known it all along; she said it because it was true and it felt painful and heart-breaking to admit, but it was what she had asked to know.

"That's right. You are half Danaan, not faintly connected but a full half. You are capable of some of the purest magick if you choose to learn to master it. That is why Elsen sent you here. That is why Meredith married your father in Velgrave, to protect you. It's why they made you a child of the South... if anyone knew this and the Consortium found out, you'd have been handed over. Meredith's gift to you was her status: she was high-born and able to protect a small child, so she took you both in as her own. It's why, when she was gone, your father moved you away."

Adrienne breathed heavily into her folded knees, slowly and heavily as the tears continued to fall. She wept for her mother, for both of them, for her father, for herself and for Lorcan. She wept as she'd not been able to weep until now, moons and moons of it spilling out of her onto Alexia's patterned carpet.

Finally, after what felt like a long time, she breathed a heavy breath and lifted her head. Only now, with the relief she felt, did she realise what heaviness had been weighing on her for so long. She closed her eyes and sighed repeatedly until she felt her body relax. The rest was a blur, but

Adrienne woke the next morning asleep on the sofa in her room, with the faint memory of someone carrying her.

Chapter 25 - The Captive King

He blinked and looked around for the familiar figure, the one that appeared to him every time, but this time there was no one to be seen. Just the shadows on the wall playing tricks with his vision as shapes began to appear on the cracked paint. Phantoms and figures were dancing across the space, playing like puppets and dreams. Then there was a tap on his shoulder, and with that, a chill crept down his spine - it was time.

Decanté, Adrienne wondered. *Where have I heard that word before?*

The Decanté people of Black Isle Cove are one of the oldest houses left in their world. They are not rich or powerful. They are people of the sea: fisherman, traders, and occasionally player s ships. Black Isle is home to one of the old world temples that still worships the gods of old."

Adrienne was sitting in a chair in the corner next to a golden lion statue, browsing through a selection of books that had been left there by its previous occupant. She put the book down in frustration. It had been days now, and as grateful as she was for Alexia's lessons - they'd started working on her connection to the Channel - she hadn't heard from Lorcan or been told what they were training her up for.

In need of a change of scenery, she took a walk down to the market town to clear her head. She browsed some of the stores, enjoying the bustling energy of the mismatched marquees and the voices sprawling out across the walkways. She stopped by a bench and sat down to watch the people passing by. She found it soothing to see that the world around her was carrying on, though she herself was stuck in a stalemate. It wasn't at all that she was discontented to be surrounded by so much knowledge in such a beautiful place as this, as many could want for nothing more. It was the lack of certainty with no end in sight; the constant, endless limbo. Finding out where her father or Lorcan had gone was so far out of her reach that the thought of it made the last few days feel like an unsettling stream of repetition.

She pulled out her piece of Stair Book paper, which she'd been too scared to look at before now. She didn't know what would be worse: seeing a message from Lorcan or the paper being completely blank. He'd evidently taken the paper with him, as it was not there when she'd returned to find the rooms empty, and surely he'd use it if he really needed her? Surely he'd tell her if he was in trouble? But then what good could she really do? She was in the middle of what was arguably the most prosperous organisation of people in their world, and yet she felt trapped and powerless. She looked at the empty pages of paper before her and resisted the urge to tear them up altogether and throw them into the fire. No news was better than bad news, but that might be all she ever got, and the wait was unbearable.

Adrienne spent a couple of afternoons in the hidden hall, sifting through books and chronicles and searching for anything that might reference the Danaan or the Seldelige. She also attended private lessons with Alexia in his office, where he made her concentrate on accessing the Channel, much as her father had. Whilst doing so, Alexia faffed and fiddled, marking books, making notes and tidying up his desk. He was, for want of a better phrase, a nuisance to her concentration levels, and yet in all other counts a committed and rigorous teacher. His actions felt utterly counter-productive to her progress and it frustrated her.

The lessons drew mainly on the same things her father's lessons had, but were unsurprisingly more finely tuned. Adrienne longed for the more familiar distractions from days passed on the island: their dog barking in the woods, the rattling of pots and pans from the kitchen, something wild and beautiful happening with the weather outside, or the low constant simmering of the stream that passed by their house.

Another similarity between this time with Alexia and her time on the island was how frustrating it was not to progress any further. She longed to learn how to go deeper into the Channel like she had that time in the woods outside of the Danaan camp. That was where she needed to get to, it was where she would be able to harness her connection to do useful things. Most of her time was spent meditating and listening to a low buzzing noise but not being allowed to go in any further. Alexia assured her that this was how it was meant to be and that this is what would gain her the control she needed to stay in one place and therefore move freely within the Channel. Adrienne found this to be a lesson in patience more than anything, but it was also a safe, familiar activity, and one that she hadn't revisited in what felt like a very long time.

She was browsing the bookshelves the next morning when she came into a curved corner, which was almost completely divided from the rest of the room. A man with glasses and an unfamiliar uniform, made of green velvet, was sitting in one of the chairs, piles of books on the small table in front of him. He seemed completely unfazed by the fact that someone else had entered the space, as she guessed that he'd already been there for hours. This corner seemed to house older books, many with fraying edges and dehydrated leather. The books had odd titles like *The World's Turns, Ancient Archives* and *Historic Dates of the Central Lands*. The text in these books was small, hard to read and often in ancient Senelin or another language that she barely knew. She bypassed these and made a note to come back to them, opting instead for a curious looking note on a stand. The note was lit up by a small Keeper's lamp and came in the form of a letter. Below it was written 'from Lord Arible of the Gedogin, to his lover, Arabella of the Danaan clan of South Galania (now Velgrave) in the year ten thousand and ninety.' The note read:

I have been working on a theory, which allows us to harness our work into vessels for later use, compressing it into a condensed form. Not only can this be stored to create usage for unskilled folk, but we could, in theory, use it to transport correspondence. If we can recreate the signals that transport energy, then we can use that process to send moments in time, words spoken and images to a vessel in another place. If the vessels match then we can manipulate the energies so that the message too is replicated, and the balance kept when the original message is dissolved. The beauty will be that anyone can use it.

She gasped and looked up to realise that the man was now watching her, "Sorry if I disturbed you," she muttered.

The man in the green velvet suit was short, no taller than the chair he'd been sitting in. He chuckled at her horrified expression, and put down his book, "Something startling you?"

"I am sorry," she said, "I just read something that I found a little surprising," she said.

The man looked amused, "Pray, do tell. I love a good surprise," he said.

"Well, you probably already know," she said, "I was always taught that not everyone can harness powers as the Danaan do, but this says otherwise. If someone has developed a method that only those with the skill can use, and yet everyone is able to use it, then surely everyone can be taught the skills?"

"Ah yes, the eternal debate. Tell me, what do you think vessels are for?" he asked in a haughty Laten accent, "It's down to more than being able to access the Channel. We all came from it and are a part of it, but that is not the point as I understand it. It is more to do with what your body is capable of. It's a physical thing, you see? For instance, the eyes... If you need to be able to see more things, then your eyes need to be powerful, and that is why the eyes of Danaan seem so big and... how do you say?... mysterious? It is similar to my people from the Laten Islands: we survived for many millennia on our small island, where resources were few, but where great medicines were developed using the resources of the island's caves. We live long, healthy lives, we are just shorter because we had to adapt to what was around us. The people of Black Isle are strange to us as well, for they are seafarers from the north, and they need to handle great ships. They also need to survive journeys with little food and still have the strength to unload cargo and occasionally fight. Who do you think the ones who thrived were? The ones who were tall and muscular of course. We adapt to our needs, yet sometimes our bodies adapt to our abilities, and our abilities adapt likewise... but forgive me, I have been rude indeed. My name is Hercel, and I am a... guest... of Lady Tosia."

"Pleasure to meet you," said Adrienne.

"I am sure I will be seeing you again," said Hercel, and with that, he put back his books and bowed to her before he left the room.

A full seven days had passed since Adrienne had arrived at Keeper's Cove, and her strength was growing thin. Not knowing what was being done to recover her father was a constant source of anxiety for her, and being assured over and over again that everything that could be done was being done, or that the best thing she could do was train, was not helping. Not only that but Alexia was going over and over the same things with her, and the more she did it, the less interested he seemed in her progress.

He would move around, getting things out of boxes and arranging them pointlessly on the desk. At one point he started reading a book and called for his dinner whilst she was mid-meditation. How was she meant to concentrate on listening to the Channel - something she'd only managed a few times before - when Alexia seemed to care more about what he was eating and what order his pens were in? It grated on her so much that this particular afternoon, a full week after she'd arrived, she lost her patience with him. There had been a particularly unwelcome set of distractions today, including Alexia leaning out the window to have a conversation with a passing magickian, and it was too much to stomach.

"I've been learning about these things for so long, Alexia," she said in the middle of a vibrations meditation, "I've been learning them for as long as any of the Danaan folk in your class. Why can there not be some progress somewhere?"

Alexia didn't seem phased by her frustrations at all, in fact, he seemed to find them amusing, "Surely by telling me this you are also telling me that you think you're further along than them?"

"But how am I meant to show you that when you're not even paying attention? It's like trying to meditate in a storm!" spluttered Adrienne.

"Let me ask you," said Alexia, "when are the times that you perceive you will need the Channel the most?"

Adrienne thought for a moment, "If I wanted to invent something new, or if I was trying to be efficient..."

Alexia shook his head and the gold earrings hanging onto his silk Gedogin robes shook dramatically, "No. These are the times when it would be useful, but when will you need it the most?"

"When I'm in danger," said Adrienne, "Like when I called the Danaan."

"Correction," said Alexia, "It was the Danaan who heard your call, they did most of the work. Now if you're in danger, perhaps with split seconds to make a move, perhaps you need to act purely on instinct whilst there are attackers all around you, or flashing lights and shouting, or a circus boat in the midst of a tempest... you may need to Channel your powers then, and it will certainly be the most challenging of circumstances when it does happen. Agreed?"

"Agreed."

"Then," said Alexia with a shrug, "do you not think it would stand to reason that we give you some distractions of your own now?"

That evening, Adrienne went down to one of the taverns in town. Tomorrow was Tamh day, so there'd be no lessons for her then and the Omphalos would be shut to those who weren't in the Alliance. She ordered a glass of spiced wine and sat in a corner, close to the music playing in the main room. It was strange that everyone in the castle seemed to know who she was: it wasn't every recruit who was given an audience with Tosia upon arriving at the keep, so naturally, word had gotten around. Some greeted her kindly, but she felt their eyes on her back as she turned away from them nonetheless. It wasn't exactly cruelty or fear of the children from the island, but she still felt exposed. With all that weighing her down, it was soothing for her to escape to the town, where no one knew of her. To sit, listening to the musicians play familiar tunes on unfamiliar Northern instruments.

A hand stretched out from the table opposite into the corner of her eye. She looked up to see green, velvet sleeves and caught the waft of strong, mulled cider from the table: it was Hercel.

"Well, hello Miss Adrienne, so lovely to find you here," he said, whimsically, "May I join you?"

They were interrupted by another voice, "Your grace, another mulled cider?" said the kitchen girl.

"I don't think I will just yet," said Hercel, "Need to let the first one cool."

The girl nodded and scrambled back to the bar. Adrienne was staring at him in astonishment, "Your grace? I apologise, I had no idea."

Hercel shook his head rebelliously, "All frills and whistles my dear, not that they mean anything anymore. I'm a prisoner of war you see, I have no power here. Hercel I am, better known as King Hercel of the Laten islands, or better known lately as the king with no castle."

Adrienne scolded herself silently for not putting two and two together, "I saw you once, I think I was quite small, but we visited the Laten Islands when I was little, and I know that was your name, Hercel, the 4th of his name."

"Do not fret, I have never been a stickler for custom, and I am really starting to enjoy this lack of... ceremony? No one in the castle knows what to do with me of course. They, of course, bow and scrape before me, and yet they often whisper Radan in my wake," he said, blowing on his cider, "This is incredibly hot... yes sorry... I am captive in the castle, an unfortunate casualty in the dispute for the Laten islands between the squabbling kingdoms, a cause in which I have no interest. We were neutral you see, in all things up until this point, but the blasted south came and occupied our beaches. There was a race between all sides to gain our favour and therefore an advantage over the war. I do fear I've been a rather awful king, but we've never needed to deal with such things. We are a very small nation, I'm practically a mayor. Anyway, rather than fight on the land and lose all our natural resources in fire and blood, there was a compromise: the heir to the Laten Empire - me - was to be exiled until further notice. The island is to temporarily be governed by the crown's council, and no change of allegiance will be made for the remainder of the war, which is, by the way, what we were doing in the first place."

Adrienne knew this must have been Rainou's work, so it appeared there was a reason her name was on that door.

"So, as a result of this, and before anyone else could claim me to use for their own purposes, Lady Tosia offered me sanctuary, on her terms. I am what they call… a prisoner with a tavern tab," he said, "Well, I am trying to make it catch on anyway."

What followed was an evening of relief for Adrienne; something about Hercel's relaxed nature, his determination to enjoy himself in the midst of extreme adversity, gave Adrienne permission to do the same. They couldn't be more different, he an old foreign King, and she a small girl from a homestead in the middle of the sea: two banished outcasts, watched day and night in a grand castle, but both invisible amongst the locals, hiding at the centre of everything. Plus, she'd finally found a willing partner to play Sailor's Squares with. She'd gotten quite good at it since she and Lorcan had found the board in their rooms that first day, but had been seriously lacking in games partners. This was how Adrienne passed her final evening in Keeper's Cove, playing Sailor's Squares by a fire in a tavern with a foreign King. When all is said and done, it is these small seeming moments that feed our strength in the darkest of times.

Chapter 26 - The Changing Light

It was always the same way since they'd taken him. He would use up all his strength to remember, and when he finally did, it would always be too late and the cycle would start once again. But this time would be different. He was too close now for them not to try, not that it would make any difference in the long run, they had him now, and any remnant of hope had died days ago. At first he imagined the scenes outside of the room, where he watched himself fall prey to their plans. How long had he been with them now that he couldn't bring himself to face the truth of what was about to happen? These are the symptoms of isolation, he tells himself, but it's no use. If he could reach her, he could tell her, warn her. But how? He was too weak and she was too far away. The hand pulled him up and started walking them towards the door, towards oblivion, they must be protected, he thought, she must find them, they must find her, or we are all lost.

The event Adrienne had been waiting for came the next morning: a Revolter message from Tosia, and an invitation for Adrienne to join her in the gardens of her private quarters.

The summer flowers in the north were different from the ones in the south, with purples and dark greens sunk low to the earth. The wild flowers grew up through long grass and the planes beyond it stretched out to the horizon with mounds of moss and rocks tumbling down to the coast.

Adrienne was sitting next to a lightly lit wood burner, which had lasted since the night before, under a fur blanket that had been given to her by one of the young Gedogin women she had been training with. It wasn't that cold yet during the day, but she had needed something extra to protect herself from the unfamiliar northern winds. After her drinks with Hercel at the tavern, she had gone alone to the beach to watch the Tor routes. When she got inside she was freezing, and the girl, whose rooms were opposite hers, had given her the blanket for 'next time.'

"I am about to tell you something that not many people understand, Adrienne," said Tosia, "The Gedogin are sworn to protect the Tor above all else. All nature is in a delicate balance, the manufacturers based at this castle only create vessels where energy can be replaced. The reason many of our people fear the Consortium is that they wish to create objects that will change the way of things, perhaps causing great gains for the balance of wealth, but everything has a price, and our resources will drain the Channel if not managed properly. Our world simply cannot survive without it. We work to find other ways to look after the commoners, but the truth is, it's this war that is causing the famine out west, a war that was orchestrated by the very people who are appealing to them for support now. It's wretched."

Adrienne looked around at the grandeur of the building they were sitting outside of, and as if pre-empting her thoughts, Tosia redirected them, "There are other areas of this world where the wealth is condensed much more than me and my kin," she said, "Do not be fooled by a marble and gold skeleton."

Adrienne tucked herself into her fur as the crisp, cool breeze of the morning drifted past them and blew away the dying heat from the wood burner on the decking, "Rainou said the same thing," she said, "there's something that's been puzzling me about her. Sometimes she can seem... quite distant. She seems older than she is. I cannot put my finger on it."

"She is older than she seems, but more importantly Rainou's life has not been simple," said Tosia, with something like regret seeping out of her, "She was captured by the Consortium whilst she was still in training with us, tortured for information, and then, when they started experimenting on Danaan to create the Seldelige, she was one of the first. After a week or so of unimaginable pain and torture, she managed to escape and found her way back to us, but she was never the same. I fear that if it had been any longer they would have succeeded in turning her into one of them. She can still access the Channel, and she has gained some of the heightened skills that the Seldelige have, but she is still human, her actions are guided by her essence."

"Poor Rainou," said Adrienne, "I can't believe they'd think to turn Danaan into Seldelige. They are complete opposites! It should be impossible. It's cruel."

"You can turn anyone into a Seldelige, but many will die in the process. To turn a Danaan is to harness something truly powerful. That's a good word for it though, cruel," said Tosia, "It is also why the Danaan are the only beings in all of the Central Lands who can take them on, and that is why they must be hidden, now more than ever."

"If you'd told me even a season ago that Danaan were real, or that the Seldelige were human, I would not have believed you! I believed the stories, that it was sorcery."

"I am sure that a person from another world, who had never encountered a Revolter or a Stairs Book, would call that sorcery," said Tosia, "Everyone has heard of the Seldelige, but just as with the Danaan, they are rumoured to be something they are not: great warriors who come from the sky, with powers that defy the laws of magick, feeding off chaos. The minute you understand how something works, the mystery is gone. These things are both logical and rational, and we understand how they work, but that is not what they are. Why shouldn't a Danaan cloak, soaked in the waters of the forest pools and glowing with the light of the Channel, be a mystery?"

"Astair didn't go into details about what the Seldelige do with the Danaan," said Adrienne.

"Astair is pained by it, deeply, though she would not show you. When the Consortium broke with the Gedogin they spun stories to use the authority of the northern and southern kings to persecute the Danaan kind. The story goes that many disappeared into the hills and others were hunted down. Settlements were destroyed, families torn apart. Some hid, disguised their heritage and lived lives as normal folk, some with success, their traditions lost in generations to come. These days it's less about having Danaan blood, anyone who displeases the Consortium or the crown gets banished to the forests."

"How sad," said Adrienne, "To be told that your family went through such torment."

"To be told?" said Tosia, incredulously, "Astair remembers, Adrienne!"

"Of course, I forgot that Danaan can live a long time," said Adrienne, "I thought it was part of the legend and not actually true."

"It is not that she was there in person," said Tosia, "but that the Danaan can access the memories of their ancestors through the Channel."

"Can they see them?"

"No," said Tosia, "I believe it is more of a feeling, like the intuition that we follow, when we are listening for those spirits to guide us."

Adrienne ran her thumb over her wrist and pressed down for a pulse, her veins were visible under her pale skin.

"The key thing in understanding why the Seldelige have not yet been stopped is in understanding what the Consortium wants: there are some who support the Seldelige, and think they are the next step in evolution; to give up unknown parts of yourself for the sake of progress and prosperity. It is important to know that those people are just as common as those who support the Gedogin, and they have their reasons as much as we."

"Vallecian of Alba gave up his ability to feel love to take down an empire, and in *All Along The Road* the farmer's wife sells her soul to a warlock in exchange for powers," said Adrienne, and then she reconsidered as if thinking out loud, "but it tends to end horribly for the characters."

"There are universal truths in those tales, but how you interpret them is up to you, and much more to do with given circumstances than you might think."

Adrienne covered her knees with a woollen blanket to protect her small frame. The view from this side of the castle was wilder than the front; insects danced around the garden as the sun rose behind the trees, and beyond the low stone walls were unknown wilderness and sea.

"Tosia, have you found my father?" she said, out of nowhere, "I'm sorry, but isn't that why you called me here?"

"Adrienne, I want you to understand the circumstances in which your father was captured. I know that must be frustrating for you beyond measure, but I need you to trust me that we're doing everything we can to recover him, and part of that is training you up. You need to have the knowledge and skills to attempt to fight the Seldelige if they attack you again."

Adrienne was puzzled, "How am I meant to protect myself by meditating?"

"Exactly how you did before when you found Astair in the darkness," said Tosia. "If you can access it, then you can block their access to it, and it will weaken them."

"I don't feel ready for that."

"Good," Tosia seemed satisfied, "I'd be worried if you did feel ready. Very good."

Adrienne was nervous now, almost reluctant to ask her next question, but she had to, "My father," she said, "do the Seldelige have him?"

"Yes," said Tosia.

"Are they going to turn him into one of them?"

"It's most likely."

Adrienne put her fists over her eyes and managed a deep and heavy breath in.

" If we can't get to him in time then they will turn him," said Tosia, "and when that happens he will spill more information than we can afford to spare."

"I need to help! Something, anything... please! I can't just sit here and do nothing!"

Tosia looked at her, expectantly.

"I know you know we're running out of time," said Adrienne as she reached into her pocket to pull out the Noch, which was shining crimson, "It's changed colour again, that means they're close to making another Seldelige. You must know this too."

"I do," said Tosia.

"Then you need to let me help you," said Adrienne, "Surely there's something I can do."

Tosia pulled a Noch out of her own pocket and placed it on the table in front of them. It too was crimson.

"That is exactly why I called you here."

Chapter 27 - The Decanté

He was led down a dark corridor into a smaller room, where a man in a dark robe was sitting waiting for him. He gestured for him to sit down at the table, where a spread of meats and cheeses was laid before them.

Eat," he said, The procedures will have taken a lot out of you; this is the time to refuel." He briefly considered refusing the food in protest, thereby prolonging the inevitable or perhaps even a more finite solution could be found if he could keep away from sustenance for long enough. It was no use though, his body caved into what might be his last joy, his last human meal. Through the window he saw a familiar skyline, the majestic Velgrave clocktower beamed up into the evening sky and he could just about make out the birds that made their home behind the clock face, circling around their territory as freely as ever. He braced himself.

Lorcan was awake again after being given time to sleep in one of the empty cabins. He was sitting in a chair, blank faced, pinning down his captor's eyes through muffled vision. He had been given a cloth and bowl of hot water to wipe his cuts, and one of the cabin boys had brought him a shot of whisky.

Noah stared back, but was the look pensive or pitying? Lorcan couldn't tell. He was fiddling with a small, gold object, twiddling it back and forth through his fingers in a way that both unnerved and irritated Lorcan.

"Where's Thomas?" asked Lorcan.

"Why did you run?" asked Noah.

Neither answered, but the sound of the metal working its way through weaved fingers filled the silence.

"You were going to hand Adrienne over to the Consortium," said Lorcan.

"We were doing nothing of the sort!" said Noah, bitterly, "Why would you think that?"

"I heard you talking about how she was a threat and what to do with her," said Lorcan, scowling, "You were going to lock her up! Don't deny it. You used her for whatever your selfish plans were."

"She had something in her possession that, if it fell into the wrong hands, would do great damage where she was going," said Noah.

"And what would you know about that? It's hers to keep and do with as she wishes!"

"It's not actually," Noah stood up and walked to a drawer, putting the metal object inside, he then turned back with a grave expression on his face, "You have no idea what you've gotten yourself mixed up in, Lorcan."

Lorcan realised he'd gotten so wound up that he was halfway off his seat, he sat down again and offered his ear freely this time, yet still shaking his head in disbelief, "Go on."

"He was going to talk to her that night, Thomas that is," said Noah, "The Consortium are always trying to trick young people into working for them, doing their dirty jobs, thieving or worse... we wanted to help her."

"Why didn't Thomas say something?" yelled Lorcan, fuming now, "I was the closest person to her on that boat, I should've known."

Noah looked at him with regret now, "I guess he thought that I could..."

"You betrayed her! You led them straight to her!"

"It was to protect her."

"If you thought you were protecting her, then how could you have let her go?" yelled Lorcan, startling Noah with the sheer force of his rage.

"Who said I let her go?" yelled Noah.

Noah was holding Lorcan by the shoulders now, piercing his eyes with a serious, earnest stare, asking to be understood. Eventually, he released him and sat next to him on the cabin bed. Lorcan nodded his head slightly and looked up at Noah.

"Fine," he said, "Who the hell are you people?"

Chapter 28 - The Seldelige

"Have you ever wondered how Seldelige are created?" asked the man in a low, piercing whisper, By Revolter, yes, and you ve had a taste of that already, but do you know how we... become?" He gave him an empty smile, his vacant eyes mimicking concern.

The Consortium succeeded in one single invention without the help of the Gedogin: a Revolter like no other. We keep it downstairs in the great hall. Your final destination so to speak," he smiled again, his cold, thin lips almost disappearing with the weight of it. Simply put, it is the largest Revolter in the world. When you are transported in it, you arrive on the other side only seconds later, and you are free. Of course, we cannot do it with just anyone. You need to be accustomed to it first, or it will wipe you out completely. That was the mistake we made the first time, but you have been prepared, you re halfway there already."

He spat at the man and reached forward to grab the meat knife in the centre of the table, but he wasn t quick enough. A guard had taken it from his hand as quickly as he had picked it up.

You are still you, but stronger," the hooded speaker continued, unfazed, Your memories and secrets are intact, but you can roam the earth without anything or anyone standing in your way. You ll be free of the loyalties and dated thinking that binds you to your secrets, and you will finally be able to share them with us for the greater good. True, if you had the abilities of the Danaan you d be of more use to us, but one thing is certain, you will be free of all the doubts and pains of mankind, free to commit yourself to our common cause. You will be stronger, sharper, and you will never need a revolter again, you will become the Revolter. Your past life will be but a dream, and you will rejoice in sharing the secrets of the Keepers with us. It s a small price to pay for freedom, and we have made that choice for the greater good," he said.

The man paused and watched his prisoner breathe a sigh of relief, for he did still have his soul, at least for now.

For everything you choose, you give something up as well," said the hooded man, The Seldelige are fighters, trained to protect the important ideals of the Consortium, and it is my job to find like-minded individuals who would join the cause... I know you think that isn't you, but that's because you can't see what I can see."

He shook his head, but even without the weight of the man's next words, he knew there was no fighting it, he was going down to that hall sooner or later.

"Will you join us, Kernavin?"

Adrienne awoke late the next morning. The autumn leaves had started to fall in the gardens, and outside her window the walls were covered in thick red ivy, complementing the scene as much as the golden sun that hovered to the east for most of the morning. She stood on her balcony overlooking the town, three magpies were perched on a rooftop in the distance towards the coast. She smiled and she watched them dance from brick to brick in the light. She looked to the east, where the mountains flooded the horizon and any evidence of the shore was gone other than the sound of fizzing waves and gulls in the background. There were four magpies scattered on nearby hedges in the gardens of the castle. That made it seven.

She took breakfast in her room and washed her face before checking her travel sack. She packed up the food she'd been saving from her meals over the last week. She had hoarded things that would last a long time, like bread, cheese and apples, not knowing how or when she would leave Keeper's Cove. One of the servants in the kitchen had also given her a meat pie the night before, and a skin flask of damson wine.

She checked her pack and saw that she was starting to run out of space. Since arriving at the keep, she had gained a new pair of brown leather shoes, a compass from Alexia, an inlay for her cloak from the woman who'd made her shoes (it was colder in the north and she hadn't thought of such things), and a gold pen that she'd picked up in the market. She also had the two small Stairs Books that she'd bought on her first night. She'd lost most of her belongings when she left the island, and purchasing the Stairs Books and pen had felt like a small achievement upon arriving at her destination, but it now seems a little naive. She'd spent money that she hadn't needed to spend, and she had little use for one, let alone two, and not a lot of room to pack them in. She took one down to Hercel's rooms, and he promised to use it to write down all the medicinal remedies he knew, as well as winning Sailor's Squares combinations for her to try when she next saw him. She left her room and walked the long walk from her side of the castle to the leader's quarters.

Alexia's office door was slightly ajar and a strange smell of musk and spice was drifting out of it. Alexia was standing in the garden outside his rooms, on a terrace, facing the horizon. She watched him for a moment, he took a deep breath and shook his hands down, as if dusting them off from some intense activity that she'd been too late to miss.

"And the day has come," he said, "When you leave us."

There was a fresh pot of rose tea on the table, and he poured a cup for them both.

"I wanted to thank you for your patience with me," said Adrienne, taking a cup and sitting down on a stool.

"It is my job to be patient, Adrienne, no more and no less, but you are welcome all the same."

Alexia sat down in the same chair that Adrienne would stare at during her lessons. It might be possible that every time she tried to connect to the Channel in the future she would (involuntarily) see this chair. She'd stared at it so hard sometimes that she knew every crack, every tiny stain, every inch of the pattern and where the material folded over. She'd coloured it in with her mind, connected the dots and unfolded the material, filling it with air. She'd mastered this chair like she was sure she'd not mastered the Channel, but it was all she could do to hope that when the time came that she needed it, it would have been enough.

Alexia was looking at her curiously, he cocked his head to the side, "What troubles you, Adrienne? Other than the obvious."

Adrienne didn't answer.

"I couldn't help noticing that your little friend has long since vacated the castle," he said.

Adrienne's energy shrunk with these words, "We had a fight," she said, quietly.

"And now you're worried that if you leave here he won't be able to find you?"

"Yes," she said, though she had a growing suspicion that it wasn't just the link to Lorcan she was worried about losing, in spite of everything.

"He has his own journey to go on I suspect," offered Alexia, "I believe that your paths are meant to collide again threefold, if not then there is a lesson here waiting for you in plain sight."

"I don't... love him, if that's what you were thinking," said Adrienne.

"Oh," said Alexia, without changing his facial expression or moving at all.

"He is kind, and we understand each other, even though we're so different. I think somehow we were meant to meet, but that's all it is," she said, honestly.

Alexia now had a look of recognition on his face, and the sun through the window reflected in the light of the flowers overlaying the wooden decking, making his face look yellow and ethereal. "That's *all* it is?" he asked, "Some people are meant to meet, and that is a great thing, even if it does not feel that way to *you*. Perhaps he was meant to play a part in your journey, or perhaps it is that you were meant to play a part in his. Sometimes we aren't the ones who feel the effects of an encounter as strongly, but the encounter has been great all the same."

The door to Tosia's rooms was firmly shut and guarded by four Gedogin guards, who immediately stepped aside as she approached them. Tosia was sitting at her desk, looking over a map of Velgrave, but it was different: there were extra streets that Adrienne had never seen printed all around it in a dark blue.

"I am sorry to have kept all this from you, Adrienne. I wanted to avoid dragging you into this unless it was absolutely necessary, but it seems I have no choice. This is a tremendous ask," said Tosia.

"I know, but I asked as well. I want to," said Adrienne, with as much courage as she could muster, though she felt her hands shake.

"We have found your father," said Tosia, "So we must act fast. When the Consortium were first experimenting they found that many people, no matter how healthy and strong their connection to the Channel, would die of the shock of being put straight into a Revolter. In fact a strong connection was a detriment to the task and often did result in death or severe damage to their mental state. So in order to create a Seldelige they have to ease a person's body into the process of transition."

She was loading up the Revolter with power and writing in coordinates as she spoke, "They've been moving him around from place to place, that's why we couldn't do anything until now. The minute we had a lead on him he would disappear and we'd have to start the search again. We knew that the most likely place where he'd be kept for a long enough window of time would be at the end: when they finally bring him to the headquarters, where their ultimate Revolter sits, and where he'll take his final turn."

"I still don't understand why you didn't tell me any of this before?" said Adrienne.

"We needed to keep you a secret. The only reason we've been able to track him all this time is because they had no idea that we knew he'd gone missing. As far as they know, they left no one alive in that house. If I'd have told you that we knew where your father was, but that we had to wait for an opportune moment to rescue him - where it may well already be too late - would you have listened? We couldn't risk you trying to take things into your own hands."

Adrienne took a breath to protest but then stopped. That was exactly what she would have done, exactly what she was thinking about doing, only she had no idea where to run to, "I would have understood," she said, half believing it.

"I am sorry, Adrienne," said Tosia, "It's a lot to take in, and now I am asking you for the impossible, but will take a leap of faith here and trust me?"

Adrienne breathed in deeply. She breathed down the shock of the attack on the island, the pain of having to carry Elsen out into the woods, the scorching heat and ash of the fire that burned her to the Channel, and the aching that she'd felt in her heart and body. She breathed down the fear and uncertainty, the anger that she now felt towards her father and mother for lying to her, the lost moments with her real mother, the frustration that she'd felt at not being able to let it all go when she knew that there was a reason for everything, that everything that had happened to her was part of some bigger plan, that it was not about her but that in spite of that she was somehow still loved. She breathed it all down, for there was no time.

She took all that negative energy and she turned it into something else, because it was the only way, because she had no choice. There was no space for worry or doubt. It was electric now, it filled her from the brim and spilled out into the ether, and her pain was her power. She stood up a little straighter and locked eyes with Tosia, "I'm ready."

Adrienne watched as Tosia loaded up the Revolter and something clicked in her, the realisation hit her in a split second. She jumped back, "You're sending me via that thing?" she screamed over the noise, "I can't!"

"It is the only way to get you there in time," said Tosia, "I will use my power to shield you from as much of the pain as I can. One journey alone will not take away your soul, Adrienne, and Rainou will be waiting for you on the other side."

Adrienne stared in horror. Her breath quickening, her body tense, "Another last-minute detail you failed to mention?"

"I know I ask a lot of you," said Tosia, "But you must trust us. If we're going to get your father back, this is the only way."

Adrienne nodded. It was never or now. She stepped forward to the machine, which was now buzzing and whirring loudly. Tosia stepped forward and handed a crossbow to her along with a small dagger, "Let's hope you don't need this," she said, and took Adrienne's hand.

Then the world went sideways. She had a feeling like blood rushing to her bones, except backwards, and something like air filled Adrienne from her toes and upwards until she felt pulled apart completely. Tosia's hand disappeared, she reached out but she couldn't find her own hand. Her eyes were blurry, she saw nothing but whiteness and felt space where her body once was. There was a sharp crack and then... a moment of peace, blissful euphoria, for one tiny moment until everything went dark.

    She woke in a house full of dark mahogany antiques and busy, patterned carpets. It was much like the houses that she'd frequently visited when she was younger, perhaps like the one her mother and her aunt lived in, though her memory of that time was, at best, a mismatch of images. The bright, Velgravian sunlight was reaching through from the balcony and curling around her feet, as the rest of her body shivered in the light breeze coming through the shutters. Her eyes adjusted as she drank in the warmth. She'd missed the Velgrave weather. But the moment was brief until her heart sank, and suddenly there was an overwhelming feeling in her stomach and a sense that all was wrong with the world.

    Rainou was standing above her holding a glass vial, which she poured into a gold cup full of fruit water on the table. She handed it to Adrienne, "Drink this, quickly."

    Adrienne took the vial and downed the contents. It seemed to stick to her throat, and its sickly taste masked something bitter and sharp. However, it did its job, and within seconds she was starting to feel herself again.

    The house they were in belonged to a small, elderly woman called Dominique, who was not a member of the Alliance but had freed up her home as a safe house for those in need. Dominique swiftly guided them out of the house and down an alleyway, where the entrance to a small tunnel lay hidden behind a derelict wall.

    They went into the tunnels and the old lady closed the door behind them. As the key turned in the lock, Adrienne looked into the woman's eyes. She was old and frail, but she looked tough as old boots. Adrienne wondered what it would be like to live your life without fear of mortality. The woman gave her an affirmative nod, and Adrienne nodded back. There was no turning back now, and there was only one way out - through the Consortium. The tunnels were dark and cold, the walls painted white, and remnants of the streets were evident all around. They passed the underside of some steps and numerous potholes, and entered from room to room as if they were exploring attics in a block of houses. This must be what Tosia had been looking at in her office. They were not sewers, more a backwards shell of the buildings above: the city's basement.

They came to the door of a large room, as large as the Omphalos, maybe bigger, with four wide columns stretched periodically across the centre of it. They peered around the corner at two guards who were standing on either side of a set of stone steps.

"No one knows about this route in," whispered Rainou, "but we recently had intelligence from a defector on their side... this is our one shot. Up until now it's only guarded by a couple of men, but once they know the entrance has been leaked they'll make a lot more effort to protect it and it'll be as hard, if not harder, than breaking in through their front door."

The men were completely at ease, which gave Rainou and Adrienne an advantage, but they were still heavily armed and it wouldn't be an easy fight.

"They're most likely holding a single-use vessel that communicates a breach of security to the headquarters, but it won't work if we can disrupt them. I'll fight them, but I need you to concentrate on blocking the Channel until I can at least disarm them. Can you do that?"

"I don't know how," said Adrienne.

"You'll know, reach the Channel, and then use your energy to keep it exactly as is until I say stop," said Rainou, "Try now."

Adrienne closed her eyes and concentrated as hard as she could, but nothing happened. She opened her eyes and looked at Rainou, who as ever did not flinch. Then she remembered what Alexia had told her, that when she really needed it, it would be there.

"Do not doubt that it's there, Adrienne," said Rainou.

She closed her eyes again, just as she had before, blocking out all fear, all anxiety just as Alexia had taught her to block out everything else around her. She was in, her vision went great like the times it had before, and she started to see thin coloured lines in the air, only this time it was different. Her head tipped forward and she felt the connection grow throughout her body, and suddenly the grey was a bright light, she opened her eyes and her vision was a wave of intensity, crisp and vivid like never before. And then she saw it: energy, travelling everywhere, colours that she'd had no idea even existed before, patterns and movements that all made perfect sense, all in unison. A green light moved from Rainou and Adrienne moved towards it. But, strangely, she wasn't moving towards it, she was moving it back, back into Rainou, where it simmered but didn't grow any further. She let go and looked up.

"Well done," said Rainou, "I'll see you on the other side."

Rainou wasted no time and took out her crossbow, aiming it at the first man. It hit him square in the chest and he fell back onto the cold concrete with a thud. She then moved to attack the next man but he was onto her before she could release her arrow and they drew swords, moving across the room and sweeping up the undisturbed dust from the basement floor in their wake.

Adrienne focused her mind and dived in, easier this time, like stepping through a familiar door. She saw the physical world in a bright, white haze. The first man was lying on the concrete, bleeding out from the arrow that had shattered inside his chest, and breathing shallowly. He reached into his pocket and pulled out a metal ball with a handle on one side. He flicked the switch and it started to give off a light that became a hazy green, and started to move like a fog, slowly at first and then speeding up. Adrienne pushed back, drawing energy from all around her and moving the haze back towards the object. The man noticed nothing as he lay there, gripping the object tightly to his bloody chest.

Rainou was grappling with the guard in the corner of the room. She ducked as his sword crashed into the wall behind her, kicking his shin with her full force and causing him to fall back. In the blink of a second pulled out a dagger from her boot and plunged it into his lower abdomen. As he collapsed in agony, she reached into his pocket to pull out another metal ball. She sliced off the handle with her dagger and threw the ball through the door they'd just come through.

"You can stop," she said to Adrienne, but the girl was in a trance now, her eyes rolling back into her socket.

"Adrienne!"

Adrienne snapped back into the room, dazed.

"I should have warned you," said Rainou, taking Adrienne by the shoulders, "I'm sorry... try to stay grounded. If you get lost in there, you may not be able to hear me come back. Are you OK?"

"I'm fine," said Adrienne, checking herself, "Maybe a little dizzy."

They walked out into an empty hallway with bare stone walls and sealed windows. There was no one else to be seen, but their light footsteps created echoes that disturbed the emptiness and made Adrienne flinch every time her feet hit the floor.

"We need to get all the way around the building to enter the hall right above the one we came from," whispered Rainou.

She signalled for them to move to a corner but jumped back when she saw a guard standing at the centre of it, facing away from them. Rainou slowly moved behind him and slipped her hand over his mouth. He struggled but it was no use, she pulled out another vial of liquid and poured it into his mouth. He fell limp.

"It won't kill him," she whispered, "He'll wake in a few hours and won't remember a thing."

They moved out of the corridor to another set of stairs that encased the right outer wall of the building, climbing to the top in haste without interruption. There was a guard at the top, and Adrienne pulled out her crossbow to aim, but before they could do a thing, he'd already been shot with Rainou's arrow.

"I had him!" said Adrienne.

"Not unless it's absolutely necessary!" said Rainou.

Suddenly there were footsteps on the stairs below them, and something flew past Rainou's shoulder and landed in the wall: an arrow. A soldier was pelting her way up the stairs, Rainou surged forward to meet her but the woman was too fast. She jumped forward and grabbed Rainou's arms, pinning her back against the railings. Rainou had her hands around the woman's neck, but the guard pulled out a dagger. It was a battle of strength as Rainou's hands pushed back against the hilt of the blade and willed the woman backwards, causing her to lose her balance. Without thinking Adrienne lifted the crossbow and willed the arrow straight into the woman's neck. She stopped still and cascaded over the railings down the stair passage with a loud thud. Rainou stepped back from the ledge and looked below, there was enough space to fall five floors in the gap, "That was necessary," she said.

The next hallway was as vast and empty as the first, except for two guards on either side of the main entrance to a large room in the centre of the building. They stopped behind a corner and watched, it didn't look like they'd heard them. Rainou signalled for them to change direction. Once they were far away enough, she showed Adrienne the map, "You see," she whispered, pointing at the sketch of the Consortium building, "This walkway goes all around that hall, and there's a door on the other side. Getting out, however, will be a different problem altogether."

The door on the other side of the building was locked. Rainou concentrated and placed her hands on the door. She leant forward and supposedly pushed something forward and out of her, which was followed by a click. *So that's it,* thought Adrienne, *if you learn how to control the Channel's energy, then you can use it without a vessel.*

The four pillars inside the hall were spaced out across the room, just as they had been in the basement, but there was one difference - the pillars on the two furthest sides stretched out like tree roots at the bottom, and inside the arches of both were two great stone compartments that were big enough to fit a person, and big enough to fit a Seldelige. There was no question of it, these Revolters had been specifically designed for one thing and one thing only. In a chair on the edge of the room, leaning against the wall with the most light, was a crumpled figure of a man. Adrienne's heart stopped in its tracks.

She rushed forwards and started untying her father's wrists, which were bound to the chair. There were bloody cuts where he'd tried to free himself from his restraints, and bruises on his wrists, "It's me," she said, "We've come to rescue you."

"No!" He said, "Adrienne... it's not what you think."

"He's talking gibberish," she said to Rainou.

"That's fine," she said, bending down to undo the other wrist, "let's get him loose."

Suddenly the Keeper's Lights on the walls lit up all at once, and the doors on either side clicked as the locks turned.

There was a sharp crack and a man appeared on the steps. No, it wasn't a man. He was wearing dark robes that covered his pale skin, and his eyes were both evil and void of humanity. It was a Seldelige. Without warning both Rainou and Adrienne were grabbed from behind and pulled back by the two guards they'd left in the corridor, leaving the weakened Kernavin to fall to the floor.

"Thank you," said the Seldelige, "For that impressive show. Kernavin and I have been happily anticipating your arrival, but for a moment there I didn't think you were going to make it in time!"

Adrienne looked to Rainou for an explanation, but the Keeper looked equally bewildered.

"My name is Haid, and you are?"

In an uncharacteristic moment of rage, Adrienne spat on the floor and head butted the man behind her. Not in an attempt to escape, just to irritate. It felt good. Even in this critical moment, Rainou couldn't help but look amused.

"Now, now," said Haid, unbothered by the insult, "Of course, you're right, I know exactly who you are. Your father and I have been getting to know each other. It's so nice to have two potential Danaan recruits come to us for once, Rainou, we always knew you'd come to your senses." As he said this Rainou flinched and struggled with her man, "I'm sure we can do wonders with you in our new programmes, we've improved things since you last stayed with us. The thing is, we're getting so close to understanding your abilities, but the recruits always seem so reluctant to stick around. They keep dying on us, you see, and we often have to begin turning them before they get to that point, such a waste of life otherwise. But you two seem very determined. You might just make it long enough..." He smiled a disturbing smile that made Adrienne shiver. She tried to concentrate on the Channel but he immediately slapped her down, the sting burnt down her face making her eyes water. She looked up to see Rainou shaking her head at her.

"You don't think I know when a Danaan is trying to manipulate the Channel?" Haid screamed at her, wildly.

"Now," he smiled again and put his weathered hands over Kernavin's head, "He's a tricky one you see, this prisoner. Normally, when we get them to the great stone Revolters, they're practically begging to be turned! Anything, they'll say! Anything Haid, to take away this awful despair! Please, please, please. And of course, I oblige..."

He let go of Kernavin and started towards the Revolter, "But this man seems to be holding onto something, and what it is that we need to fix the problem, well, we show him what he's holding onto - and we take it away."

The guard holding Adrienne pushed her towards the stone pillar, holding her by the neck so she had no choice other than to comply. Her crossbow was taken out of her hands and thrown across the floor. It smashed as it hit one of the pillars.

"You see, he'd been crying out his daughter's name in his sleep. Of course, you were briefly reunited on the road, which I'd imagine helped him hold onto the memory of you... that did set us back a bit."

'What are you talking about?" said Adrienne, raging.

"Oh, you must remember? Come on! Think Adrienne, think! Don't they teach you people to think for yourselves anymore? What a waste," he laughed his cruel laugh again, which echoed into the vacuous room.

She thought back to her journey on the road: the man they'd seen, half-starved, covered in dirt, naked and barely human. She hadn't seen his face properly, she couldn't get close enough, or had she just been too afraid to look? Her heart sank and her eyes filled to the brim with tears that she daren't let fall, not now.

"We knew that the only way the Danaan could possibly hope to bring him back from this was if he could see his daughter, and that might just bring him back from the darkness," he said this as if it was some trivial game, "but they didn't count on what would happen if he got to watch her be torn apart by the largest Revolter in the world."

Adrienne started to struggle now, fighting off the guard with every inch of her being, trying to move the energy around her, but it was no use. Haid reached his arm out casually and somehow made her go limp, as if he'd knocked the energy out of her body. Suddenly she was being forced inside the stone box, the door locking the door behind her.

In that same moment, Rainou had taken advantage of Haid's focus being elsewhere and broken loose from the guard. The second man quickly clocked on and attacked her from behind. She was fighting them both now, warding off their attacks with quickness of foot and nothing more.

Adrienne was held in place inside the stone machine, watching Haid move towards her. It was unbelievably cold, so she pulled her arms inside her cloak, and then she felt it. The Noch was in her pocket, where it had been this entire time. She pulled it out under her coat and looked for its crimson light, but it wasn't crimson anymore, it was changing to a luminous green like the roots of the Tor. Slowly then all at once. She didn't think, she didn't have a plan, but she trusted that the way was there. She closed her eyes and focused.

The room went grey and the paths of light appeared, then the brightness came. The light from the Noch was brighter than any of them. Her senses were heightened, she was completely aware of everything around her and yet in a completely different realm of existence to it.

Somewhere in the present world, Adrienne felt the Revolter start churning and vibrating as Haid revved it up, but it was as if she were watching her dream.

The luminescent light inside the Noch started to move. At first, it grew and trickled out of the object like a stream, and then it grew into a straight line, which moved with Adrienne's thoughts, as if she were directing it, or part of it. She turned it to the door of the Revolter, which smashed open and crashed onto the floor in front of her.

She stepped out of the door just as Haid was reaching out his hand to knock her down. This time she saw green wisps of light flying towards her, but nothing happened. She felt the impact of his attack as if a gust of wind had merely brushed her cloak. Some part of her in another plane might have been shocked at this, but she barely acknowledged the thought. Haig pushed his hand with all his might and a crimson wave flew at her, but she held out the Noch and it sucked the energy in, then she pulled it back and let it fly forwards out of the tip of the shell. Haig was knocked backwards onto the floor, skidding and hitting the wall several metres behind him. Adrienne turned to Rainou and whipped the weapons out of the hands of both guards in two foul swoops of the Noch.

Rainou, cut loose from her trap, rolled across the floor, narrowly dodging an energy attack from Haid. A burnt mark appeared on the wall behind her, cracking a hole in the stone walls, and causing rubble to fall to the floor. She threw an attack back at Haid but it narrowly missed. Behind her, the guards had found their feet and were coming at her until she swiped at the first man, knocking his axe out of his hand, and thrust her sword into his belly before knocking the other clean out on one of the pillars.

Haid was reaching for Kernavin now, but Rainou propelled the guard's axe forwards through the air in his direction, which scraped the side of his head, causing blood to weep down his face. He looked furious. Adrienne tried to attack Haid again with the Noch, but it had stopped buzzing and gone back to its normal light. She fell back as the sight left her.

Haig was preparing for his moment now, the power balance clearly falling back in his favour. Rainou eyed something across the room and looked at Adrienne, who nodded. As Rainou ran forwards with her sword, Adrienne leapt behind the pillar and reached her arm out for her crossbow, which was underneath a now lifeless guard. Before her, Haid and Rainou were clashing swords, sparks flying out of the ends like fireworks, the room flooding with bright cracks of light. Adrienne pulled at the crossbow, but it was lodged underneath the man; she pushed his body with her feet and pulled again. The weapon came loose, and Adrienne leapt to her feet, crossbow in hand.

What happened next happened in a matter of seconds. Adrienne pulled up the crossbow to her chest and swung around to face the fighting. Haid had kicked down Rainou, who ducked out of the way but was blocked by the stone table behind her. In a split second, Haid swung his sword round in the direction of Rainou's neck; she lifted her dagger and thrust it up to counteract the blow. Adrienne aimed the arrow at Haid's head and willed it forward. Haid turned his head mid-swing to see the arrow. It made a small crack, and then silence.

Rainou slid down the side of the table and gasped in relief, unashamedly cursing. They were, for now, alone in the silent room. After a moment of bewilderment, Adrienne ran to Kernavin and started untying the rest of his constraints.

"Can you hear me?" she cried.

Rainou pulled out another vial like the one she'd given Adrienne back at the safe house and fed it to Kernavin.

He accepted it and fell immediately into a drowsy trance.

"He'll be fine," she said, "but we have to get out of here quickly."

The two of them pulled him up by either side and moved as fast as they could out of the back door, but the stairs at the other side of the building started to fill with the noise of footsteps. They pulled him out of the door, locking it behind them, and hurried down towards the basement below. "You must stay awake," Rainou said whilst pulling Kernavin upright, "You must try!"

He opened his eyes as wide as he could, but his head was spinning and the floor was somehow getting closer...

Kernavin woke in a brightly lit room, on a bed, with layers of blankets weighing him down. As his eyes adjusted to the light, he saw patterned carpets and disgusting old furniture that reminded him of his father-in-law's house. Beside him was a bowl of untouched food and a jug of water. He reached out to grab the jug, but his arm was too weak.

"Careful there," said the voice of an old woman, "you're still getting used to being in your body, there may be some adjustments. I believe it's been described as an extreme sort of pins and needles for those who have experienced it, though I wouldn't know. I suppose you'd like to see your daughter now?"

He mustered a nod, and the woman departed the room. Moments later Adrienne walked in. She looked taller.

"You're awake."

"Just about,"

"I thought you were dead."

"I thought I was too."

There was a brief moment of silence between them as they observed each other.

There was something about the way his daughter was now holding herself that seemed alien to him. She was taller, for sure, but there was something in her manner: a confidence or capability that he'd not seen before. One of her eyes looked brighter than the other, which looked like it was carrying the weight of something heavy and dark.

"You disappeared," she said, stoically.

"I'm sorry."

"I had to burn her body, you know, because there was no one else left to do it. My mother..."

"I could have prevented it... I could have... I tried to stop it," Kernavin gestured forward for his daughter but she was standing just out of his reach.

"You can't protect me from the world," she said.

"No, of course, I can't, but I wanted to protect you for a while. I wanted you to have an easy childhood because I knew that your life would not be."

"You could have at least told me about the Noch," she raised an eyebrow a little at this.

"That was... yes," he said, resigned, "The true Nochs were created to sense the Channel and its disruptions, and when a real disruption came, they had the power to counterattack what was causing it... in the right hands."

"...and what could be more of a disruption than a Seldelige?" said Adrienne.

"Yes."

"Rainou says that this one is rare, that most of them don't do that, that these ones were destroyed a long time ago because they were so dangerous."

"That's right," said Kernavin, "And I was meant to look after that one, so I hid it where no one would look. With you. I didn't think you'd end up in the headquarters of the people I was trying to hide it from. How did you escape the building?"

"The truth is, we were lucky," said Adrienne, "The Seldelige sent guards to block off the exit, but by the time we got there, they'd already been taken down by five or six members of the Alliance who Tosia had contacted in Velgrave."

He nodded, pensive, "I don't think I can take you home Adrienne, I'm sorry."

"I don't think I want to go home anymore," she said, "I've seen too much. I feel different. Apparently, you're to report back to Tosia in Keeper's Cove when you're feeling better, and I'm... not allowed to go back yet. Apparently, Tosia doesn't want me returning to Keeper's Cove until I've decided what I want to do: if I want to join them, or if I want to live apart... what does she mean by that?"

"She means that because I decided to leave upon becoming a Keeper, you may choose not to go that way as well."

"You left?"

"Not completely," he said, "But becoming a Keeper entails a lot of responsibilities that not everyone is prepared to take on. I think given your connection to me, Tosia might be hesitant to invite you in until you're absolutely sure."

She sat on the bed and poured the water into a cup, which she handed to him. He took it and gulped it down, coughing after he rushed to swallow his final mouthful.

"I'm going with Rainou to Senelin City," said the girl, "She has business there, and I can fill in my aunt on everything that's happened."

There was a brief pause.

"...Rainou?" Kernavin, "Yes, I remember. She was very young when I met her."

"So you knew many Danaan once upon a time..." said Adrienne, "Like my mother."

"Ah," said Kernavin, completely thrown and utterly apologetic, "Adrienne, I'm so sorry you had to find out like that. I had hoped that I would be the one to..."

She looked at him with a sullen stare, and out of that came a brief moment of raw, helpless vulnerability that broke Kernavin's heart.

" I know why you did it," she said, "But I'm not quite ready to talk about it yet."

Chapter 29 - The Keepers

It had been five days and counting since Lorcan had been brought back against his will to the Player's Circle. The crew that Lorcan did see, when delivering food or taking his chamber pot away, seemed to have noticed nothing out of the ordinary. They'd apparently departed Keepers Cove for the Laten Islands nothing short of a bit later than scheduled, and they barely took notice of the fact that the kitchen hand had displeased the management. It made Lorcan wonder what else he'd managed to miss aboard the ship all those years, what other mischief had Thomas passed under the radar of so many? Lorcan wondered what they'd been told, but it was hard to gauge; so far he'd barely been allowed to leave the cabin, which had so graciously been bestowed upon him by Noah, assuring him that he was no prisoner but that he was still, in fact, a valued member of the crew. Thomas, who he had yet to see, had requested time to discuss certain matters with Noah and other senior members of the crew before Lorcan could be let out. Lorcan felt that, despite these assurances, he was exactly like a prisoner. He made a habit of making his feelings known, scowling and occasionally throwing things at Noah - the messenger.

That morning, a knock came at the door. Lorcan jumped out of his bed and into the chair opposite as the door swung open. Thomas entered, holding a bottle of brandy and two shot glasses. He sat opposite Lorcan on the side of the bed and filled up the glasses.

"Drink this," he said, handing Lorcan a shot. "You'll need it."

"Where are we going?" asked Lorcan, standing and reaching for his coat.

"Nowhere," said Thomas, "Sit down."

Lorcan did as he was told.

"We have a lot to discuss, a lot of things you couldn't have known," said Thomas, "And a lot of things that we've had to think long and hard about sharing with you."

Lorcan tried to speak but something about Thomas's intensity and stern expression stopped him in his tracks. Resolved, he waited.

"You've not been with us long, most of our crew starts out young, but they usually come from Black Isle. I have a tendency to make exceptions. People like yourself and Noah with nowhere to go. I take you in, not just because I have a soft spot for people with nowhere else to go, but because you'll owe me, that means I can trust you to be loyal. So far, you have proved the exception to the rule. Even so, people in your position don't usually learn what you're about to learn, what Noah has already learnt. Do you understand?"

"No," said Lorcan, flippantly, and then, "Yes, so far."

"It took a lot of convincing to get me to let you onboard, Lorcan," he said, "A lot. We'd already taken in Noah, we had no need for anyone new, but when I found you that night, half-starved, weathered by whatever you'd just escaped from, I couldn't leave you there."

"I know," said Lorcan. "But all the same, you seemed to let Adrienne on without any trouble."

"We'll get to that," Thomas replied, sharply. "Do you know much about Black Isle Cove?"

"I know they have great boats, the most trusted seamen in the Central Lands," said Lorcan. "That's about it."

"It's true," said Thomas, "but they're a small island, maybe smaller than the Laten Islands. They can't make great ships like this one, but they can man them."

"Are you telling me that... you're a Black Isle crew?"

"Not just a Black Isle crew," said Thomas, "I am a Decanté, of Black Isle. Technically I'd be in line to the throne if we still had one, not that I'd be interested in any of that."

"What?!" Spluttered Lorcan, "Why is this a secret? Surely this would work in your favour? A royal line of Black Isle running the most famous players ship on the Central Seas?"

"Are we in need of any more prestige?" asked Thomas. "No, it wouldn't be worth the risk, given what we are and what we know. Tosia's entire operation runs on us being off the Consortium's radar."

"You work with the Gedogin!" gasped Lorcan, beyond repudiating.

"We're off their radar, you couldn't find us in any of their red books. We are kept separate from their laurels and accolades though we're Keepers, in our own way."

Lorcan shook his head in disbelief, "Why should I believe you? You tried to kidnap Adrienne... you nearly killed me. How do I know this isn't just a ploy to get information out of me?"

Thomas sighed and poured another shot of brandy for both of them, "When you arrived at Keeper's Cove, Tosia disappeared for a few days. Where do you think she went?"

Lorcan necked his brandy, "Well if that was the case then why didn't she tell us then and there?"

"We weren't sure if Adrienne was who she said she was. We sent scouts down to Wiberia to confirm Kernavin was missing, and they found the ashes of the Danaan woman, but we found no evidence of the girl or the path she took. If you were imposters, Tosia didn't want you getting wind of our suspicions and running away. The Player's Circle is, to all intents and purposes, invisible. It wouldn't have been fitting for Tosia to then tell Adrienne of our existence, even if she does intend to train her up."

"Adrienne doesn't want to be trained up," said Lorcan, somewhat unconvinced. He then raised his hands to ask the obvious question, pointing at himself.

"You on the other hand," said Thomas, "are a liability. It's pained me these last few days to decide what to do with you. We could either kill you - believe me it would have been the simpler option - or bring you in further. You're a smart boy, Lorcan, but you've been led astray by your circumstances. You've seen a lot of suffering."

He shifted in his chair and leaned forwards towards Lorcan, "In order to live a life of purpose, sometimes we have to forget the things that don't serve us. I know your feelings regarding the Gedogin, but the part they've had to play in your life is nothing compared to that of the Consortium. There is no good or bad but thinking makes it so, and there is no choice that isn't wrong to someone somewhere, but I am telling you that there is more to learn. You must find ways to process your energy for good, and I'm giving you a chance here to make something of yourself in all this, but it comes with a caveat: next time, there will only be one option."

Lorcan was let out of his room that morning and allowed to wander around on deck. His eyes darted from face to face as they passed him, wondering who knew what he'd been told that morning. The Laten Islands were now looming nearer on the horizon, their endless cliffs stretching over the waters and gulls flying overhead. A fortress loomed out of the mountains, sewn in like a patchwork quilt into the granite, and in the distance, a soaring volcano towered over the highest peaks. Even after seeing it many times before, the sight never failed to take his breath away.

The shows playing that day were comedies and not something that Thomas or Jill needed to be part of. Noah too was kept behind, allowing for the cabin boy understudies to take up the main roles and have a go at taking centre stage.

After the players had departed, Jill came to Lorcan's cabin. She was dressed in casual workers' clothes and a black cloak, which hid her long frizzy hair from the relentless island winds. She picked up Lorcan's coat and handed it to him. "Come on then," she said, in her familiar, mothering tone.

They walked along the beach to an empty clearing. Stood by the cliff base were two hooded figures. They walked up to join them, and to no surprise Lorcan saw that it was Noah and Thomas, standing in front of a dusty fire. They gestured for Lorcan to sit and joined him, facing the easterly sun.

"There's no going back after this," said Thomas, "Are you absolutely sure you want in?"

Lorcan shut his eyes and took a deep breath, letting it out slowly, "I am," he said.

Thomas nodded and dropped his hood, whilst he manipulated the breeze in the fire using his hand. The dust settled under his command and the fire began to blaze enough to warm them. He spoke, "There were once four clans and now there is only one."

Lorcan nodded, recognising the old folk tale at once, "There were once four clans, a long time ago when the world was different; the Seers; the Healers, the Warriors, and the Seafarers. There were once four clans that guarded the door to eternity, until the day it would be locked forever.

But what few know is that there are still four clans: those who see beyond what the eye can see, the Danaan; those who use nature to create great healing, the Laten Islanders; those who fight to keep the Tor protected, the Gedogin; and those who guard the seas, the Decanté.

We are waiting, below the surface, biding our time until we're needed again. And it seems that soon we will be, finally, as the world takes its final turn once more.

We are the knowledge holders.

We are the alliance.
We are the Keepers."

Chapter 30 - The Winding City

Rainou and Adrienne arrived in Senelin two days later under nightfall, and so as not to seem conspicuous, Adrienne lodged in a lady's boarding house, aliasing as an artist from the south. Many of that profession took the pilgrimage to visit the masters of the city, to see its great architecture up close, in all its cascading levels and bridges. Rainou had business in the Gedogin's outpost on one of the higher levels of the city, and Adrienne's aunt was to liaise with them there.

Adrienne checked in to the boarding house, which consisted of a quaint living area filled with mismatched upholstered chairs upon which sat other unaccompanied women taking tea and playing cards, and a small bed chamber for each of them, with four-poster beds and a wash basin. She met Rainou in the street outside. It was nighttime by now, but the city was not asleep. The aroma of Elkien trees graced the upper levels of the city where she stayed, and she took a moment to gather some scrapings from their bark. Elsen had taught her that these trees only grow in the north, and their properties of healing are invaluable to anyone who has been taught how. She wondered then how Elsen had learned of her own heritage as a Danaan, being fostered on the Laten Islands, and who then was it that protected her from the outer world? *That is not a question for now*, she thought.

The clanking of wine glasses came from restaurants and clubhouses that populated the streets outside, and a faint soundscape of noise came up through the storeys of streets below - a reminder of the polarisation that had plagued the city for many years. Adrienne imagined a young Noah playing in the night air several tiers down, and her chest felt a little sore. She leant over the handrail and peered down, but the overlapping nature of the levels blocked her view.

All she could see were the middle streets, trees and the raised canal that took pedestrians all the way down to the bottom. It was the only way that someone from the lower levels could see their city in full, though they would never be let off the canal path to anywhere higher than their own station.

    They began to walk down the road, and the warm night was a welcome feeling after so many weeks in the bitter north. That night, the streets they walked down were alive with candles and bright windows, the canal beside them was ablaze with lanterns, with boats and nighttime strollers on the walkways. They worked their way through the intertwined alleys, down steps to the second level, which led to a narrow walkway that passed entirely below the one they'd been on before, and yet seemed in a perfectly logical place with the structures around it. Round, compact houses that would have been small in any other place, reached the height of castle turrets. Houses that should be grand and majestic were wedged into smaller slots amongst each other on the street, minimised in size to give a doll house effect. Every corner was a visual feast, until eventually, Adrienne's eyes softened to what they saw, like a full stomach only halfway through a Midmoon feast.

    The Gedogin outpost was in the midway point between the upper boulevard and the ground alleys, and though not the official building of the Gedogin in this city, it formed an inconspicuous meeting point for Keepers, and meetings of a sensitive and less public nature. But as they were stepping down into the business quarter Rainou stopped so quickly that Adrienne nearly walked right into her. She looked as if she was listening to something, but Adrienne couldn't hear what.

    "Change of plan," she said to Adrienne, "We're going to the headquarters. Something's happened."

Rainou had as little time to explain as they hurried back to the upper boulevard. Adrienne had seen Rainou fight for her life, she'd seen her hurry, but in these moments she saw something in Rainou's expression that she'd never have expected: fear.

The headquarters was a large yet inconspicuous looking building, with a triangular arch and tall white doors. It could quite easily have been a temple built by one of the new religious sects or an overpriced schoolhouse. However, the familiar marking of the crest on the large double doors told otherwise. As they walked up the stone steps, they saw the first clue that something was amiss: it was not guarded. Rainou closed her eyes and raised her hands out in front of her. She stepped forward, shaking her head, "The defences are down," she said.

They opened the outer doors and cautiously stepped inside, "It could be a trap," said Rainou, "Adrienne, now would be a good time to use that Noch of yours. Tell me if you sense any interruptions."

Adrienne pulled the Noch out of her pocket and held it up in front of her, but there was nothing, just its normal faint white light.

They walked through the main hall to an auditorium, and before them the great doors were swung wide open. The room had seating and a walkway ending in a raised area, like a lecture hall. The windows were blocked off and the room was barely visible through the darkness. The lecture stage was broken in half and in front of it, facing away from them, was Adrienne's aunt, a short woman with dark hair in a dark purple cloak, shorter than Adrienne had remembered. Next to her was a Laten man in green velvet attire, like the outfit that Hercel had worn. They were staring up at an image on the wall. Rainou clicked her fingers, causing the lights in the room to blaze up in an instant. As they grew closer to the woman, the horrific truth reached them. There were days old dead bodies lying at the foot of the raised stage, their rancid smell causing them to wretch and cough as they passed them. The place was entirely ransacked, but whoever it was who had attacked this building, whatever they were looking for, they hadn't found it. Neither the man or woman standing at the front were fazed by and of this, they just kept staring at the wall.

    Rainou and Adrienne joined them at the front, and their eyes followed theirs to whatever it was that had stolen their attention. The wall originally had an illustrated image of the Keeper's crest, just like one on Tosia's wall, with the four pictures leaning to the symbol in the middle, but there was something else, something new. In dark, clear writing on the wall above were seven words:

    This time, the chain will be broken.

Shanaki - Epilogue

"My oh my! Would you look at the time, I've quite overrun today," chuckled Shanaki, waking his audience from their trance. At the back of the room, shop tenders stood with the guardsmen who were waiting, impatiently, for the story to finish and the crowds to depart.

"I will have to save the rest for another day," said Shanaki, standing up from his seat, "and let us perhaps give Adrienne a break from all this going onwards, for she too needs to process all that has become her this day." Shanaki oof'ed and sighed as he pulled himself up, refusing help from any of the nearby folk.

Slowly, the crowds started to evacuate the menagerie, stopping to thank Shanaki and drop money in his box as they did so. As the contents of the menagerie dispersed, a young girl was staring into the window of one of the shops, and as she did she kept turning to look at Shanaki through the moving crowds. Eventually, the only sound in the space was that of shopkeepers tidying away their goods and counting their change, and the guardsmen pulling down shutters to lock up for the evening, but the girl was still there.

It was getting dark, so Shanaki picked up his book and walking lantern, and walked to the door. He stopped behind her when he noticed what she was looking at through the window. The object she was looking at was tattered and torn, and lightly priced at ten silver coins, ostensibly due to the fact that it no longer worked to serve its purpose. It was a small stone case, the shape of an arched doorway, with a round circle in the centre, and its markings were faded.

"Will Adrienne ever see Lorcan again?" said the girl, "I thought that part of the story would be longer."

Shanaki smiled at this, "We are all the centre of our own world," he said. "That is all for Adrienne to learn and for you to find out. There are so many stories going on in the world at any given time, and we are continuously playing a part in other people's lives and we never even know it. Sometimes our part is small, and sometimes it is bigger, but that doesn't make it any less important. Sometimes when we meet someone new, we try so hard to figure out what we're meant to learn from them. We forget that it might be ourselves who have the gift to give. It's only when we remember to learn together that the lessons come. So the question is, why were they meant to meet and what is their parting worth?"

    The girl went silent for a moment, pensively looking in at the items in the shop window.

    "None of them work anyway," she said to him, pointing at the stone box, "My mother had an old Revolter. She used it for storing meat and milk in the summer because it was so cold inside."

    "We have found other ways to fulfil the same role of these tools," said Shanaki, gesturing at the ice truck outside.

    "But they weren't ever real, were they?" she asked. "The vessels, they were made up in the myths. These are just collector's items, that's what they say... made for temples and museums, or to frighten people into believing in the Channel. I saw one play an old message once, in a sideshow at a circus. It was from a long time ago, and it was crackly and dark, but I saw it... anyway, it was just a trick."

    "Did the trick work?" asked Shanaki, and she shrugged.

    He pulled out a small lantern from his pocket and exposed the wick to the air. "You can understand what you're made of, how the magickal reactions in your brain take place to form you, an entirely unique being in the world, but that doesn't mean that that is what you are, does it? Surely seeing that they do work makes them more believable, not less?" As he said this, he squeezed two fingers onto the wick of his lantern, and smoke started to emerge from underneath. He lifted his fingers from the wick, blowing at it ever so lightly, and slowly but surely, it lit up.

Thanks to my agents Luke Chandley, Adam Rushton and everyone at AROL. To my publishers, Rebels of Summer. To all the people who have championed me, sometimes utterly silently, in their own ways (you know who you are). To my partner, Chris, for his unfathomable patience in riding out all the neurosis that comes with writing something of this magnitude. To anyone who took the time to read, skim over or discuss draft 1, 2, 3, 4, 5... not to mention my extraordinary mother, to whom I owe all the thanks in the world for reading every single draft. To Emma, the strongest, most wonderful human, without whom I would be lost. And to my dad, for always being there to talk me through the difficult bits. Thanks to Oliver for the wonderful map! As for the rest, a thank you for all the visits to Middle Earth, Temerant, Oxford, Narnia, Westeros, Avalon, Hogwarts and Earthsea that have kept me believing

K L Murray is the pen name for writer Kate-Lois Elliott. She has written for online and print magazines as well as stage, screen, and radio for over 15 years. In 2022, she was nominated for a British Writers 'Guild Award for the comedy series How To Be Maggie: With Maggie P. Her debut novel, The Inner Channel, was longlisted for the Merky Books New Writer's Prize in 2021, the Penguin Random House company fronted by British artist Stormzy.

Published in partnership with Rebels of Summer.
www.rebelsofsummer.com
Instagram: @rebelsofsummer
Facebook: Rebels of Summer

Printed in Great Britain
by Amazon